Zero

Warriors Series, Book 8

by

Ty Patterson

Acknowledgements

No book is a single person's product. I am privileged that *Zero* has benefited from the inputs of several great people.

Gary L. Bristol, Hank Halstead, Donald Hoffman, Richard Lane, Jim Lambert, Jack Willis, who are my beta readers and who helped shape my book, my launch team for supporting me, and Donna Rich for her editing and proofreading.

Books by Ty Patterson

The Warrior, Warriors series, Book 1

The Reluctant Warrior, Warriors series, Book 2

The Warrior Code, Warriors series, Book 3

The Warrior's Debt, Warriors series, Book 4

Warriors series Boxset, Books 1-4

Flay, Warriors series, Book 5

Behind You, Warriors series, Book 6

Hunting You, Warriors series, Book 7

Warriors series Boxset II, Books 5-7

Zero, Warriors series, Book 8

Available on Amazon, Nook Books, Kobo and iTunes

Sign up to Ty Patterson's mailing list on his website, *www.typatterson.com* and get the ebook copy of The Warrior, free. Be the first to know about new releases and deals.

Dedications

To my parents, who taught me the value of a good education. My wife for her patience, and my son for listening to my jokes. To all my beta readers, my launch team, and well-wishers.

To all the men and women in uniform who make it possible for us to enjoy our freedoms.

To a true Warrior, William S (Billy) Brown, Jr, of Manteo, NC. Leader, Husband, Father, Friend, HERO.

Chapter 1

Washington D.C. is the center of the political universe.

There are other cities that generate more traffic and business; New York or London for example. There are other countries that wield as much economic clout as the United States. If China sneezes, the world's stock markets catch a cold.

However, when it comes to global political influence, the United States is still the foremost world power and its capital is at the heart of that.

Due to that singular white residence which is recognized the world over; it is also one of the most secure cities on the planet.

It is not just that residence that calls the city home. There are various defense, intelligence, and investigative agencies that are headquartered in the city. Many of those agencies carry three-letter acronyms. Some of those agencies are unknown to the taxpayer and are hidden under layers of deception.

Not far from the city is another singularly recognizable building, this one with five sides.; the largest office building in the world. It's an office of course, but it's also much more than that.

Washington D.C. is small compared to other world cities. It is less than sixty-four square miles and has a population of less than seven hundred thousand.

In comparison, New York is just under three hundred and five square miles, with over eight million people. London is well over six hundred and seven square miles and has a similar population to New York.

Despite such a concentration of agencies and political power, security in the Washington D.C. isn't obvious.

Gun toting police officers don't hang about on street corners. Cruisers patrol the streets of course, but if they are bristling with men and guns, it isn't apparent.

But the security apparatus is there, hidden, tucked away and part of it springs to life when that motorcade emerges.

Then helicopters, numerous patrol cars, with motorcycle outriders appear and shut down streets and suddenly you can see uniforms, weapons, hard stares, and dark shades all over.

The city resumes its normal state when the motorcade disappears.

The Presidential View Hotel caters to select tourists,

businessmen, politicians, and that particular life form that's all too common in the city – lobbyists.

It's a small, intimate hotel, just over hundred rooms, a Michelin-starred restaurant adjacent to the lobby. The restaurant is well known in the city and one always needs reservations.

The reason for the hotel's name is apparent if you step outside and face it and turn right. You'll see that white residence, the American flag flying proudly on top.

The more famous Jefferson Hotel is just a stone's throw away, diagonally opposite, on Sixteenth Street.

The president frequents the Jefferson occasionally. It is said there are tunnels that connect the Jefferson with that famous residence. Obviously, no one is going to confirm their existence.

Washington D.C. hasn't been attacked by terrorists in a while. In a time when TV and newspapers air atrocities committed every day in various parts of the world, *a while* doesn't mean much.

They came to the Presidential View in twos and threes. Most of them were clean shaven, the few who had facial hair, were neatly trimmed. One of the facial hair wearers sported a moustache. A brown one. Another had a French beard and glasses.

They wore jeans or tracksuits and dark windbreakers. Some wore ball caps.

They all carried gym bags. They were heavy, but all fifteen of them carried their bag with ease.

Two of them came into the restaurant, lugging their bags, hung around as if waiting to be seated.

They drifted away when it looked like it would be a long wait. Both of them casually eyed the seated patrons, about thirty of them.

Neither of them saw the group of nine in the far corner.

Zeb saw them. He saw their bags. He saw their eyes run past his group. He read their body language. They hadn't come to be seated. They had come to see how the restaurant looked or felt.

Tourists. He half expected them to click pictures, but they didn't.

He turned his attention to his eight companions, who, along

with the ninth, formed the Agency.

The Agency didn't have a three-letter acronym. Few people knew that it existed. Of those, only a handful knew of its true purpose. Those who knew, had security clearances that were off the scale.

The Agency took direct and proactive action against threats to the country. It went in where other deep black agencies hesitated.

Terrorists, organized crime, drug traffickers, armaments dealers, missing nuclear and chemical warheads – those and many others were the Agency's targets.

It had taken out bad guys in Syria, Iraq, Iran, Somalia, Indonesia, Pakistan, Afghanistan, France, Britain, Nigeria, and many more countries. It went where the threats were, regardless of national boundaries.

It had its own intel network that rivaled the best in the country; a network that Zeb and Broker had built.

Zebadiah Carter, Zeb, was its lead agent.

A seat away from him was Broker, the handsome, elderly one. An intelligence analyst who ran the logistics, the planning, and the intel for the Agency.

Broker was flanked by Bwana and Roger. Bwana was as tall as he was dark. He looked frightening. He was frightening when he was in combat mode. He was as gentle as a kitten when he played civilian.

Roger could have modeled for the luxury couture brands. Instead he chose to be a Special Forces operative and that resulted in his joining Zeb.

Bear, as tall as Bwana, but with a thick beard, sat with Chloe, a petite brunette. They were a couple, in work and in life. They were the best close protection people Zeb had come across.

Meghan and Beth Petersen, twins, sat next to Chloe. Brown haired, attractive, vivacious, and extremely intelligent. They supported Broker. They virtually ran the Agency and reduced Broker to lounging around on a couch.

Most of them were ex Special Forces operatives, except Broker who had come from the Rangers, Chloe, who was from the 82nd Airborne, and the twins.

The twins were daughters of a celebrated cop in Jackson Hole. They had bumped into Zeb a while back and worn him down till he made them part of the crew.

At the head of the table sat Zeb's boss. Clare. She reported only to the President. She had never let the Commander-in-Chief down.

Zeb's crew was in town to celebrate Clare's birthday. She was in her late forties, the same age as Broker, but didn't look it. Her grey eyes were usually cool.

They were mirthful that day. All of them were. It was one of those rare periods of downtime for them.

The plan was to have a leisurely breakfast that would merge into lunch.

Some alcohol would be consumed. Broker and Roger were wine connoisseurs and never lost an opportunity to try new wines.

Zeb had turned teetotaler a year back. Always a rare drinker, giving it up had been easy.

The twins had followed suit. They stuck to organic drinks and took the gentle ribbing from the rest of the crew with good grace.

Zeb turned to the entrance, smiling in response to a joke from Broker, and saw the two men departing.

He noticed their tracksuits first.

They didn't belong in the restaurant.

Tourists aren't known for their dress sense.

He then saw the gym bags. One of the men adjusted the bag on his shoulder; it tightened and for a moment straight lines and angles stood out in relief.

Must be some sporting team.

He laughed absentmindedly at something Meghan said.

Sports teams don't stay in this hotel. Which kind of game requires something straight or angled?

Ice hockey? Nothing going on now. Not in this part of the country. Field hockey? Not played here.

He ran the various sports in his mind, looking down at the table.

No game came to his mind.

When he raised his head, all of them had gone silent, were staring at him.

'What?' Meghan asked him.

He shook his head. He was overreacting.

'What?' She persisted.

He told them.

Broker rose. 'I'll have a look outside.'

He returned a few minutes later, looking relaxed from the outside, except for the pinched look in his eyes that only they recognized.

'Three men outside, all dressed similarly. Three gym bags. I collared a bellhop and asked him about the men. They aren't staying in the hotel.'

Mumbai.

The thought flashed in Zeb's mind.

In 2008 a bunch of terrorists had breezed through the city, shooting at will in a busy railway terminus and other public places.

In addition, they had shot through two high profile hotels. They had killed a hundred and sixty-four people before they themselves had been brought down.

Every security agency in the world had planned and prepared for Mumbai-style attacks, since then.

It's Clare's birthday. Don't go looking for threats when none exist.

He forced himself to relax, reached out for his glass when the look on Broker's face stopped him.

'I *accidentally* brushed against one of the bags. It sounded metallic.'

'Where is he?' Zeb asked Clare urgently.

She knew what he was asking, pulled her phone out and made a brief call. Her shoulders relaxed. 'He isn't in town. No one is staying or visiting this hotel today.'

The warmth in her eyes disappeared. 'Let's deal with this. It could be nothing, but let's be sure.'

'If we approach them, they might just cut loose. The hotel's busy. Even the presence of cruisers might set them off.' Chloe, pragmatic, calm, collected.

'I don't think they're on a killing mission or a suicidal mission. They would have opened up by now.' Bear added. 'This looks like a hostage deal.'

Zeb agreed and came to a decision. 'Broker, can Yuri hack into the hotel?'

Yuri was their friendly East European hacker, one of the best in that business. On another mission they had come across him and had offered him a deal.

Work for them, or take a bullet. Yuri took the former. He was loyal, never seemed to sleep, and had become one of them.

Broker sniffed. 'I could, if I wasn't here. I'm sure he can too.' He made a discreet call, laughed once and ended it.

'He'll get onto it.'

'Ask him to penetrate the camera system. He should take it over only when I say so.'

Broker nodded, fired off a text.

Clare opened the menu which ran to several pages and flipped to the end. The hotel's layout and fire escape plans were marked in red on the last page. She studied it for a moment and turned it around to Zeb.

'How would you do it?'

Zeb had thought about it; the moment he had spotted the two men. 'I think they'll have around ten or fifteen men. You don't need a lot to shut down a hotel. Once you control the entrance, the parking lot, the service entrances, you've taken it over.'

'This hotel has seven floors, fifteen rooms on each. Maybe about three hundred guests.' He had looked its details up before booking the table.

'All rooms were booked when I inquired,' Beth said.

Zeb nodded, carried on. 'This restaurant is the only dining room they have. There's a gym and swimming pool next to the basement parking lot.'

He paused, laid it out in his mind, continued. 'One man on the roof. Nothing there, one man will do. Two men on the uppermost floor – one in the corridor, one in the stairwell. Such pairing every few floors, right down to the ground floor.'

'Control the cameras, take over the phones, computers and security, shut down the entrances, and the hotel is captured.'

'People get taken in by the size of a hotel. They think such a large building will require an army. It isn't size that matters. Entrances, exits, and communication lines. That's all there is to taking over a hotel.'

They sat in silence mulling it over. None of them objected. They had experienced hostage situations before, knew capturing such a hotel wasn't difficult.

'We should've brought in India-style hotel checks,' Bwana commented darkly.

After the Mumbai attacks, every major hotel in that country had installed bag scanners. Every visitor to the hotel was frisked.

Zeb waved the comment away. No point in dwelling over *should haves*. 'How many of you are carrying?'

All of them were except Broker. 'I don't need guns. My brains are scary enough,' he said loftily.

Bwana and Roger collected the women's handguns and their magazines under the cover of the table and distributed them.

'You got your earpieces?'

All of them had them. Gone were the days of speaking into a collar mic or a wrist mic.

These earpieces doubled as mic as well as speaker and were near invisible. They weren't available commercially.

'Bear, Rog, Bwana, the four of us will conceal ourselves till these guys show their hand. We'll then play it by ear. Broker and the twins will be our eyes, at least in the restaurant.'

'Those two might have noticed the nine of us,' Beth objected.

'Which is where Yuri comes in. The moment we disappear, Yuri should show our SUV exiting the parking lot. That's their proof that we have left.'

'Broker, Yuri should loop the camera feed the moment these guys reveal themselves. That will lull them, will give us cover to move.'

'Where will you hide?' Meghan's voice was even, but the concern in her eyes was apparent.

Roger grinned, a smile that had captured many hearts from coast to coast and in many countries. 'It'll be hard for me since I stand out, naturally. These guys, they look like furniture. They'll be okay.'

'Ignore him,' Bear rumbled. 'We'll be fine. Chances are these guys will leave and we'll return, feeling foolish.'

None of them believed his last line. They all had finely-tuned inner senses. Each one's was pinging.

There was an immediate threat nearby.

Zeb went to the men's restroom.

Six stalls. Sink counter. No place to hide.

He turned to leave when his eyes drifted to the roof.

Suspended ceiling tiles.

He checked the stalls. They were empty. He locked the restroom from the inside, climbed on top of stall, drew out a dinner knife and poked at one of the boards. It resisted, but gave way when he applied pressure.

He moved it cautiously and peered in the dark space.

It had pipes and tubing and AC ducts.

There was ample space for a body that needed to be concealed.

He dropped down, unlocked the restroom, and took a swift look outside. No one was approaching it.

He climbed up the stall and squeezed through the small opening, drew in his legs and placed the tile back in place.

He inserted his knife in a crack between two tiles and widened it. Now he had eyes to the restroom.

Hopefully small enough to escape detection.

He waited. That was the easy part. He could wait for hours, days, weeks. Lie motionless for hours on end, just his eyes moving.

Waiting came naturally to him and to his team.

'I'm in,' he spoke softly. 'In the men's restroom.'

'So am I, in the laundry room, on top of some kind of giant dryer.' Bear.

Bwana checked in. He was in a janitor's closet, perched uncomfortably on a floor-to-ceiling tool chest. The chest didn't quite reach the ceiling. Bwana had twisted himself to fit in the narrow space.

They waited a while for Roger to come in and when he did, they heard female voices in the background.

'Don't ask where, but my handsome self is hidden to the world.'

They waited. Zeb hoped the wait would be in vain and they could resume their celebrations.

Clare didn't do birthdays. The Agency was her life. It was precisely for that reason that the twins had planned the surprise get-together.

Minutes merged. Men entered and exited the restroom. Toilets flushed.

Ninety minutes later, just when Zeb was thinking of overreaction, an assault rifle went off.

More firing followed, in different parts of the hotel. A stunned silence and then shouting and screaming began.

Rifles chattered high up in the hotel. The panicked voices died down.

A burst of noise came through.

From the restaurant.

Two shots sounded. More screaming, but this time it was muted and then silence.

'You were right.' Broker's voice was grim.

'Those two guys in the dining room, they came prepared. They lost the gym outfit and are now sporting combat trousers and black tops. They shot in the air first. Then they randomly picked one man and woman from the crowd and shot them.'

'They didn't speak a single word. Just walked up and finished them.'

'They've got control. Total control. Not a single hostage will go against them. Not here at least.'

Zeb knew it was unlikely other captives in the different parts of the hotel -- the kitchen staff, the guests in their rooms – would offer resistance.

People in a crowd behaved differently. The mob gave them courage. That courage had been stamped down brutally by the killings.

There could be more dead in other parts of the hotel.

The beast in Zeb came to life. It filled him. It prepared him.

Unknown number of hostiles. Around four hundred hostages, including guests, staff, and diners.

Just four men to counterattack.

It was zero time.

Chapter 2

'They've got a jammer. My phone has no signal.' Bear's voice was soft, calm, even, as if he was discussing the weather.

'Mine's dead too,' Roger checked in.

'So's mine.' A growl. Bwana.

'They're professionals. You heard those rifles? They are silenced. Traffic will drown their sounds.' Roger's voice came over a cracking sound. His knuckles.

Zeb eased to one side and cautiously stretched out his legs. 'What's happening out there?'

'They're grabbing our wallets and phones,' Chloe whispered and stopped broadcasting when one of the gunmen approached their group.

'Women and men are being separated. Teenagers too. Men in one corner, women in another, male teenagers in a third, female teenagers well away,' Meghan spoke, behind Broker's back.

'Oh, they brought in the hotel staff. About fifty of them. The manager, waiters, cooks, cleaners, bellhops. All of them are here. They too have been separated and made to join the male and female groups.'

She followed Clare, Chloe, and Beth, and moved to their corner where they joined a bunch of terrified women.

Three other gunmen came inside the restaurant and shut the entrance.

Five gunmen and nearly a hundred hostages in a sealed room.

Broker eyed their weapons. *Kalashnikovs and AR-15s. None of them is masked. That's troubling.*

He knew what that usually implied. He brushed it away. There was no point thinking about it.

All of them average in looks. You wouldn't remember them for long.

He glanced in Clare's direction and breathed out silently in relief at her imperceptible nod.

She had managed to send a text message out just before wiping her phone clean.

A password and a swipe activated a program that erased

all data on their phones and filled it with innocuous phone numbers and messages.

'One of them is going through our bags. Two are at the entrance, another is at the kitchen's entrance. That too is shut. The fifth is walking around.' Beth took over from Meghan, her lips barely moving.

'None of them has said a word. All of them look alert, competent. And dangerous.'

Forty minutes had passed since the takeover.

Forty minutes for courage to return.

Broker's heart sank when an elderly man, well dressed, in a suit, stepped forward and approached the three riflemen.

'Hold up, friend,' Broker spoke softly, urgently.

The white haired man didn't listen. He marched to the entrance, a determined air on his face.

'Who are you guys? What do you want? You can't kill us all, you know.'

The gunmen watched him silently and when he was ten feet away, one of them raised his AR-15 and fired a single round in the man's head.

The man dropped. Screaming followed a split second of stunned silence.

The shooter pointed at the ceiling and fired a single burst. The shouting ceased. A woman rushed forward toward the body. She was restrained by other hostages.

She collapsed in their arms, weeping quietly.

Silence fell, but for the soft sounds of crying, praying, from different parts of the room.

The shooter pointed at two men. They came forward hesitantly, grabbed the body and dragged it against a wall.

'They killed one more. Not a single word, still, from the gunmen. These guys aren't your wild-eyed killers.' Meghan's voice was clipped.

Bear peered through the crack between the doors of his hide.

The laundry room was empty. It had one set of doors that connected it to the rest of the hotel. Those doors had opened and a gunman had surveyed the room when the firing had broken out.

They were now closed.

It was a huge room and smelled of detergent and freshly-washed clothes.

Steam hung from the ceiling and a bank of machines at one end gurgled and murmured as they turned and washed and rinsed and did whatever they were programmed to do to deliver freshly-laundered and ironed clothes to their guests.

Another end of the room had clothing hanging from several lines. Drying.

Bear was cramped in a small service area, behind a set of whitewashed doors. Cables ran behind him, switches were mounted on walls.

He inched his doors open with his left hand. His right hand was curled around his handgun.

The laundry room remained empty.

He remained in his hide for a moment.

There were cameras in the room. They could be monitored. A gunman, or two, could burst through the door to investigate why a service door had opened.

Long minutes passed.

The connecting doors stayed closed.

Yuri. He must have worked his magic. He must be looping the tape.

Bear stepped out, used the cover of a washing line from which hung white blankets, to check the room out.

It was a hall. A large rectangular room whose sole purpose was to wash, dry and iron.

An entrance on one side led to another room, the ironing room

The giant presses were silent, awaiting commands from their operators.

A single camera shone in the ceiling.

Bear ignored it and walked the length of the room, to its rear, where he had spotted a door.

It was secured from the inside. Cool air came in from underneath it. A small window to its right revealed a well-manicured lawn.

Rear of the hotel. Service facilities.

He went back to his hide and checked in with Zeb.

Zeb couldn't reply.

His restroom was no longer empty.

A gunman stood on the tiled floor and glanced about. He was dressed, incongruously, in an overcoat that almost reached his ankles.

There was nothing incongruous about the AR-15 around his shoulder. His left hand gripped its stock loosely, easily.

He checked each of the stalls, looked at the ceiling, looked around seemingly aimlessly and came back to the center of the room.

He seemed to be in no hurry. A headset was wrapped around his face. His lips didn't move.

He was of average height. Five nine, Zeb guessed. Clean shaven, wearing clear glasses. Short hair.

Combat trousers and combat boots beneath that overcoat. Are those Vibram? Vibram soles were widely used in the military and special forces. His crew and he owned several pairs.

The hostile glanced at the ceiling.

Zeb slowed his breathing, willed his pulse to a near standstill, then commanded his inner self to flatten and compress itself.

He became one with the ceiling. He was a part of the suspended tiles. His *chi* merged with that of the hotel and became indistinguishable.

It came naturally to Zeb, it required no conscious thought.

He had once lain within touching distance of a bunch of hostiles in Somalia, in their hide in Mogadishu, concealed in a crawlspace above the bathroom.

He had spent two weeks there, without their ever realizing there was another human in their small quarters.

The bespectacled man turned when the door opened and another hostile entered.

They spoke, their voices muted and too low for Zeb to overhear.

He gave up trying to listen and focused on body language.

Leader, follower. Is Glasses the ring leader? He certainly has the air.

Glasses looked around one last time and then followed the gunman out.

The door shut behind them, but Zeb didn't move.

Fifteen minutes later, the door opened suddenly and Glasses peered in.

His eyes ran searchingly for a moment and then his head disappeared and the door closed.

He didn't return.

'Sitrep,' Zeb asked softly.

'A gun toting dude poked his head in my closet, shined a flashlight. He didn't see me.' Bwana grunted.

Bear and Roger echoed his tale of surveillance.

Zeb nodded in the dark. The attackers had double checked to make sure the hotel didn't have hidden guests.

'They took our names, details, like where we worked. Why we were in the hotel. When we arrived, how we arrived.' Meghan replied.

Someone will cross check that. Tally the vehicles in the parking lot with the hostage statements.

'They spent more time with the teenagers. The male ones. A few of them broke down crying. We were too far away to hear anything.'

Zeb thought for a moment. *Hostages?* He hadn't recognized any of the patrons in the restaurant. He knew Clare hadn't either, and she moved in more rarefied circles than he.

If they were after hostages, they didn't have to take-over an entire hotel.

'Anything happening outside?'

'Nope.' Broker, this time. 'It's an hour now, things are still normal, at least from what we can see. No cruisers, no FBI teams. Nothing. Usual D.C traffic, outside.'

'They haven't made demands?' Roger interjected.

'Have they declared themselves?' Bwana asked.

'No and no. What part of *not a single word spoken*, didn't you get?'

Just because they were being held hostage, facing an uncertain future, possibly death, wasn't reason enough for Meghan to lose her feistiness.

Zeb couldn't help smiling in his cramped hide. 'Bwana, Roger, any hostiles that you can see?'

'Not a danged one,' Roger replied disgustedly.

'One.' Bwana's voice became grim.

'My hide is diagonally opposite a conference room on the ground floor. There was some kind of corporate shindig going on. Two gunmen came in, shut it down. Sealed the room. One shooter remains.'

He paused.

Zeb kept quiet, knowing there was more.

'Sometime back he opened the door, called a woman over and manhandled her for a minute.'

No one said anything.

They knew Bwana well. If he had his way, the molester wouldn't be seen again, alive.

Conference room could hold another hundred. So five hundred hostages in all.

Five gunmen in the restaurant. Two that Bwana's seen. Two in the men's restroom. Nine. Zeb counted silently.

There will be more on the higher floors.

'Chloe, did your five leave the restaurant at any time?'

'No.'

'When did the three others join?'

'Twenty minutes after the first burst.'

'One of those could be from the two gunmen I saw.' Bwana's voice was dubious.

It's possible, but more likely that they have separate teams. That's how we would take-over a hotel.

'Bwana, can you take that guy and interrogate him?'

'It'll be a pleasure.'

'Broker, Beth, you need to visit the restrooms and get a feel for how they are deployed.'

'What about Rog and me?' Bear's voice was almost plaintive.

'Wait up, till Broker and Beth return.'

If it was us, our command post would be in the center, which would be the reception.

He made his plans while waiting for Broker and Beth to make their move.

They could shoot first, but I'm betting they won't. Broker can talk a mountain lion down. These gunmen shouldn't pose a problem.

I hope.

Broker looked across the room at Beth. 'I'll go first.'

She blinked in acknowledgement.

He raised his hand casually, removed his earbud, pocketed it and took a step forward.

The three gunmen at the door turned in his direction.

Another step. The patrolling shooter watched him.

A third step brought him to the center of the room. Behind him was the hostile, still going through various bags, briefcases, and purses.

To his right was one shooter.

Ahead were the three men guarding the entrance.

Broker raised his hands. 'I need to visit the restroom. I can't hold back any longer.'

A gun barrel rose and pointed at him.

'Sure you can shoot me. What'll that achieve? I'll just soil my trousers and create a stink. You could kill me. That'll get everyone restive.'

He was close enough now to look into the green eyes of the gunman who had shot. The eyes were flat, impenetrable.

They surveyed Broker.

The gunman held a hand up. Broker halted.

He spoke in his headset, his eyes never leaving Broker's face. His finger was curled around the trigger.

A knock sounded on the door. Three raps, a pause, two more.

The door opened and another gunman entered.

He was different.

He wore glasses and the five gunmen in the room seemed to lean toward him.

Glasses conferred briefly with Green Eyes and approached Broker.

He circled Broker once and came close.

'You are not scared. Why aren't you? Who are you, friend?'

American accent. No particular geographical influence. Native English speaker.

'Why should I be scared? You're not here to kill us.'

Glasses was amused. 'What makes you think that?' He gestured behind his back. 'We have already killed.'

'You killed for effect. If you wanted to kill us all, you could have done that quite a while ago.'

'We could still kill you.'

Broker didn't answer.

'Who are you?' Glasses asked him finally.

'I run an oil intelligence business in New York. I look at oil markets, analyze trends, prices, political developments and send briefings to my clients.'

Glasses made a hand signal. One of his men came forward with a card.

Broker's business card. It was one of the covers he used.

Yuri would have taken down their consulting business website the moment Broker had messaged him. In its place, he would have inserted a bland business page.

Standard operating procedure.

Glasses studied the card briefly and raised his head.

Broker returned his gaze. 'We are probably more valuable to you as hostages for whatever you plan to do. You'll get more cooperative hostages if you allow comfort breaks.'

'You realize we'll watch you closely, now.'

Broker nodded.

Glasses signaled to another man, whispered instructions and left the room.

Two gunmen approached. One headed to the male hostages and shepherded a bunch of them to the restroom. The other kept watch.

Broker joined the men, who walked slowly, darting nervous glances at the shooters.

The cloakrooms were set back from a hallway that led from the restaurant, passed the reception area and disappeared down a corridor.

The corridor led to guest rooms and the conference room facility.

The reception area had five men.

Glasses was in front of the desk, with a clear sightline down the corridor. Two other men ranged near the entrance, the fourth was at the far end. A fifth was pacing in front of the reception area.

That hallway will eventually lead to the kitchen, the laundry rooms, other service facilities. That's where Bear is.

Funny, all five are wearing those overcoats. Are they concealing something beneath?

Broker didn't have any more time to observe. A hand behind his back propelled him inside the restroom where he joined the waiting line.

The restroom gave the illusion of privacy. It bolstered the courage of a couple of men.

They whirled around on the single gunman watching over them.

They didn't complete their turn.

He didn't shoot.

He stepped forward and rammed his barrel in the first man's midriff.

The man collapsed forward in a grunt.

The gunman stepped back smoothly, turned his gun around

and hit the second man in the head as if it were a baseball.

The second man crumpled without a sound.

There was a stunned silence in the restroom, the rest of the men looking at the bodies on the floor and back at the gunman.

He returned their looks impassively and when he gestured with his barrel, the hostages turned to the stalls.

The male hostages returned to the restaurant, half-dragging the two men.

Another gunman stepped forward, corralled the women and led them away.

Broker looked around casually. No one was paying attention to him.

He described the men in the central lobby and what had gone down in the restroom.

Beth, back from her visit, described what she had seen. She hadn't noticed anything different.

'Your Glasses and one of those dudes, is who I saw in the restroom,' Zeb spoke when he had finished.

'The lanky one, I think, he was in the corridor,' Bwana chimed in.

Ten men. Zeb thought furiously. 'Broker, where's the office?'

'Behind the reception. There's a curve in the wall which conceals a door.'

'They'll have one or two men there. They'll have taken over the cameras, the phone system, everything.'

'A couple of things happened when Broker was away,' Meghan's voice was barely audible. 'They took our phones, bags and wallets. One man questioned the teenagers again. He wrote their names – I'm guessing – on a sheet of paper.'

'They're scared. Many of them are crying. Heck, several adults are crying. But all of them are cowed. They won't go against the gunmen.'

Clare broke her silence for the first time. 'Zeb, these guys aren't checking in regularly with Glasses or anyone else. I have been observing them. They speak in their headsets only if spoken to, or to ask something.'

'Feels like a tightly knit team. Total trust, that kinda stuff,' Bear rumbled.

'That has a downside though, doesn't it, Zeb?' Bwana asked

hopefully.

Yes, it has. Zeb weighed his options. *If they're aren't checking in, and the men are isolated*--.

'It's a go.'

Chapter 3

Bwana peered through the crack. The solitary gunman was pacing in the hallway.

He disappeared for five minutes to Bwana's right. Returned, stopped in front of the conference room, opened it. Peered in for a few seconds and then disappeared to his left.

He was alert. He never spoke in his headset. Not when in Bwana's sight.

He's got his AR-15, handgun, and a thigh-holstered knife. Spare mags in those trousers pockets, I'll bet.

All I have is my Glock and a spare handgun.

It's enough.

The hostile would be most distracted when he had his head inside the conference room.

If I take him then, there's no knowing how the hostages will react.

Better when he's turning around.

He timed the gunman's moves.

Return from the left. Pause in front of the conference room. Listen. Move down the hallway.

He should've been less predictable.

Bwana waited for one circuit to be completed.

The shooter had disappeared to his right, on his next circuit, when a thought struck him.

That hallway leads to the central lobby. Anyone standing there has a clear sightline.

He let another circuit complete and for the man to disappear from his sight, to his right.

Bwana dropped to the floor and cracked open the door, wider.

The hallway was empty but for the lone gunman.

In the far distance, the central lobby was unoccupied.

He rose silently, shut the door, and waited.

The gunman returned.

He opened the conference room door.

Peered in.

Shut it.

Turned.

Bwana struck.

He was a blur of motion. Ebony-colored speed and silent

fury that hurled from the now wide-open closet.

One hand went around the gunman's head and jammed his mouth shut.

Another hand grabbed his throat and squeezed.

One moment the gunman was on his vigil.

The next, he was slumped on the floor in a cramped closet, a large, black man, looming over him.

His eyes grew wide. His mouth opened.

Bwana stuffed a wad of cloth down his throat and thrust a knee on his chest.

The man gagged. Bwana eased.

'You shout, you die.'

'You talk, you live. Maybe.'

Bear watched through a window for a long while.

No gunmen came his way.

Why should they? They have camera control. The cameras show nothing out of the ordinary.

The hallway from the laundry room wended through the unseen parts of the hotel, linking to several utility rooms, offices, branching out to the kitchen, a staff room, generator room, and several others.

Bear checked each one out.

They were all empty.

Beth said all staff have been taken to the restaurant.

The last room he checked was the kitchen.

It was enormous. It gleamed of white tile and stainless steel. Food lay on counters, in various stages of preparation. Gas burners flamed, heating empty air.

Bear looked around, spotted a hallway and followed it.

It led to an enormous store and freezer.

The store smelled of raw vegetables. The freezer smelled of meat.

The freezer didn't have meat alone.

Five bodies were hidden under strips and chunks of raw meat.

Each body had a single hole in the head. The bodies were aproned, in the universal uniform of chefs.

Bear snapped their pictures with his phone and notified the others.

'Five dead. Possibly cooks.'

Zeb finally responded. 'Search the rest of the kitchen.'

Bear searched. There was nothing to be found. Nothing that wasn't out of place.

'I'm going up.'

'I'm joining you,' Roger replied.

Up was the rest of hotel, where they figured there would be more men.

Zeb came on. 'Go down first. Secure the basement and the gym.'

Bear paused. An elevator ran down to the basement parking lot and the gym.

Elevators were out of the question.

Roger read his silence. 'There should be a flight of stairs. The same stairs that go up, should go down.'

Broker spoke heavily. 'They don't. There is a flight of stairs, but they are behind the office. Access is impossible. The gunmen are thick on the ground around there.'

Bwana broke the silence.

'My guy spilled. Glasses is indeed the ringleader. He is a merc. There are eighteen of them, spread out across the hotel.'

'There's one in the basement, one on the roof. A couple on the seventh, and two more on the lower floors. He doesn't know how they are spread out in the lobby and the restaurant.'

'They are all mercenaries and killers. Glasses is tight with a bunch of four other men. The five are like a core team.'

'The five with the overcoats,' Beth muffled her words in a cough.

'That's right. We have a problem though.'

They waited for him to continue.

'My guy doesn't know anything about the plan. He doesn't know why they are here. He has no idea of how they'll exit. All that info is with the core team. His job is just to follow orders.'

'All he knows is that exit is in the next forty-five minutes.'

'Once Glasses orders *EVAC,* he is to bring out all the hostages from the conference room to the central lobby.'

'To be executed?' Zeb queried.

'He doesn't know.'

'He confirmed there is no check-in routine. No special code for the guys to communicate with. They wait for orders from Glasses and act accordingly.'

'That's it? That's all this dude knows?' Meghan couldn't hide her incredulity.

'Yeah. He's worked with Glasses before. Glasses has always been good to him. That's why he signed up.'

'He has a name? Who Glasses is? Where he's from?' Broker, this time.

'The guys are a mixed bunch. Glasses is American. My dude is Colombian. Ramon Borra. He was in their army, previously.'

'What's the ringleader's name?'

'Borra is no longer talking, unfortunately.' Bwana didn't sound remorseful.

'Change of plan.' Zeb was expecting something like that. Bwana didn't take kindly to women molesters.

'Bear, Roger, the two of you go up, take out whoever is up there. Let's forget the basement for the moment.'

'Bwana, you stay put. Wear that headset and warn us if you hear anything. I'll come closer to the central lobby. '

'Broker, any change at your end?'

'Only three gunmen in the restaurant now. The other two left a while back. Maybe they're in the central lobby.'

'They've pulled down the drapes, here,' Chloe added. 'We can't see the street now. However, there doesn't seem to be any change outside.'

They all knew that wouldn't last much longer. Ninety minutes had elapsed since the first shots.

Friends, relatives, co-workers, business partners, would have called the hostages' phones. They would keep trying. Someone would raise an alarm.

Once that happened, only Glasses and his core team knew what would happen.

'We have forty-five minutes. Let's make the most of it.' Zeb signed off, grimly.

The access to the flight of stairs was concealed behind a pair of swinging doors that were painted to blend with the rest of the wall.

The doors were in a passage that also had another pair of swinging doors that went to the kitchen.

The passage was not in the central lobby's line of sight. It didn't have a guard. It probably had one when the attackers opened fire.

The hotel was in their control, however. There was no need to waste manpower. Besides they had camera control.

Roger joined Bear when he rounded a corner.

They bumped fists silently.

Bear raised an eyebrow. 'Where was your hide?'

Roger grinned. 'Next to a boiler in a staff restroom. The women's restroom.'

They approached another corner.

Bear signaled to Roger, got to his knees, put his face to the floor and looked around the corner.

Roger covered him from behind.

Clear, Bear signaled.

They darted across the open space, guns at the ready and approached the swinging doors cautiously.

It didn't have a window.

Roger shrugged when Bear looked at him questioningly.

He placed a hand on one door.

It opened without protest. Noiselessly.

The passage behind it was empty. It led to the flight of stairs.

They climbed it. Bear ahead and to the right. Roger behind him, a couple of steps below.

Bear in the front, since he offered the larger target. He would be the magnet for attacking fire.

It would buy them a second for Roger to counterattack.

The stairs went upwards in a square spiral.

Between two inclines was a landing. At the end of the third landing was a floor.

Fifteen steps to each incline. They could run up and down all those stairs all day, without breaking a sweat.

They reached the first floor.

Bear didn't pause this time.

He swung open the doors that led to the floor.

A gunman was standing right opposite, his hand on the stock of his Kalashnikov.

'Got a light, buddy?' Bear asked him, conversationally.

All friendship and good cheer. Like how two gun toting men behaved.

The shooter blinked.

His mouth opened.

His rifle rose.

Bear dropped to the ground.

Roger fired from behind him.

Two shots. Muted by a rudimentary suppressor – a plastic bottle that contained potato wedges, fashioned by Bear – at the end of his Kimber.

The gunman slammed back and was caught before he could fall, by Bear.

They stripped him of his weapons. Roger donned his headset, Bear took his knife and handgun and his Kalashnikov.

They resumed their climb.

Special Agent in Charge Sarah Burke leaned out of her window to see what was holding up the traffic. A line of school buses, cars, and courier trucks snarled back from Dupont Circle to Florida Avenue NW.

She had to get to the Presidential View hotel for a meeting that would start in half an hour. She was already running late.

Well, not really. Her meeting was due to start in *forty-five* minutes, but Burke was a control freak, a punctual freak.

Why arrive on time if one could arrive early and be prepared?

The meeting was important. It was with a banker who promised to reveal everything he knew about insider trading and price manipulation at one of the largest Wall Street banks.

Burke led an elite team of investigators who handled high profile cases, difficult cases, hotter-than-radiation cases. Investigating Congressmen? Burke handled it.

Going after international drug kingpins who were protected by foreign governments? The case came to Sarah Burke.

Dealing with messy-and-surrounded-by-media-frenzy, kidnappings and murder? Burke was on call.

Serial killers, rapists, child traffickers, white slavery rings, international and domestic terrorists – Burke had cracked them all wide open.

She was a star in the FBI, not that she regarded herself in that manner.

She knew she was a fine investigator, and that was good enough for her.

Her last case had gotten her promoted.

She had saved a small town in New Hampshire from being

taken over by a violent criminal gang. That had won her more headlines, more national press coverage, than she had ever received in her life.

Her promotion meant she handled an additional team. An HRT, Hostage Rescue Team, based out of Quantico.

In the dark of the night, Burke wasn't sure about her promotion. There were wrinkles to that last case that only her investigators, the FBI Director Pat Murphy, and Deputy Director Bob Pierce, who was her boss, knew of.

She had refused the promotion. Pierce had tried to convince her and when he had failed, he had referred her to the director.

'I don't deserve it.' She had repeated her explanation to Murphy. She went on to explain the details of the New Hampshire case to him. Details that he was well aware of.

He halted her flow of words.

'Do I look stupid to you?'

She blinked. 'No, sir.'

'Do I look like I reward people just because I like them or I think they are pretty?'

Sarah Burke knew she was attractive, and yet that had never been a factor in her meteoric rise in the FBI. Her co-workers, some of the best investigators in the country, saw her as their lead investigator. Her gender didn't matter to them.

She had never been inappropriately approached in the FBI.

'No, sir.'

Director Murphy bent his head to a sheaf of papers on his desk.

The interview was over.

Burke accepted the promotion, smiled gracefully at the good wishes showered on her, met her HRT crew and bonded with them.

The line ahead cleared and she jammed the pedal before any other vehicle rushed into the gap.

Finally.

She circled the Presidential View Hotel twice, frowning heavily, when she saw the entrance to the parking lot was closed.

In fact the hotel's grand entrance itself was shut. Something she hadn't seen before.

She parked illegally, near a fire hydrant, placed her FBI card on the dash and exited. It wouldn't save her from a ticket – meter maids ruled the world -- but she could try.

She approached the hotel and tried the door. It didn't yield.

She searched for a buzzer. There wasn't one.

Such hotels didn't have buzzers. They had doormen.

The doorman was absent. In fact there was not a single person in front of, or around the hotel.

She called out, feeling foolish.

No one responded.

She looked to her left, to her right, and stepped gingerly onto the neat lawn to her left and approached a large window.

It was curtained and she couldn't see through it.

She banged on it.

Nada.

Frustrated, she pulled out her phone and called Mark Kowalski. Kowalski was in her investigative crew. He was her mentee. He was bright. He was sharp. He had an irreverent sense of humor.

'Yo, boss. You need the traffic cleared?'

She gritted her teeth. 'I need the number of the Presidential View Hotel.'

Something in her voice stopped him from further banter.

She heard keys clicking. He recited a number a second later.

She tried the number.

It was dead.

Her radar started tingling.

If she strained her neck, she knew she would see the flag on that white building in the immediate distance.

A hotel as prominently located as this didn't shut down in the middle of the tourist season.

She continued left, round the hotel, as far as she could go. No clues.

She crossed the entrance path and went to the right.

More large windows. More drapes.

She banged them again.

She peered through one window.

She saw her own reflection.

She went to the next, and then the third.

She jumped back, startled, when she saw the face.

It was a woman's face.

It was tear streaked. Her lips were moving, but Burke couldn't hear through the thick glass.

She recognized the expression on her face, though.

It was one she had seen thousands of times.

It was blind panic.

Her phone appeared in her hand as if my magic.

Kowalski's number came up.

'Hostages at the Presidential View Hotel.'

'Roll out the HRT.'

Chapter 4

Twenty-five minutes had passed since Bear and Roger had taken out the hostile on the first floor.

The airwaves were clear. No one had spoken over the dead men's ear pieces.

Twenty minutes left.

Bear and Roger upped their speed without conscious thought.

The second floor was empty.

So was the third.

A gunman was climbing down when they turned a corner.

This one was more alert.

His eyes sharpened. The momentary puzzlement in his eyes fled when he didn't recognize them.

His AR-15 rose smoothly.

His finger curled and depressed the trigger.

It slackened and the rifle slipped when Bear's throw buried a dinner knife in his throat.

Roger grabbed him, before he could fall, ripped the headset from his face, and stuffed a wad of cloth in his mouth.

He hunched down to question him, but it was too late.

Bear's knife had been straight and true.

They picked him up, went back to the previous floor and dumped him in a service closet.

'One more down,' Roger whispered in his mic.

It was the movement in the air that alerted Zeb first.

Particles danced and vibrated.

Sound then followed.

A chopper.

He was still cramped in his hide in the men's restroom.

The plan was for Bear and Roger to clear the upper floors and return to the central lobby.

The two of them, along with Zeb and Bwana would then take on the gunmen in the central lobby.

It wasn't much of a plan.

It was the only one they had.

The sound grew louder, and then other sounds drowned it out.

Sirens.

'The cavalry has arrived,' Beth and Broker said simultaneously.

'What's happening? Keep talking.'

Zeb made a snap decision.

The arrival of the police would distract the gunmen, however briefly.

He looked down one last time through the pinhole, slid back the tile he was on, and jumped down.

One second to allow circulation to return.

Another second to cautiously open the door and survey the hallway.

It was empty. It wasn't quiet.

It felt like a crowd had gathered outside the hotel.

He heard bullhorns. He couldn't make out words.

The hotel seemed to tremble in anticipation.

'Three men left with us. Everyone else in the central lobby. Restaurant locked from inside.' Beth. Sharp, short sentences.

'One man to the right, watching the men and women, another to the left, watching the teenagers' groups, the third at the door.'

'Can you take them out?'

A louder voice came from outside.

Meghan's voice came, breathless. 'Yeah, we can. The three were distracted for a second. I ran across the room and joined the younger women. Chloe and Beth have edged closer to the door. Broker is not far from the third gunman.'

'Attack only when they are distracted. Don't approach them. Use a chair, plate, dinner knife, whatever is at hand. Hurl those at them. Plan what you're going to use. Memorize the steps. And then execute.' Zeb warned them.

'Yeah, got it. We've been through this before, Zeb,' Meghan replied softly, impatiently.

They had. There had been a couple of missions where they had overpowered their attackers in precisely the same manner. They perfected their moves during training with SEAL teams, Delta teams, and other elite special forces groups.

Zeb knew his crew were ready.

He also knew they didn't need to be told of the danger.

Taking on experienced gunmen, while unarmed, usually ended badly.

But his crew weren't usual.

'We can take them out. Give us the word. Quit acting like

an old woman.' Chloe's voice was tinged with humor.

'Bwana, you ready?'

'Bro, just give me the word.'

'Roger?'

'Got that. We're approaching the fourth.'

A voice came over the gunmen's headsets and with that, events changed.

'Prepare for evac. Round up all the residents. Send them down.'

Bear, Roger, and Bwana heard acknowledging grunts in their headsets They grunted in unison.

Bear relayed the order over their headsets.

They digested it for a second, then Beth continued her commentary. 'They're bunching us together.'

'We still have our positions. These three guys look uneasy. But still competent.'

Roger queried. 'Zeb, what do we do with that order?'

Perhaps the plan is to flood the ground floor with residents. Use numbers to negotiate. Or even a mass execution on live TV and then start with their demands.

'Move people down, from the fourth to the first. Seal them inside the first floor. Ask them to use the stairs. Those who can't walk, ask them to stay in their rooms.'

Another thought came to him.

'Bear, Roger, one of you go to the fifth floor. Seal that door so that no one can enter or exit.'

'Won't the dudes then know something's wrong?'

'They'll find out sooner or later. We've to prevent the higher-up gunmen from entering the fifth.'

'What about the residents on the higher floors?'

'Summon all the elevators to the fourth. Jam them open.'

'Gotcha.'

Roger looked at Bear critically, at his beard, his bushy brows and his thick, unruly hair.

'I'll go to the rooms,' he declared. 'Looks matter. They'll take you for a thug. We don't want any elderly people having a stroke from seeing you.'

Bear grinned silently in acknowledgement.

Fifteen rooms on the floor.

He called the elevators and when they arrived, used fire

extinguishers to rig them to stay open.

He then sprinted down the hallway, knocked on each door and when heads popped out, he used his command voice.

'Listen up, folks. I'm the good guy. We're dealing with those gunmen. However, for your safety, you need to move downstairs. To the first floor.'

A babble of voices broke out. Someone cried out in relief.

Roger silenced them with a raised hand.

'We've no time to discuss this. Those who can't move, please stay in your rooms and emerge only when the cops announce themselves. The rest of you, move, NOW!'

They moved. In twos and threes initially, and then in a bunch, tightly packed.

Roger opened the service door for them, took them down the stairs.

Bear brought the rear up.

'We're heading down.'

'They have bunched us close to the door now. No gunmen behind us. Not that there is anywhere to go. Two at each side, one near the door,' Chloe briefed them.

Burke swung toward Bubba, the improbably named head of the HRT.

He read her expression. 'No one's responding.'

His team was in position. Snipers on rooftops, armed men crouching behind cover, a smaller team ready to penetrate, yet another team in the chopper, ready to abseil.

But they needed a *go*.

A Go could not be given without some kind of response from inside.

'We've deployed Doppler radar, thermal imagers, some fancy see-through tech. We know where the bandits are.'

'A bunch of armed men in the central lobby. Five of them. Three in the restaurant. One opposite the conference room. Two on the seventh. One on the rooftop. One in the basement. There could be more. Tech isn't perfect.'

'Hostages in the restaurant, in the conference room, in the guest rooms. Hostages all over.'

He ran his hand over his bristly hair and turned when a team member ran up.

'There's movement.'

Burke joined them and huddled over the screen.

A mass of people, orange, green, and yellow blobs, were moving slowly.

'That's a feed from a chopper at the back. I reckon that's a stairwell.'

He pointed at two shapes. They held something long and angular in their hands.

'Guns. One gunman at the front. One at the rear.'

'Why are they bunching them together?'

Bubba didn't answer her directly. 'If we have to breach, it has to be now, before they come to the ground floor.'

'How will you do it?'

'Snipers will take out any possible bandit. A team will blow open the front door, but that's a decoy. Teams from the top and rear will be the main attacking force.'

'It'll be messy.'

'Yes, ma'am.'

Burke held off giving the Go. There was no way they could breach without civilian casualties.

The gunmen hadn't made demands. They didn't seem to have killed any hostages yet.

There was still time. Possibly.

There was no time.

Bwana, still in his closet, heard a voice call out.

The voice repeated again, impatiently. He inched the door open.

The voice was calling for Borra.

'Zeb, someone's calling for Borra.'

He didn't have to explain anything more. Things would come to a head soon.

Zeb positioned himself behind the restroom door.

He wouldn't be in the line of sight of anyone who opened it.

'Bear, Roger, where are you.'

'Nearly there. Hostages are on the first. We've sealed it.'

He heard a clatter and a curse.

'We're on the bottom landing.'

'Borra? Where are you?'

The voice yelled. Footsteps came near.

'Borra?'

A gunman came in front of the crack, looked around, poked his head inside the conference room and withdrew it quickly.

'Borra's not here.' He yelled in his headset.

A silence.

'EVAC, NOW!'

'Go!'

Zeb burst out of the restroom, Glock ready, Glock searching.

Bwana flung open the closet, a panther leaping for the kill.

The gunman caught the flicker of motion.

He turned.

He went down, when Bwana felled him with a single blow to the head.

A fraction of a second to check he would no longer be a threat. Another fraction to grab his AR-15 and sling it over his shoulder.

Bwana moved forward, hugging the left wall.

Bear and Roger burst through the swinging doors, uncaring about the noise.

Noise was good. Noise was shock. Shock was their friend.

They fanned out, their assault rifles covering the hallway.

They spotted Zeb.

He spotted them.

He gestured them forward.

'BREACH, NOW!'

The voice came over the gunmen's headsets.

A split second of silence.

An explosion rocked the hotel.

Chapter 5

A second series of explosions followed. Light, sound, and smoke drowned their senses.

The gunmen in the restaurant flung open the doors.

They shot in the air.

'OUT. MOVE.'

The hostages moved, screaming, panicking, toward the open outlet that promised escape.

They were directed by bursts in the air.

They were guided expertly to the breached entrance of the hotel.

Another blast sounded.

Smoke, thick smoke filled the central lobby.

The lights went out. Rifles chattered.

The screaming became a roar.

The hostages stampeded.

Smoke grenades.

Zeb dropped to the ground, squinting, trying to see through the dense darkness.

He felt movement beside him. Bwana, Roger, and Bear.

He crawled forward swiftly, reached the opening of the central lobby.

A swift glance.

It was empty.

He wiped his streaming eyes and looked again.

It remained empty.

'Broker? Meghan, Beth? Chloe, Clare?'

His voice was flat, cold.

There was no response.

The crowd was thick around the front of the hotel.

Hostages milling around, trying to get through, shouting, swearing, screaming, crying.

One body was indistinguishable from another.

Male and female looked the same from where they were.

He couldn't see any bandits, any raised guns.

'Chloe?' Bear called out, urgency in his voice.

'We're here,' she shouted in their ears.

Bear sagged imperceptibly.

Bwana gripped his shoulder for a moment.

Their crew was safe.

'We're in the thick of the crowd.' Clare's voice was raised over the commotion. It was still calm.

Someone moved.

Zeb turned, saw Bwana run down the hallway, rip the shirt off the dead gunman and return.

He tore strips, handed one to the each of them.

They fashioned bandanas, spread out and checked the central lobby.

It didn't have a living person.

The restaurant had the bodies of the hostages.

The kitchen was clear.

The crowd around the entrance was thinning.

Searchlights pierced through the smoke.

The bullhorn came back.

Red beams cut through, seeking, searching.

Zeb flung his gun away.

His crew followed suit.

They raised their hands in the air and waited.

'What the–'

Sarah Burke took cover when the blast sounded. The explosion rocked the vehicle she was behind.

She looked at Bubba.

'Did you– '

'Not us,' Bubba interrupted her. 'Hold on. Let me get a sitrep.'

Burke peeked over the vehicle she was behind, ducked again, when another set of explosions sounded.

An agent darted to her and handed her an armored vest. She nodded her head gratefully and donned it.

Her hands stilled when she heard the shooting and the screaming.

She glanced up and froze momentarily at the sight of the hostages flooding through the hotel.

'Bubba, what's happening? Who's shooting?'

She rapped out another order. 'Kowalski, guide them, count them, take their details. Get medics to attend to them.'

'On it.'

'Bubba, what's up? There was firing.' Her voice was strained. She didn't care.

'The breach was from inside. The shots were from there too. These folks are hostages from the restaurant. The rest of the hotel's residents are still inside.'

Bubba chewed furiously on gum, his eyes flicking between the hotel, a screen in his hand, one hand cupping a headset.

'They detonated smoke grenades. We're trying to get more details. We have lost *eyes*.'

'These hostages are too tightly packed to distinguish bandits from good guys.'

He waited for a lull in the shouting. 'I figure they shot a few hostages.'

'Or fired above their heads to start a stampede. The gunmen could still be inside. They could also be among this lot of hostages.'

'Kowalski, you heard that?'

'Yeah.' A laconic reply.

Her crew had dealt with hostage situations before. 'Some of Bubba's men are with me. Our crew is here. Medics are on hand. The cops are here as well, lots of them. We've got enough manpower and firepower. If they're in this bunch, we'll get them.'

Her phone rang. The director. She took his call, briefed him with whatever she knew, which wasn't much.

Pierce called. She briefed him too.

She set up a communication channel, assigned a team member to manage it, broke away when Bubba signaled her.

'I've some good news. A sniper took out a gunman on the roof. Two more on the seventh floor have surrendered. They made contact using a guest's phone.'

'Smoke's clearing. We are getting sight back now. You'll like this.'

Burke waited.

'Four bandits are on the ground floor. In the central lobby. They have surrendered. They're hands are raised. They're waiting.'

Burke closed her eyes in relief.

They snapped open suddenly.

'It could be a decoy.'

Bubba nodded. 'Figured that way. We've got the hostages surrounded. We're moving them in single lines, taking their details.'

'There are more hostages in the hotel, on the upper floors.

My teams have gone in.'

Burke saw men rappelling from a chopper on the roof.

Bubba followed her gaze. 'More teams have breached from the rear.'

Burke nodded, turned to look behind her.

The street was thick with people and vehicles.

Spectators drawn in by the live action being played out. Media vultures in their vans. Both sides of Sixteenth Street were jammed as far back as the eye could see.

Choppers circled the air, most of them police and FBI, but there were media birds up there too.

She ran a palm over her forehead. It came away damp.

'Kowalski,' she barked. 'You got crowd control in place?'

'Yeah. D.C. cops have that well in hand.'

'What about air control? We don't want those birds running into one another.'

'That too.' Kowalski got back. 'It wouldn't be bad though, if those media birds tangled.'

A commotion caught her eye. A group of hostages milling around a cop. Gesticulating, arguing.

'What's happening there?'

Kowalski ran toward the scene.

A bullhorn came on, dragging her attention back to the hotel.

Bubba, ordering the men in the hotel to walk out slowly.

He moved to get a better line of vision, spoke in his headset. 'You got them in your sights?'

He nodded unconsciously at the reply. 'Shoot them in the legs if they make a wrong move.'

His voice sharpened. 'What's that? Seventh is secure? Great. Sweep each floor.'

He listened for a long while and then nodded. 'Keep checking.'

His face was grim, his jaw hard.

'What?'

'We found bodies. Both hostages and gunmen.'

Before Burke could reply, the gunmen from inside the hotel, appeared.

They were masked, strips of cloth crudely covering their face.

Four of them.

A surge of electricity went through everyone.

The crowd seemed to move forward involuntarily.

The four men were surrounded by cops and disappeared from her view.

Burke motioned for Kowalski to join her, skirted FBI agents, vehicles, cops, and neared the four hostiles.

They were standing in the cover of an armored FBI vehicle, away from the gaze of prying eyes and cameras.

Their ease struck her.

There were guns pointing at them. Their faces had been captured by the world's media, even if they were masked. D.C. cops and FBI agents surrounded them, but the four men stood casually, their hands still in the air.

Three men visible. The fourth is behind that giant.

The giant was a black man with close cropped hair, muscles bulging beneath the top he wore. Next to him was an equally tall man, thickly bearded, with the same kind of muscular build.

Standing behind, yet visible, was the third man, probably an inch shorter, leaner, but with the same tightly coiled physique her HRT crew had.

He's smiling behind the mask. His eyes are amused, she noticed with a slight start.

She turned around to make sure they were hidden from cameras and reporters.

They were.

'We got the other gunmen too. The hotel's secure. Residents are being checked.' Bubba spoke in her ear.

A cheer went up from the watching crowd as the news spread.

Sarah Burke ignored them.

There was something about these gunmen that niggled at her.

'Remove your masks.' She used her interrogator's voice.

Something flickered at the edges of her vision. A shout.

She half turned and watched a tall man approach at a run. He was the same height as the third captive, older, and good looking.

Great looking, she corrected herself absently.

From behind the man, two women became visible.

Similar features. Similar hair.

Twins?

That niggle became persistent.

Yet another woman joined the running contingent.

A fourth emerged, a couple of feet behind the man in the lead.

The fourth woman wasn't running.

She was grey-eyed and moved with an invisible force field that made the FBI agents and cops fall away.

Sarah Burke stared at her dumbly for a moment. Kowalski gasped.

She whirled to face the captives.

The fourth man had come up from behind and when she saw him, she felt as if she had been punched in the stomach.

He had removed his mask and stood lightly on his feet, his brown hair shifting slightly in the light breeze.

His hands were still raised, he was unarmed, but Burke still felt the coiled beast in him.

She knew him.

Zeb Carter.

'You?' She blurted stupidly.

Before he could reply, the grey-eyed woman reached her. Burke knew her as Clare, didn't know anything else about her except that when she spoke, her director listened.

'Stand them down.' Her voice was soft, audible only to Burke and Kowalski, but there was no mistaking the steel in it.

'Stand down. They're our guys.' Burke ordered her agents. Kowalski relayed the instructions to the cops.

'You are releasing them?' Bubba couldn't contain his disbelief over the airwaves.

'Yeah, I know them. They are the good guys. I'll explain later.'

Her agents lowered their guns, but the D.C. cops still trained theirs on Carter and his crew.

His crew. Who else could they be? Who else would have that indifferent air of silent menace?

Clare finally asked for a phone and made a call when Kowalski gave her his.

'Did you get them? They make any demands?'

A call came in before Burke could reply.

She turned her head away when one of her agents spoke in her earpiece, listened quietly, her face tightening, her body straightening.

'Are you sure?'

'Yeah. It isn't looking good. The usual politics of inter-agency finger pointing has started, but luckily, we weren't responsible for it.'

'Any others?'

'We're still tallying that up. It's a madhouse, out here.'

Burke, gazing at the scene, agreed.

There were close to a thousand people packing in a tight square on Sixteenth Street. Hostages, cops, FBI agents, medics, Secret Service – they had turned up too. Choppers flying low, bullhorns going off every now and then.

On top of that were the media scrum and the spectators, held back by a cordon of police, but loud and vociferous with their demands.

'You know what to do. Double check and come back to me.'

'Yeah.'

She ended the call, jerked her head to a vehicle which was outfitted as an office and strode toward it.

Carter and his team followed her.

She crossed her arms, leaned against a desk and glared at Carter, once Kowalski had shut the door.

'Care to tell me what's going on?'

Carter told her in brief sentences, not a word wasted. His top was matted with sweat, his face had smudges, but his voice was low, strong.

Burke flicked her eyes to his crew, looked at Kowalski, who nodded and produced a jug of water and plastic glasses.

He passed them around.

Burke used the momentary silence to summon Bubba. 'You should hear this.'

Bubba arrived a few minutes later, an air of reserve around him; not disbelieving Burke that these guys were the knights, but not believing her either.

He joined Burke and Kowalski and took his first good look at the *hostages*.

He had barely settled his backside against the desk when he sprang off.

'Bwana?'

The black man cracked a smile. 'Came close to being *the late Bwana*.'

The two men hugged, thumped each other on the back and when Bubba returned, he explained. 'That mountain trains with us occasionally. He's never said who he works for, but you're right. He's one of us.'

Burke nodded, not understanding, and swivelled to Carter. No explanations came from him.

As if he has ever explained anything, she thought sourly.

Carter ran through everything again, this time to pin drop silence, and when he had finished, Bubba nodded.

'There were eighteen gunmen in all. Your tally of those dead matches what my teams found. We found the bodies of the hostages, in the same places you mentioned.'

'On top of that, we found five dead gunmen in the office behind the reception.'

Carter looked at his men. They shook their heads.

'It wasn't us.'

'Didn't think it was. I'm guessing they were shot by their own men.'

Zeb looked at the FBI agents. There was something in their posture. Something that didn't look right.

Broker couldn't hold back any longer. He voiced what was on top of their minds. 'Did you get them?'

Burke's shoulders dropped imperceptibly.

'We got three, who surrendered. They are the only ones we have in custody.'

Her lips thinned. 'We have reports of five cops helping the hostages, directing them.'

Of course. He waited for her to speak, knowing where this was going.

Beth came to the front and glared angrily at the FBI agents. 'Only they weren't cops, were they?'

'No. They disappeared in the confusion. We have raised an alert, every cop is on the lookout.'

'You don't have any descriptions however, and with all that's going on out there,' Beth waved a hand, 'you don't know how they escaped.'

Burke inclined her head.

'Have they made any demands? Are all hostages accounted for?'

'No demands were made. In fact they didn't make any contact at all. We are tallying the hostages up, still.' An expression flitted over her face and disappeared just as fast.

She briefed them on how she had discovered the hostage

situation. 'We are the lead agency on this, but will work with the D.C. cops and other investigative agencies.'

'Our role—' Zeb began.

'Will be covered up,' Burke interjected. 'Luckily your faces were covered and your team were part of the hostages. We will have to explain the four of you, however. The media pressure on this will be hyper.'

'Give them the truth. As near as you can,' Clare's eyes were amused. 'That these four were do-gooders, who saw an opportunity to take down the hostages. They were army buddies who happened to be dining in the restaurant when the take-down happened.'

Burke frowned. 'The vultures will want to know their details. Who they are, where they are from, where they served. With respect, ma'am, this is the biggest story on the planet for the media. A hostage situation minutes from the White House. Ex-army guys trying to take out the gunmen. They'll lap it up and want more. Much more.'

'Leave that to me.' Clare smiled briefly.

Bubba frowned as he looked at the two women. 'You can do that? Just who are you, ma'am, and who are these guys?'

He looked accusingly at Bwana. 'You left a lot untold, buddy.'

Clare's smile became a laugh. 'Ask Pat.'

Kowalski took pity on Bubba. 'We came across Clare and Mr. Carter on a previous investigation. That feeling of frustration you feel? We've both felt it.'

'And if you find out anything about them, please tell us, Bubba, because we don't have a fricking clue,' Kowalski said drily.

Conversation died down as they waited for Burke to finish a call.

She straightened, asked a question, answered in syllables and when she faced them, Zeb knew.

This is it. This was the gunmen's game plan all along.

Burke's face was pale. She moistened her lips and at the second attempt, words flowed.

'They have got the Veep's son.'

Chapter 6

'How did this happen?' Deputy Director Bob Pierce asked for the umpteenth time, his face red, his voice raw with anger.

No one replied to him. Pierce was venting. Replies weren't required.

They were gathered in a large conference room in the FBI's Hoover Building. FBI, NSA, Metropolitan Police, several other agencies, were gathered in it. Clare sat quietly at the table, behind her ranged Zeb, Broker and the others.

The meeting was chaired by Sarah Burke and had been immediately convened after confirmation that James Barlow, fifteen-year-old son, the only child, of Vice President Terry Barlow, was missing.

He was not the only hostage unaccounted for.

Along with him was Shawn Fairman, his close friend and school classmate, of the same age.

All other hostages were accounted for, as were the hotel staff.

The hotel had four hundred and eighty people including staff, residents, visitors, and restaurant customers. Eighteen hostiles took the total to four hundred and ninety-eight.

Four hundred and ninety-one were accounted for.

Burke had swung into immediate action. She had arranged for photographs of the two boys to be circulated to all law enforcement authorities.

Electronic sketches of the gunmen were circulated; created after a hasty briefing with Zeb's team and other hostages.

Dulles and Ronald Reagan airports as well as all other airfields, in and around Washington D.C. were locked down.

Bus terminals, taxi companies, and car rental agencies were shut too.

Checkpoints were set up in the city to slow down and inspect traffic.

So far, there were no reports of the seven.

The inevitable turf wars for lead agency status ensued but were put out swiftly by Director Murphy.

Kidnapping was a Federal crime. This was no ordinary kidnapping.

The FBI would lead the investigation, Burke the point person.

After furious consultations with various agencies and a hushed call with the White House, Director Pat Murphy had arranged a press conference and had gone public with the news.

The media went into frenzy. It became furious. It turned hostile.

The highest profile kidnapping in the history of the country. A siege, explosions and gunfights, a stone's throw from the White House. All this, and the FBI didn't have much to go on.

The Secret Service was criticized.

How was it that James Barlow and his friend were unaccompanied?

How was it that their whereabouts weren't known to anyone?

Murphy explained that the kidnappers had used mobile jammers. That Barlow had evaded his protection team.

His emails and text messages revealed that he and his friend had planned this for a while.

James Barlow had wanted to spend some *normal* time.

The media was sympathetic to the Second Family, but was ruthless toward the law enforcement agencies.

It ripped, chewed, tore, and raged at Director Murphy.

Director Murphy received his bruising with equanimity. It came with the territory

He knew the Secret Service would be investigated. James Barlow's protection detail was already suspended, pending an investigation.

His own agency, the Metropolitan Police, other law enforcement agencies, would be held to account.

All that would happen in the background.

Finding the missing boys was the immediate focus.

In less than an hour after the press conference, every household in the country, every person owning a cell phone, knew what Barlow, Fairman, and the kidnappers looked like.

Hotlines were set up to deal with the calls, most of them crank calls.

Sarah Burke was given unlimited manpower and resources. The three gunmen who had surrendered were led away for interrogation. So far, they hadn't spoken.

The ten dead gunmen were being identified. They were photographed, printed, DNA sampled. Those details would be fed into supercomputers.

Fingerprints would be cross-matched for verification..

Burke didn't hold out much hope. This was a smoothly executed kidnapping. Glasses – they adopted the nickname Zeb's crew had given – wouldn't have used those with a record.

A red-faced reporter asked about motives.

The investigation had just started. All motives were being investigated, however, kidnapping seemed to be the apparent one.

Burke was calm under pressure. Composed under hostile questioning.

Zeb watched her sum up, answer questions, assign tasks, handle those senior to her, with ease.

He knew she felt she had been wrongly promoted.

He also knew she deserved it.

If there was anyone in the FBI who could find the boys, it was Special Agent in Charge, Sarah Burke.

She, Bubba, and her agents had made him reconstruct the events. They had interviewed him and his crew, individually, and then jointly. The Metropolitan police had interrogated them.

Their stories matched.

The hotel's guests were questioned.

Their accounts matched those of Zeb's team.

Their guns were taken; the rounds in the dead gunmen were compared.

Match.

Their earpieces were investigated. Their origins were questioned.

'Just who are you?' More than one interrogator yelled at them.

Zeb stonewalled them.

Clare and Pat Murphy ensured their anonymity remained. No record of their presence, no trace of their names, would exist.

Murphy had squeezed his shoulder once; there was history and deep friendship between the two of them. Murphy, alone in the FBI, knew of the Agency, and Clare and Zeb's role in it.

Murphy didn't thank him for helping out; there was time for that once the boys had been found.

Zeb watched the proceedings for another half an hour and then leaned forward to whisper at Clare.

She nodded. They could leave. This wasn't Agency business.

Zeb rose, caught Director Murphy and Sarah Burke's eyes, nodded at them and left through a side door, his team trailing behind.

They exited Hoover Building through a service exit and hailed a couple of cabs.

Bear, Chloe, Bwana, and Roger in one, the rest in another.

A couple of men shouted and ran toward Bwana just as he was ducking into his.

They wore suits, carried briefcases, and were hard eyed.

'Buddy, we hailed that cab before you. It was stopping for us, not you!'

Bwana looked at the driver, who shrugged.

Bear climbed out. Chloe and Roger followed, and the suits entered the cab.

The second man turned to Bwana. 'You got to learn manners in this town, boy.'

Boy.

Bwana didn't speak. He didn't move. He looked at suited man for a long while, felt a presence behind him and stepped back.

Gone was Roger's smiling visage. In its stead was a cold-eyed man, angles and edges on his face.

He bent close to the suit.

'Leave, before you get hurt.'

Suit slammed the door shut with a yelp and the cab moved away.

They got another cab and headed to their hotel, which was on Pennsylvania Avenue, a few minutes' walk from the White House.

They gathered in Zeb's room somberly. The twins flopped on the bed and turned on the TV.

No one spoke.

Broker sprawled on a couch. Chloe perched on a settee next to Bear, while Roger and Bwana parked their behinds on window sills.

Their eyes were drawn to the rolling coverage on the television.

The Presidential View Hotel was mobbed by camera crew and onlookers. Reporters were interviewing residents and hotel staff. Choppers still circled the air.

The residents on the fourth floor described two men who had directed them to the first. Mystery surrounded these two men. No one knew who they were. The FBI or the cops had no answers.

The FBI had put out a story that they were likely to be do-gooders and had requested the men to identify themselves, to help the investigation.

No one had come forward.

'We should have killed them all. We should have gotten to the central lobby sooner and taken them out.' Bwana turned away from the screen and looked at each of them.

They didn't reply.

Broker made a call from the room phone. They needed equipment. New phones, earpieces, handguns.

'Gulfstream will be here in an hour.'

They owned the airplane, a gift from a grateful Saudi royal whose daughter they had rescued. The aircraft was piloted by two ex-servicemen whom they trusted.

Zeb allowed his team to wallow in self-recrimination for another half an hour and then strode to the refrigerator, drew out bottles of water, and handed one to each of them.

He took the remote from Beth and turned off the TV.

They looked at him.

'This isn't an Agency investigation. That doesn't mean we shouldn't look into it.'

'Status?' the voice barked.

'We've got them,' Glasses replied. He was used to the man's bark and abrupt manner.

The man at the other end of the call was the paymaster. He was entitled to his idiosyncrasies.

Glasses, who went by the name of Chip Merritt, walked into the kitchen of the house they were holed up in, filled a glass of water and drank deeply.

The house was in Lighthollow, a city of twenty thousand people in the state of Virginia. Merritt had researched various towns and cities before settling on that particular city and that house. It was two hours away from the capital city and about an hour away from Chantilly and Winchester.

Merritt liked drives of an hour. They were short enough to get from point A to point B; they weren't long enough for fatigue to set in, or mistakes to be made.

They had reached Lighthollow after a brief halt in another location, to change the appearance of their vehicle. That location was an hour away, too.

Lighthollow had a high percentage of transient population since it was close to a few large construction projects. A new big box store was going up an hour away and an office complex was being built on the other side of the city.

The house itself had neighbors on either side, but was private and had everything that he wanted.

'I should hope so; otherwise all this TV coverage is for nothing,' the voice replied sarcastically.

'You left a few bodies behind.'

'They won't be identified. They have no records.'

'So it's just the five of you?'

'Five and the two kids,' Merritt confirmed.

'How are they?'

'Not good. One of them has panicked. He's barely coherent. He keeps babbling, praying, begging us to let them go.'

'That's not unexpected. Hostages tend to behave in that manner.'

There was no humor in the voice. 'What about the other one?'

'The other one seems to have lost his memory. He doesn't remember his name. Nothing of what went down.'

'He's faking it,' the voice snorted.

'I *asked*,' Merritt emphasizes. 'He isn't.'

He recalled an earlier attack, in another place, in another country. 'It looks like a fugue. A fugue's a –'

'How do you know it's a fugue? Do you have medical experience?'

Merritt described the other event. He and his crew had gone after an entrepreneur in Brazil. They had gunned down his security detail and had manhandled him, only for the hostage to lose his memory temporarily.

'He didn't recover for a month. That operation was a failure.'

The paymaster cursed for a long while, uncaring that Merritt could hear.

He quieted down after a while and thought for a moment. 'That changes things. How secure are you there?'

'Very. We can hole up here for weeks.'

'Good. I'll find a doctor, someone who can be involved.'

Merritt went to the first floor and checked on his men. Two of them were standing guard outside two rooms. Two others were sleeping.

Both guards gave him thumbs-up. All was under control.

Merritt went downstairs. 'Don't. I know one doctor. I have used him in the past.'

The voice rose. 'He needs to be a specialist. The boy needs a psychiatrist.'

'Relax. I know one such guy.'

'He needs to be controlled.'

'He will be. He won't return alive.'

'Question the other boy too.'

'I will. Let them rest first and feel safe.'

The voice hung up abruptly. No 'good-byes,' no 'take-cares.'

Merritt was used to the voice. He didn't mind the abruptness. He preferred it to pointless verbosity.

Chip Merritt wasn't his real name.

He was born Dale Johnson, on a farm in Kansas, and had fled his home the day he turned eighteen.

He had joined the Army and had been immediately deployed to Iraq. There, he had developed a taste for killing.

His skills had gotten him into the Special Forces and saw him in various hotspots in the world. He then moved into the NSA and worked in a special ops group that took on missions only a handful had heard of.

He concealed his killing instincts from his team. It wasn't difficult. In the heat of battle, in special ops missions, a maimed body was easily explained.

Dale Johnson died in a mission in Iraq. A raging fire consumed his team's hide and attracted enemy fire.

Of the team of four, only one survived and made it back to

the States. The three team members were buried quietly, the way deep black agents were.

Johnson had faked his death. The fire, attributed to enemy insurgents, had been started by him. Johnson's body was an insurgent's body.

John took on the identity of Chip Merritt and ventured into the private sector.

He built a reputation, a legend, for solving problems for those who could afford his services. The problems almost always included extreme violence. Sometimes they involved killing.

The more jobs he completed successfully, the more Chip Merritt's legend grew. He advertised, initially, in the dark internet but after a period of time, he got clients by word of mouth and references.

Merritt didn't go through middle men. He had a strict policy of dealing with only the paymasters who also *had* to be the clients. No cut-outs. No brokers. No intermediaries.

There was a risk to that of course. His clients could finger him.

Merritt was no fool however. He had inhabited the dark world long enough to master his craft. He had enough smarts to mitigate those risks. He had killed a couple of clients who had the temerity to go against him.

He had killed them slowly and brutally, and had posted pictures and videos on the dark internet. It was a message for other potential clients.

More than fifty killings. Not one ping on the radar of any law enforcement agency in any country.

He worked with his four-man crew, and when necessary, hired more bodies from a close network of contacts. He usually killed all extra hires after a job. They were disposable. The less people who knew about him, the more successful he was.

The voice was the only client for whom he had executed several jobs. There was respect between the two and when the voice had come calling with the latest job, Merritt had leapt at it.

We kidnapped the Veep's son and his friend. Right from under the Secret Service's noses.

He chuckled in the silence of the house.

The voice had mentioned the probability of kidnaping a

high profile person, eighteen months back. He hadn't given more details, except that the victim could be a boy, and the grab could either be at home or at a hotel, or various public locations. He mentioned the grab had to be spectacular.

Merritt liked spectacular.

In that time, he put together the moving parts, recruited the various teams needed and trained for all eventualities.

The voice had then given another clue. There could be two boys.

Later, he gave the boys' details and asked Merritt to look into them.

Merritt looked. He broke down their lives, inhabited their online presence, came to know them better than even their parents, and reported back to the voice.

The security around the boys wasn't hard to overcome, despite the presence of the Secret Service. In a dummy run, he had even bugged their phones.

It was simple to pull off. A crowded restaurant. The boys at a table. The security detail at another. One of Merritt's men dressed as a waiter, another as a cleaner.

A hip against the table. Food, drinks, and phones spilling to the floor. The phones opened, the batteries slid out.

The cleancr rushed up. The security detail rose, and then subsided. Clumsy waiters weren't uncommon. The cleaner replaced the batteries with bugged ones.

The phones were returned. The waiter asked the boys to check the phones. The boys turned them on and inadvertently activated the bug.

The bugs went everywhere the boys went. Teenagers and their phones were never apart. Merritt heard everything that went on in their lives and homes

Merritt smirked. Everyone thought they had the best security, till the time they came up against Merritt.

Merritt could have grabbed the boys at any time. He planned for various scenarios and drilled his team till they could execute at short notice.

He then waited. The voice said the time wasn't right.

The hotel appointment came up in the boys' text messages. The boys said how they would escape the protection detail. It was an adventure, the kind of thrill, boys indulged in.

He informed the voice.

The voice came back.

It was a go.

The plan had worked flawlessly.

All my plans do.

He rinsed the glass in the sink, went to the study where he was joined by two men.

One of them sat in front of a laptop, opened a screen and typed a single command.

'It's time.'

Merritt couldn't contain his eagerness.

'Yeah, it's show time.'

Chapter 7

They got the call when Beth was narrating everything that she had seen at the hotel.

Zeb was making all of them run through the entire hostage taking again.

Repetition after intervals of time made recollection easier. Brought back small nuggets that had previously been forgotten.

The room's phone rang stilling Beth in mid flow.

No one but Clare knew where they were.

Zeb lifted it and straightened at the voice on the other end. 'We'll need gear,' he said finally.

He turned and saw expectant faces.

'James Barlow's phone was activated fifteen minutes back.'

They met Burke, her agents, and Bubba's crew at what looked like a dilapidated warehouse in Foggy Bottom.

Bubba silently handed them Kevlar vests and handguns.

'You are coming strictly as observers. You are the only folks who have seen the gunmen. Don't use those weapons. This is our show.'

'Sure.' Zeb adjusted his vest and gun and looked up when Burke approached.

Her face was expressionless, but he could see she was almost vibrating with nervous energy.

'You said they used jammers?'

Zeb nodded.

'Well, they seemed to have killed all your phones too, since not a single phone registered on the networks.'

Kowalski joined them, laptop in hand. 'Except for six phones.'

'Barlow's and Fairman's. An elderly couple's who were vacationing in the hotel. A couple of businessmen.'

Broker strapped his vest and helped Bwana. 'All in the same location?'

'Nope.' Kowalski opened the laptop and on its screen were four red dots.

'This is a program we have that grabs data from the network and extrapolates the phone signals.'

'Two phones are in Virginia. The couple's.'

'One phone is right here, in Georgetown. One of the businessmen. The second executive's phone is in Mechanicsville, Virginia.'

'Barlow's and Fairman's phones are in Maryland. In Baltimore.'

'None of the phones seem to be in use. We called them, messaged them. Nothing. Their batteries are back in them, but they are inactive. The networks show no traffic.'

They gathered around the screen and watched the red dots as if they could speak.

They didn't. The dots didn't move.

Burke jabbed at the screen with a manicured finger. 'The two executives' phones are in offices. The couple's phones are in another hotel. I've got teams checking them out.'

Broker blew out his breath. 'There's a problem.'

'Yeah, we know. They could be traps. Our men know it.' Bubba slapped his back, turned to his men. 'All right, mount up. We move fast. You know your roles.'

They left in a convoy of six SUVs, black, and fast, powered by souped-up engines.

Zeb and Broker were with Burke and Kowalski. The others had split and shared rides with the HRT members.

It's dark. More than eight hours since the rescue. Time enough for the bandits to have disappeared.

Yet here they seem to be.

'Where are the phones?' he asked Burke.

She didn't answer immediately. She replied to something, someone, on her headset and then turned to Zeb.

'It's a house. A family home. It was rented four months back. The tenants, a couple, work in D.C. We have checked them out. They are away, in Colorado.'

Broker rubbed his jaw absent-mindedly. His eyes had the faraway look they got when he was thinking furiously. 'The house is empty?'

'Yeah. Well, it was. Looks like it has occupants now.'

Zeb watched Massachusetts Avenue fall behind, then New York Avenue. Concrete hummed effortlessly beneath them, its faint resistance easily overcome by powerful motors.

'You need to get a feel for the place. Have surveillance, before we go in.'

'All in place. We have a six-man team checking the house out. It's a residential area, one of many whose sole purpose is to provide homes for commuters to D.C.'

She took another call, spoke briefly, and resumed when she had ended it. 'Small street, a dead-end. Ten homes on it. Our house is at the end of the street. It has a park at one end, a garage, parking space for two cars.'

She opened her screen and brought up a maps program.

One house opposite, another beside it, separated by a hundred feet.

Zeb pointed to the two neighboring houses. 'What about those?'

'D.C. office goers in both. One has a family of four, that's the one opposite. Mom and Dad drive to D.C. every day after dropping their kids at a local school. One child is six, a girl, the other is four, a boy.'

'The other house has a single resident. An IT geek who works for a tech company in downtown D.C.'

She forestalled his question. 'All of them have been checked out, in fact every resident on that street. All are clean.'

Excitement leaked from her voice. 'The surveillance team has drones, thermal imagers, all that fancy stuff. They report six bodies inside the house. Two of them match the build of Barlow and Fairman.'

'Weapons?'

'Looks like. A lot of them. There are angular shapes all over the house.'

'Cops?'

'State police are present, but are providing back-up only. They are discreetly hidden.'

They were on the Baltimore-Washington Parkway. Tires hummed, lights flashed when other vehicles fell behind. The inside of the vehicle was warm and smelled of leather and adrenaline.

Zeb fell silent. Broker didn't speak, beside him.

It didn't feel right to either of them.

The kidnappers went from being careful to careless. That doesn't happen. But this is the Feds' show.

They reached the neighborhood twenty minutes later, rolled up to the other vehicles which were parked in a lot by the side of a playing field.

Zeb saw a white-walled structure in the distance.

School.

Bubba handed them headsets, opened a screen and described the layout.

'You folks split up. I want some of you watching the rear of the house, the rest at the front. How you organize yourselves is up to you. Pete, Flynn?'

Two men approached.

Bubba introduced them.

'Pete will be with the team in front, Flynn with the other team. Observation only. Got it?'

Broker's lip quirked to retort. Zeb ordered him with his eyes to stay quiet. They nodded dutifully.

Bubba gave them NVGs and set off at a rapid trot.

'What's the plan?' Bwana asked as they followed the FBI agents.

'Two, three-man teams will penetrate from the front and the rear. One at the front, the decoy. The six men at the rear will do the hard work.'

'There will be snipers. Two at the front, two at the rear.'

Zeb pictured it in his mind.

Six bodies in a two-story house. Four bodies on the second story. Two of them in a room. Two others pacing randomly.

Two bodies below, on the ground floor.

'You'll attack without warning?' Bear, not even panting despite the rapid pace set by Bubba.

Bubba didn't reply. His was a member of an elite Hostage Rescue Team. They had taken down terrorists, kidnappers, badasses of all kinds.

They didn't discuss tactics with strangers, even if one of those strangers was known to them.

They filtered in the dark, passed houses through which sounds of dinner and TVs could be heard.

They reached their street, approached it from the cover of other homes.

The HRT teams split. The sniping teams took positions. Positions that Bubba had already identified.

One team was perched in a tree. Uncomfortable, but it would have to do.

The other team was on top of an abandoned shed. Both teams had a good view of the front and the back windows.

Zeb, Bwana, and Roger crouched next to Flynn, at the rear of the house. The rear had a backyard, which led to an open field. A playground.

Too quiet. Where are the dog walkers? The couples out for a stroll?

Bwana's eyes gleamed white in the dark. Zeb knew what he was thinking. Both Bwana and Roger shared his sentiments.

'This doesn't look right, Burke.'

'Only one way to find out, buddy,' Bubba replied, his voice cool, impersonal.

Far behind, about a thousand yards away, were another row of houses. All of them checked out by the state police, who were present in twos and threes between various houses, throughout the neighborhood.

A chorus of 'in position' came over their headsets.

At Bubba's command, the attack teams approached the house, from the front and the rear.

A man gave running commentary of what he could see on the screen. The screen had feeds from the drones and the imagers.

Two men at the rear unfolded a ladder silently and placed it against the wall.

'Go!'

The night burst into sound and noise.

The team at the front blasted the door.

One team at the back blew open the rear door. The second team scaled the ladder and approached the window, where the boys were.

The first shot got drowned in the ambient noise.

It found the agent approaching the window.

He fell.

Zeb whirled behind.

He heard the second pop. Faint and from far away.

A second agent fell.

'Window team down.' Zeb raised his voice over the bedlam of voices. 'Sniper behind us. He has sights on the door and windows. Bubba the other team should stay put. We'll try to get them out.'

'Don't breach,' he added. 'Repeat, don't breach.'

He ignored the rush of commands and orders, got a grasp

of their situation.

They were pinned down by one or more snipers. Two agents lay still, unmoving. The other two lay equally still, hugging the ground. They were alive. Zeb could see their headsets moving.

More pops and cracks came, many of them from the front of the house. The shots became a river.

'It's a trap!' someone screamed out the obvious.

Neighboring houses lit up. Zeb imagined heads popping out.

Burke, Bubba, or the state police should get them to stay inside.

A bullhorn came on just then, announcing just that.

Flynn rose, ignored the harsh whispers from Zeb and Roger, evaded their grasping hands, took a step forward, lurched and fell.

Bwana leapt, grabbed him before he could land, dragged him back.

A pop sounded. Something sang through the air above Bwana's bent body and impacted the wall.

Zeb half turned to see if he could detect any flash from the shooter.

He saw Bwana bring him back through the corner of his eyes.

He saw Bwana straighten after placing Flynn down.

Bwana jerked.

He fell.

Bwana!

He didn't know he was moving.

The next moment he and Roger, bending very low, had lifted Bwana, dragged him to the side, away from the sniper's apparent line of sight.

A curse left Roger. That was all the emotion he showed.

Bwana and he were like brothers, however, now wasn't the time for chest beating.

There was no cover. He and Roger lay low on the ground, Bwana and Flynn still, between them, bullets flying above them, seeking them.

Some rounds thudded into the walls of the house. A window broke somewhere.

He could hear more firing from the front.

He ignored it.

The playground didn't have cover.

The neighboring house could have hostiles.

However, the sniper seemed to shoot only at full height level.

'Third house.'

Roger nodded and bending over, lifted Flynn and ran awkwardly.

Zeb followed him, carrying Bwana as carefully as he could. He was heavy. He was a giant. Zeb would have run a marathon with him over his back, if necessary.

Roger hailed him from behind a dark structure.

It was a garage.

He ripped open Flynn's vest, examined him in the dim glow of a night flashlight.

'Flesh wound. Got him in the shoulder, above the vest. He passed out from the shock.'

Zeb wasn't listening.

He was looking at Bwana.

His eyes were open.

His forehead was bleeding.

He was smiling.

'It creased my head. A fraction to the side, and I would've joined my dad. I must have blacked out for a second, but I am fine.'

Zeb pressed him back when he tried to rise. He looked at the wound.

It *was* a crease. The round had slid past Bwana's left temple, taking away a small sliver of flesh.

The wound bled steadily, covered the right side of Bwana's face with blood.

Zeb patted his pockets, cursed silently at their lack of gear, removed his vest, ripped a strip of his shirt and bandaged Bwana.

The bleeding slowed. The rudimentary dressing darkened.

Zeb made no attempt to stop Bwana from rising. His friend knew his own body. If he could rise, he was good. Flesh wounds hadn't stopped him before. They wouldn't, this time.

Bwana touched the dressing gingerly with his fingers. They came away dark. 'Stings,' he replied at Zeb's look of askance.

He smiled in the dark. 'It should improve my looks.'

Roger snorted without looking away from the dressing he was applying to Flynn. 'Nothing will help you with that.'

The snort was a heartfelt sigh of relief. Bwana heard it and reached out silently with his fist. Roger bumped it and turned his attention back to Flynn.

They were done discussing the crease. It was behind them.

Zeb kneeled next to Roger and watched his hands move expertly, applying a pressure bandage fashioned from strips of his shirt.

'He's lost blood. He needs care. Immediately,' Roger murmured softly, worry showing in his eyes, when he looked at Zeb.

Zeb called it in.

'We are pinned down, Zeb, by snipers. On top of that we have a firefight with the shooters in the target house. We'll get to you as soon as we can. ' A clipped tone answered. Burke's.

'Krantz?' Bubba called out to the teams in the back.

Krantz answered hoarsely. 'Brody and Kirk have been shot. They are in bad shape. We don't have cover. We are on the ground, but so far no shots have reached us.'

'Hold tight, son. We'll get to you as soon as we can.'

Zeb cupped a hand around his watch. Just ten minutes had passed since the attempt to breach. It felt like hours.

Another voice drawled. 'Lieutenant Harvey here, from the State Police. We're approaching the street from the open end. We have got medics, and an ambulance. If you folks can get your injured to us, we can attend to them.'

A flurry of conversation followed. Harvey saying they could clear the sniper nests, the Feds insisting they could.

Burke cut through the turf war. 'Harvey, let us deal with this for now. Too many players will complicate matters. We have birds coming up. We will take them out. For now, please establish a perimeter around the area. These snipers aren't on suicide missions. They will try to escape.'

Bwana nodded approvingly. Sarah Burke had an excellent command of tactics.

Krantz came through again, hollow voiced. 'We just lost Brody and Kirk. Hefner and I have crawled to the side of the house. We're good for some time. There's nothing but a wall here. No chance of hostile fire.'

'Stay there, son. Don't come out in the front. Too much heat there.'

Bubba had lost two men. His voice was as if he was discussing the weather.

Good man.

Zeb tuned out and looked around. They had cover from the garage. Not a single round had come their way. However, the wounded man had to be attended to.

The FBI agents seemed to be pinned down. The state police weren't able to help.

He considered Bwana. The giant read his probing glance. 'I'm good. Honest.'

Roger joined Bwana and the two stood, like pillars rising from the earth. They bent and lifted Flynn gently, without a word from Zeb.

Zeb took their handguns, pocketed them, skirted them, and moved to the front.

Bwana and Roger wouldn't require their weapons; their hands were occupied.

Zeb would need them.

Flynn had to be taken to safety. The sniper nests at the front would need to be dealt with.

One man with three handguns against an unknown number of snipers.

The beast inside him woke up.

It was time to go hunting.

Chapter 8

Zeb peered behind the garage and saw a dark fence that ran along the backyard of the third house.

'Moving behind the third house.'

Burke acknowledged. Bubba grunted.

'We're waiting,' Harvey drawled.

'Don't shoot us. We're the good guys,' Roger chuckled. Facing sniper fire was no reason for one to lose a sense of humor.

No lights on the ground floor. Every other home is lit, but not this one.

Zeb held a hand up to pause Roger and Bwana, behind him.

The fence was a dark line ahead of him, to his right. To its left and right were large splotches of dark; the playground and the backyard.

'Bubba, Burke, which house are your snipers holed up in?' he asked urgently.

'The one next to our target for sure. There are a couple of snipers firing from a distance, behind us.' Burke's reply faded as if she had turned away, came back strongly a moment later. 'There's one more sniper whose location we haven't determined. One reason we asked the state troopers to stay back.'

'What about your drones?'

'Shot down. Thermal imagers are showing random bodies. There's an electromagnetic signal from within the house; it's playing havoc with our equipment.'

A couple of cracks sounded, shots were fired in return.

Zeb trained his NVGs on the house. He detected no movement, no bodies. The first floor was dark.

His beast was stirring. His radar was pinging. It was highly likely there were shooters in the house.

No other choice though.

He signaled Bwana and Roger to come through.

They ran, carrying Flynn between them.

Zeb ran with them, on their right, his body covering Flynn's.

The sniper would have to go through him before it reached Flynn.

They made it to the middle of the fence when the first bird came over them.

A searchlight turned on, swept on the playground, found them, and turned night into day.

'Burke, Bubba. It's got us in its light. Call it off.'

He turned to the house, thought he saw movement at a window.

It shattered and a round embedded in the ground behind them.

'We're under fire. Turn that light off,' Bwana growled.

The light turned off, the bird moved away.

More rounds came. Cracks that filled the night.

Zeb didn't tense his body. He was used to enemy fire. He ignored the shooter.

Crossing the fence and seeking the cover of the fourth house was important.

Nothing else mattered.

Fifteen feet remained.

Bwana picked the pace up. Zeb followed.

A last round tried to find them, and then they were behind a wall.

They didn't stop.

Zeb kept a watchful eye out for more hostiles.

He got a curious neighbor instead.

A portly man opened his backdoor cautiously and shone a flashlight on them.

'Get back,' Roger roared. 'Stay inside. We're with the FBI.'

The man stumbled back inside, shut his door and his house went dark.

Zeb searched in front of them. 'Harvey, where are you guys?'

Harvey guided them, behind the sixth house, where he stood flanked by several cops.

Medics grabbed Flynn, rushed him to a waiting ambulance and only then, Zeb relaxed momentarily.

The firefight had increased in intensity behind them.

Zeb turned his attention to his headset again. Bubba's men had entered the target house. They were engaged with the hostiles. All six of them.

'The boys were never here.' Harvey's lips were thin, tight,

his eyes bleak.

Zeb accepted a bottle of water from one of the cops with a nod of thanks. Drank deeply, wiped his mouth and jerked a shoulder at Bwana.

'Could your men have a look at him?'

Another set of medics surrounded Bwana and led him away despite his protests.

Roger made to follow him, hesitated, turned to Zeb.

'Go with him. You know how stubborn he can be.'

'You're going after that sniper?'

'Yeah. He has to be taken out.'

Harvey sent three of his men along with Zeb.

They had a hard, competent look.

'Stay outside. If he escapes, grab him.'

'You're going in alone?' One of them, Stuckey, asked.

'Yeah. We don't know what's inside. A family of five lives there.'

Maybe they are alive.

He went to the portly man's house after deploying Harvey's men to cut escape routes.

He opened the rear door hesitantly at Zeb's knock and command.

His eyes were fearful. They widened at his request, but he opened the door wider and let Zeb through.

'Yeah, there's a window facing that wall.' He guided Zeb through the house and to the window that he had seen on their run.

'Bob Scarrow's a good guy. We have been neighbors for a long time. I never figured him to be involved in a shootout with the cops.'

Zeb looked at him bemusedly for a moment and then the man's assumption dawned on him.

'Sir, we are sure Mr. Scarrow is not involved. It looks like he and his family are being held hostage.'

The man appeared relieved and disappeared once Zeb headed out of the window.

He landed lightly and surveyed the third house's wall. It didn't have any openings. Red bricked from top to bottom, now dark in the night, it was mostly a flat, even surface that rose from the ground, with occasional bricks protruding a bit in a pattern that was barely discernible.

The snipers wouldn't know of his presence at the wall.

They would be keeping an eye on the front and back. They would be on the second story. That offered them a prime shooting position.

However, they couldn't see what was happening beneath them, close to the walls of the house.

At least, that's what I hope.

Zeb peered around the back. The backyard was silent. Something sparkled on the mowed lawn.

Zeb squinted and then his brow cleared.

Splinters from the window, when one of them fired.

There was a rear door, three large windows at the bottom, two at the top.

The house was a box, one of thousands that had been constructed to feed the demands of the labor force.

The ground floor had the living room, kitchen, dining room, a storeroom, spare bedroom and a bathroom.

The second story had three bedrooms, a playroom, and a bathroom.

Two exits; one at the front and another at the rear. A garage that was connected to the house by a door in the store room.

They would alternate between the front and the back.

'Bubba, I'm going into the sniper's house.'

'It's all yours. We're busy here.'

'I need a favor.'

'Go on.'

'Shoot the front windows of sniper house, the ones on the bottom, at my command.'

'You heard that, Mike, Paul?'

Confirmations came back.

Zeb fell to the ground, crawled to the rear, reached the first window.

He risked a quick glance. A dining table. Chairs. Nothing else visible in the dark.

'Now!'

He heard the front windows break.

Simultaneously, he broke the rear glass with his handgun, surged through the opening, rolled to the far end continuously and crouched, gun extended.

Not an entry I would advocate.

The dining room was still. The ground floor felt empty.

He checked out the rooms rapidly. There were no occupants.

He waited for the movement again.

It felt like someone was pacing from the back to the front.

He went to the stairs and found it was blocked.

Chairs, tables, stools, and various small furniture was stacked on the steps. He couldn't go past them.

If he moved any piece, the entire lot would tumble down, alerting the shooter.

Bricks on the outside aren't even. They could offer footholds.

He went outside, and surveyed the wall.

Yes, footholds were an option.

He went behind the fourth house.

'Roger?'

'Yeah?

'How's Bwana?'

'Impatient.'

'I need you.'

Roger arrived six minutes later, at a run, his face smiling.

The smile turned to a grin when Zeb explained.

'I've heard some foolhardy plans from you, but that's the worst.'

'You got a better one?'

Roger thought and then shook his head.

'Let's do it then.'

Zeb tested a few footholds. He could climb easily and reach the window of one bedroom on the upper floor.

'On a count of five.'

Roger fist-bumped him and crawled through the window Zeb had smashed.

One.

Zeb leapt high and grabbed a jutting brick. His feet searched for and found footholds.

Two.

He took a step up.

Three.

Another inch up, within reaching distance of the window

Four.

He was just beneath the window. Gun ready. Body poised.

Five.

Roger grabbed random furniture on the staircase and pulled.

The entire lot came crashing down.

A startled shout from the upstairs. Feet rushed.

Simultaneously, Zeb powered himself up with his left hand.

He smashed through the window with his left shoulder, fell inside, rose to his feet in a liquid movement, his gun an extension of his arm.

Room's empty

He snapped a glance in the hallway.

A shadow was turning his way.

Light gleamed off metal.

Metal became a barrel.

Became a rifle.

It pointed at him

Someone screamed.

A man roared.

Zeb fired. Two shots that sounded like one, that punched the shooter back and felled him.

Someone moaned. A female voice.

A shadow appeared on top of the stairs.

Roger.

He fell in behind Zeb.

They checked out another bedroom, more rooms. Many windows were shattered.

Shooting from inside, through the windows, at the Feds.

They approached the last room.

Zeb lowered to floor level and looked.

Another hostile!

'I'll shoot all of them.' The gunman shouted.

He had a woman in front of him. She was gagged, her eyes wide and frightened. A handgun was jammed in her temple.

The room was lit, the drapes were down.

Four other bodies lay on the floor, tied and gagged, watching him helplessly.

'You take a step inside, I'll kill her.'

I know that accent.

Zeb took a step inside.

He raised his gun hand.

'I'll shoot her,' the man raged. His knuckles tightened.

'Don't. I'm putting my gun down.'

He moved deeper inside the room.

The shooter turned around to follow his body. The woman stayed tight to him.

Zeb lowered slowly, his hand going down to place the gun on the floor.

His eyes locked on the shooter's eyes.

Dark eyes. Dark hair. That accent.

Zeb's handgun was almost on the floor.

The gunman watched it.

Roger stepped in the room.

'How's it going?'

The gunman whirled, his mouth opening in a snarl.

His gun slipped from the woman's temple for a fraction of a second.

Zeb shot him.

The round tore a strip of flesh from the gunman's forehead.

The woman fell from his grasp.

Zeb shot him again, in the right shoulder.

A third shot went through his gun hand.

Zeb was on him before he could react, slamming him against the wall, disarming him, and laying him on the floor.

He tore strips from the gunman's clothing and secured him.

Roger went to the hostages and released them and stood back to give the family their time.

Zeb dragged the gunman away from the room, and down the staircase. Roger dumped the dead man in the backyard and joined Zeb in the dining room.

'Harvey? Third house is clear.'

'We are moving in. The FBI has cleared the target house. The snipers on the outside have been nullified.'

There was almost a smile in his voice. 'We got the sniper who shot Flynn and your friend. He was trying to get away. He fell right into our arms.'

'He gave up?'

'We had to convince him, gently. He's okay, but his face is disfigured, somewhat.

The mopping up took an hour and when completed, they met in Burke's vehicle. It was outfitted as a mobile office and could accommodate ten people.

Bubba, Burke, Kowalski faced Zeb, Roger, Bwana and Broker. Lieutenant Harvey thrust his head through a window. Broker, Bear, Chloe, and the twins listened from the outside.

No one spoke for moments.

Zeb finally broke the silence.

'We were played.'

Chapter 9

'How many hostiles were there?' he asked when Bubba or Burke didn't refute him.

'Six in the target house. Four snipers attacking us -- two from houses behind us, almost a thousand yards away, and the two you took down.' Burke wiped her face with a towel, hid behind it for a long moment before putting it down.

'You're forgetting the sniper at the back. The shooter who killed my men.' If voices were lethal, Bubba's voice would have killed that sniper.

Burke held a hand up, tiredly, in apology. Exhaustion lined her face. Anger and bitterness laced her voice.

'Eleven in all, of whom only three are still alive. One guy from the target house, the guy Carter captured, and the sniper Harvey's men nabbed.'

Bear, outside, changed his position against the vehicle. It rocked. The street had forgotten what dark looked like.

It was flooded with cops, FBI agents, ambulances, floodlights, and residents.

The neighborhood had never experienced a gunfight on the scale that had just occurred. Residents were shaken, many were excited, hundreds of mobile phones were working and social media statuses were being updated.

The state police had corralled the media a street away. However, they had choppers in the air, and it was one of their birds that had shown the searchlight on Zeb.

'Break it down for us. How did this,' Bwana waved a massive hand, 'happen?'

'Only one gunman is talking. The one Zeb captured.' Bubba sighed and took his time, choosing his words. The loss of his two men showed. Zeb knew there would be investigations and perhaps action against him.

He's a good guy. He didn't get much wrong tonight. He made a mental note to speak to Director Murphy.

He looked at Bubba, waiting for him to speak, and from the expression on the HRT leader's face, knew something momentous was coming.

'All but the snipers are a bunch of Muslim extremists. This was their war against us.'

Zeb heard the twins gasp. Roger didn't react. He had seen two of the gunmen, had heard one of them speak, and had drawn his conclusions.

Kowalski closed his eyes and leaned back. His lips moved but no words came.

ISIS.

Zeb knew that would be the first link that would spring to anyone's mind.

This kidnapping just became nuclear.

'Let's not make any assumptions,' Burke read their train of thought.

'This guy said he and his fellow gunmen, had no involvement in the kidnapping of the two boys.'

She briefly outlined what the shooter had spilled. They hadn't had time to question him thoroughly; nevertheless, he had told them a lot.

That he and his group were active on the darknet. They had been approached a year back to stage such a shootout.

Their contact set everything up for them. He gave them the location, arranged the logistics, the weapons, sent them the two phones, instructed them to turn them on at a specific time.

He told them how it would be played out by the FBI and the cops, and what they had to do.

Roger frowned. 'Don't these kinds of attacks have a pattern? The killers kill as many people as they can, and then either kill themselves or go down in a blaze of gunfire?'

'Those were their instructions.'

'They lost their nerve, however. I guess we should be thankful for that,' Bubba said heavily.

'He said all along they had just practiced shooting at targets. They couldn't kill the hostages in the house. They fired at our teams blindly, and when we asked them to surrender, were too scared to do so.'

'They accepted they would be killed in police fire.'

Zeb thought about it. Something didn't fit.

'So a bunch of amateur gunmen outwitted us?' Roger's Texas drawl echoed his thoughts.

'We were outwitted by this mastermind. Who these shooters never met. They just interacted with him over the internet. They had a few video calls, but he was always masked. They said he was American sounding. They couldn't place his accent.'

'Some dude approached them and they just believed him, did what he asked?'

'He made them jump through several hoops. Made them prove their commitment.'

'There was a hostage situation in New Jersey, some months back. A bunch of masked gunmen took over a convenience store, injured the owner, and escaped before the cops got there.'

Bwana frowned. 'Way I heard it, the store owner was a vet. He did some damage, which made them tuck their tails and run.'

Burke tucked an escaping tendril of hair behind her ear. 'Yeah, but those masked men were these guys. They also confessed to other hold-ups. They built confidence in the mastermind and then he gave them this job.'

'They didn't ask him to prove his credentials?'

'They did. He executed a cop on a live video stream.'

Chloe shoved Broker out of the way and thrust her head in. Her eyes were blazing in anger. 'He did what?'

'Trooper Jim Budgie of the New Jersey state police, based in Trenton, was abducted as he was getting into his cruiser. This was last year. You might recollect, there was a massive statewide and then nationwide hunt for him. He was never found.'

'Our mastermind proved his credentials by shooting him in the head, in front of these guys. He told them where the body would be found.'

Kowalski handed more bottles of water. 'They found Budgie's body buried in a landfill near the town of Edgeley, about eight miles from Trenton.

'Once they found the body, they needed no further convincing.'

'Where are these guys from?'

'Five of them are from New Jersey, three from Virginia. They met in online forums several years back, got together, became friends, started going to the same mosque every month. They nurtured this sick desire of theirs and then the mastermind came along.'

'They planned to join ISIS?'

A knock interrupted her. A trooper spoke briefly to Bubba and left when he nodded.

'Flynn will recover. A few weeks of rest and he will be good as new.' He held out a beefy hand to Bwana. They shook silently. None of them mentioned the two dead agents.

Zeb watched in silence, the uneasy feeling in him deepening.

He voiced it at last.

'That guy who downed Flynn and Bwana. Those were close to thousand-yard shots, in the dark. An amateur would have missed by a mile.'

Kowalski smiled in a night in which there wasn't much to smile about. 'We wondered if you would spot that.'

'Burke misled you at the beginning. Not all eleven were amateurs.'

'The three snipers were pros. Mercenaries. One of them was Colombian. He was the one behind the house and was captured by the state cops. The two at the front were South African. Only one of them is alive.'

'Thing is they were working to a different plan. They never met those Muslim extremists. All they knew was that there were a bunch of people inside the target house who they weren't to shoot.'

'Their job was to shoot law enforcement officers and get away. Obviously, they didn't succeed in that last part.'

This is way beyond smart. Two separate teams. No team knowing what the other is up to.

'How were they recruited?'

'He isn't talking.' He glanced at his watch. 'Not even an hour since we took back the house.'

'The lone survivor from the target house isn't either.' Bubba ran an impatient hand over his buzz cut. It rasped like a saw.

He held out a black box which had switches and dials on it. 'Seen something like this before?'

Broker reached out for it, glanced over it and passed it to the twins. 'That's an electromagnetic wave generator. You can set it to cycle through various frequencies and wavelengths. It will screw up most electronic equipment.'

Bubba nodded. 'Not the kind of equipment you can order on eBay. Their contact sent this box to them and told them to turn it on when we attacked.'

His face darkened. 'That dude, that contact; he was the puppet-master.'

No one disagreed with him.

They broke off a few minutes later.

Burke had to report to the director, Bubba had to take care of the dead agents. Procedures had to be followed, the captured men had to be transported to interrogation cells, the neighborhood had to be returned to the residents.

There was the media to deal with, on top of everything else.

Zeb watched Burke and Kowalski walk away. Three hundred odd million people in the country wished for her to succeed.

Those same people will be all too eager to criticize her. Today's operation won't help, though it wasn't her fault.

His people fanned out beside him, Broker at his shoulder.

'When's our gear arriving, Broker?'

'It's at the hotel. The pilots relayed a message to Kowalski.'

'Let's go.'

His crew seated themselves in a couple of vehicles. He boarded last, throwing a last glance at Burke.

She was standing away from the jostle of FBI agents and cops, looking at nothing in particular, cutting a lonely figure.

He didn't envy her. It wasn't just her agency that expected results from her. The media would hold her accountable.

It was eleven p.m. when they reached their hotel.

Broker signed for the several packages and when they went to Zeb's room, broke them open and handed out their gear.

Glocks and other various makes of handguns that each team member preferred. Spare mags. Specially designed armor that not even the FBI had. Jackets and shoes. Encrypted sat phones. Flesh-colored earpieces. Tablet computers.

Four pairs of keys to two SUVs parked in the hotel's garage.

They had arrangements with select garages in major cities in the country and select cities in Europe and Asia, where they stored such SUVs.

Each vehicle was equipped with armor-plated glass, steel-reinforced body, run flat tires, an arms cache and several other gadgets.

The garages - many of them run by ex-Army mechanics

- all of them vetted by his crew, dropped the SUVs in their city of operation, then took them back to be serviced and re-outfitted every mission.

Each of their jackets and shoes had GPS chips in them. Each of their phones and tablets tracked those chips. So did the vehicles. At any point, they knew where the others were and if the chips exceeded set parameters of distance, they got alerts.

'Nothing like our own gear,' Broker growled as he fired up his tablet and configured their equipment.

Zeb ushered them out and told them to rest well. It had been a long day. The coming days and nights would be equally long.

Rest would be scarce till Barlow and Fairman were found. They had to grab sleep whenever they could find it.

He stripped to his shorts, did a hundred push-ups and a hundred and fifty sit-ups to loosen his body. He followed it up with an elaborate martial arts routine that left his blood singing and his body bathed in sweat.

A long shower, a glass of water, and he was ready for bed.

Sleep didn't come easily.

He thought of the sequence of events in the hotel. Glasses' face popped in every now and then.

He didn't look of Middle Eastern origin. The gunmen in the house – were they decoys? Or were the others?

Why such an elaborate take-down to grab Barlow?

He tossed and turned, rose to drink another glass of water, and stared silently at the night through his window.

Traffic lights blinked red and green outside. Traffic should have been thin at this time of the night, but it wasn't a normal night.

Why did they stage the event in Baltimore?

An answer came just as he was drifting off to sleep.

To delay us. To consume investigative resources and effort.

His eyes flew open.

Why?

He didn't have an answer.

He grappled with it for another half an hour and then turned with a sigh and shut his eyes.

What else would they do to delay?

He rose, dressed and went down to the basement garage.

He thought of waking his people.

Let them sleep. The day has started in Ukraine.

He texted Yuri.

Where's Burke? Where does she live?

Yuri replied several minutes later, after presumably hacking into several secure databases.

She was still in the Hoover building. She had a two-bedroom apartment in Alexandria, where she lived, alone.

Zeb wheeled out of the basement and headed to the Hoover building.

His dark SUV blended well among the several similar vehicles parked on streets around the building.

He waited for forty minutes and straightened when he saw Burke's blue Honda ease into the street.

He followed, three cars behind, one of which was Kowalski's.

'Are Burke and Kowalski involved?' he spoke aloud.

He heard Yuri's fingers dance over his keyboard as he searched more databases, looked into camera images and then reply, 'Nope. Doesn't look like it.'

Thought so. She's far too professional for that.

Kowalski peeled away at Crystal City.

Two other cars came in between, one a Toyota Land Cruiser, the other a Ford Escape.

The Toyota and the Ford changed places often on the short drive, and for a few miles, the Ford dropped behind Zeb's vehicle.

The Escape's windows were tinted and Zeb couldn't see inside, but he thought he saw two shapes.

Burke's flasher lit and she hung a right off Landover Street and entered a private driveway that led to a thirty-story apartment block. Hers was on the fourteenth floor.

Her Honda disappeared behind the building, the Ford and the Land cruiser slowed, Zeb drove right past.

He saw the two following vehicles climb the driveway and when he turned a bend, he drove up the sidewalk and parked illegally.

He climbed up a grassy embankment, sprinted across flat ground, entered the small garden in front of the apartment block, slowed when he reached the entrance and pulled his cap low over his head.

There wasn't anyone in the lobby.

Three elevators faced him. Two were climbing.

One was on the fourth floor, the other was on the second.

How many people would I have?

Four at least.

He looked around, found a service door, opened it and found the stairs.

He climbed.

Second floor, third, fourth.

On the tenth floor he found one gunman.

Chapter 10

The gunman, brown haired, lean, light facial hair, turned on hearing him.

He was wearing a leather jacket, his right hand underneath it.

He saw something in Zeb's face and the hand went deeper inside and withdrew.

Zeb saw the grip of a handgun emerge.

He dived at the shooter's legs.

The gunman kicked out.

Zeb ducked just in time.

The handgun was out now, turning in his direction, the gunman's eyes were narrow pinpoints of light.

Zeb followed the swinging leg with one hand, grabbed the bottom of a trouser leg and pulled.

His grip was weak; the gunman shook loose easily.

He lost a few seconds, however, before the gun could commence its descent toward Zeb.

Seconds in which Zeb's other hand reached out and plunged his Benchmade inside the shooter's right thigh.

The gunman's mouth opened wide.

Zeb leapt up and punched him in the throat and grabbed him as he collapsed and dragged him to a side.

He secured the gunman with plastic ties, patted him down, pocketed his wallet and his gun and climbed.

There will be one more gunman just outside the fourteenth floor. The other two will approach her apartment.

The second gunman was more alert.

Zeb sensed his presence even before he saw him.

The gunman was alternating his gaze between the stairs and the service door leading to the fourteenth floor.

Zeb lay down on the stairs and crawled up, one at a time.

He saw the gunman's legs through the wrought iron bars in the railing.

The gunman wore soft soled combat boots.

The boots shifted.

A pair of bushy eyebrows peered down at Zeb's barely visible eyes.

The eyebrows rose.

The eyes became wider.

The gun straightened.

Zeb shot him.

The suppressed sound was large in the confined space of the stairs.

Zeb hoped it wouldn't penetrate to the floor outside the landing door.

He caught the shooter as he was falling. He didn't bother with ties. The shooter was beyond troubling him.

This is the B team. The A team will be on the floor.

The A team was approaching Burke's door in the hallway.

There were six apartments on the floor, two next to the elevators, two opposite, and two on each side of the rectangular hallway.

Burke's was on one side of the hallway.

The hallway was carpeted and absorbed the sounds of the two gunmen.

They flanked each other, had their guns out and were approaching Burke's apartment in the dimly lit corridor.

Zeb was prone, had opened the service door an inch and got a good view of the hallway.

The door might creak. They might hear it and turn. They might shoot, which might bring Burke out and into danger.

He could call out, but that would have the same effect.

I can shoot them both from behind, but chances are one might turn back and shoot.

He raised his eyes and ran it along the walls of the hallway.

There wasn't anything on the walls.

He turned to look at the landing he was on.

Something red caught his attention.

A fire axe. An extinguisher. An alarm and a firehose.

He looked through the crack again.

They were almost at Burke's door.

He levered off the floor, grabbed the extinguisher with his left hand, smashed the glass on the alarm and set it off.

Its loud wail broke the silence.

He kicked the door open.

The gunman had stopped just as one was knocking on Burke's door.

They whirled around, crouching.

He threw the extinguisher at one of them and dropped to the carpet.

A hostile fired at the approaching red missile.

Zeb fired, at Burke's wooden door.

The second hostile spotted Zeb.

He yelled at his companion.

They sprang apart, flame spat, a round went high above him.

Zeb shot one gunman in the leg, a second shot went in his shoulder. The shooter lost his gun. He slumped against the wall, out of action.

The second gunman took his time.

His arm was straight; his body crouching, offering the smallest possible target.

Burke's door opened.

The gunman panicked.

He tried to ignore the open door and his first shot went wild.

He threw himself to the carpet, triggering fast and wild; then he stopped when Zeb's rounds found him in the chest.

Burke's door opened wider.

A shotgun emerged and then her head poked through.

The shotgun pointed at the first gunman. He moaned softly. It went over the second.

He was beyond speaking

The shotgun moved up the carpet and found Zeb.

'Burke, don't they teach you to not let strangers follow you home?'

Her eyes widened when she saw him and the bodies in the hallway.

'There are a couple more on the stairs.'

The shotgun in her hands trembled for just a moment and then her game face returned.

'How did you know?'

Zeb didn't reply. He turned back and looked at the other apartments on the floor. 'Your neighbors don't ignore gunfights at their front door?'

'None of them are home. On vacation or work trips.'

He nodded absently and bent over the bodies and searched them.

His hands stilled as soon as he saw the earpiece in one of the gunman's ears. He raised his head and spoke urgently.

'Grab your phone and laptop. Wear shoes. We are out of here in five minutes.'

She looked at him in shock, her mouth opening to protest. The words died when she saw his face and saw him load his Glock with a new magazine.

She turned, went back inside the apartment and was out in less than two minutes, a duffel bag in one hand and her armor over her T-shirt.

Zeb summoned an elevator in silence, his ears straining to hear anything out of the ordinary.

Sarah Burke watched him out of the corner of her eye. His face was expressionless and gave nothing away about what he was thinking.

His movements were almost languid even when in the heat of action.

'You get any sleep?' she asked and then bit her tongue.

Nice, Burke. He was held hostage. *He organized a counter-attack when inside. He was then in Baltimore and subdued a few more gunmen. Now he's here, after saving your ass. Sleep? Sure, he got lots of it.*

Carter didn't answer. He watched the elevator's indicator light move up.

He didn't wait for it to approach. He indicated the stairwell and strode away without a word.

She followed him down, mimicking his silent movements, glanced once at the dead shooter, paused at the sight of the second gunman who was still alive.

This will be a ton of paperwork. He looked at her and she hurried.

She saw his Glock was in his hand and removed her sidearm, a Glock 22, and held it down by her side.

He reached the ground floor landing, held a hand up to halt her and opened the service door cautiously.

He opened it wider and signaled to her.

She followed.

They stepped into the large lobby, empty, and hurried to the exit.

She matched him for strides, her ponytail flying behind her. 'Are you expecting more gunmen?'

In answer, three gunmen rose, from behind the reception desk.

Carter reacted with blinding speed.

A hand shoved her and sent her flying behind him, to his left.

She crashed against the wall, the armor cushioning her fall.

That slow mo thing in movies. It's real, she thought inconsequentially as the first burst from her Glock went wide.

Carter was moving. He was never still.

A body roll. A burst of flame. A hostile went down.

A leap across the floor, away from her, drawing heat toward himself. His gun flashing, his hands moving without conscious thought, changing mags, the roll of shots not letting up.

She took aim and fired at one shooter who was turning toward her.

He went down. She shot again. He lay still.

The gunman Carter had shot crawled behind the desk, joined the third hostile and they opened fire.

No cover for us. They're both focusing on Carter.

Carter wasn't shooting back. He was rolling desperately, but aiming high above their heads.

She fired at the desk, anything to keep the gunmen down, and glanced up.

A chandelier, right over the desk.

A piece of it fell and burst into splinters as it crashed right over the desk.

The shooting paused for a moment.

Carter took the opportunity to run across the front of the desk, to approach the gunmen from the side.

She rose.

'Stay down.'

She lay down.

His gun rose.

He skidded and fell.

Not skidded. He's shot. The gunmen anticipated his move.

She rose, not heeding his commands this time. She poured rounds at the desk and ran toward him

Someone whistled.

Who the hell is that?

A figure came in the edge of her vision

Another figure appeared.

Carter turned on the floor to take in the new threat.

He's alive.

The explosion flung her back and rang through her ears.

She thought she had blacked out for a moment, but realized it was smoke.

Something was ringing in her ears. She shook her head to clear it.

A figure appeared over her.

She raised her gun. It was removed from her hand easily. A hand grasped her and pulled her upright.

'Are you alright, ma'am?' Bwana Kayembe's eyes peered into hers.

'Carter?' she asked hoarsely.

The dark face lightened. 'He's fine. Couple of rounds in his armor. A burn on his shoulder. It will take more than that to put him down.'

Cops flooded in, FBI agents poured through the lobby, before she could reply and the law enforcement machinery took over.

It took an hour for their statements to be recorded and for the gunmen to be hauled off.

Only one remained alive, the one Carter had knifed on the stairwell.

The men behind the reception desk had been killed by the Barrett Bwana had fired.

Roger had thrown the flashbang that had stunned all of them, Bwana had completed the job.

He shrugged at Burke's questioning look. 'Desperate times, desperate measures.'

She managed a smile and turned to meet the Chief of Police of the D.C. Metropolitan Police Department.

He asked questions, she answered and then Deputy Director Bob Pierce arrived and the FBI took over.

Outside, the five a.m. sky was streaked in orange. Inside, flasks of coffee were handed out.

Burke, ensconced in a thermal jacket, headed toward Zeb who was being attended to by a medic.

He was bare from the waist up, his shoulder was being dressed.

She went closer and drew a sharp breath when she saw the old marks on his chest and back.

Bullet wounds. Knife scars?

Someone handed her a fresh water bottle. Roger. She thanked him silently and they stood and watched his friend button his shirt.

Pierce cleared his throat. 'Someone care to tell me what went down?'

Carter told them about his hunch that the Baltimore incident was a delaying tactic. That whoever was behind the kidnapping, would try again.

'Taking Burke out – what could be more delaying than that.'

'You could have called us or the cops, once you spotted the gunmen.' Pierce's eyes were narrow.

I don't like vigilante action, his body language was declaring.

Carter looked embarrassed for the first time since she had known him. He tossed his phone at Pierce. 'Tried. It ran out of juice.' He had forgotten to charge it.

He described the events as they happened, Burke corroborating those she had been part of.

Pierce turned to Bwana and Roger who stood silently beside their friend, theirs arms crossed over their chests.

'How did you guys get here, if his phone was dead?'

'We've got trackers on our gear.' Roger pulled out his phone, swiped screens and showed the display to Pierce.

Its chime, indicating Carter was on the move, had woken him up. He had roused Bwana and the two had arrived as soon as they could.

Pierce looked at Burke. She nodded. The events made sense.

'She needs to stay somewhere else. Have protection around her.' Carter broke off and thanked an agent who handed him his Benchmade.

'Yeah, we'll take care of it. Maybe you folks should move your base, yourself.' Pierce was more relaxed now.

Maybe it's Clare's presence.

Burke had spotted her come inside the lobby and stand quietly, away from the bustle.

Her eyes had flicked once in acknowledgement of Pierce's hand wave.

Even still, and even at a distance, her presence was a force field.

Maybe Pierce knows these are her men. Not vigilantes, exactly.

They broke an hour later.

'Sleep now. We'll meet at eleven.' Burke looked at the three men who had saved her.

They acknowledged her and left with Clare.

Kowalski came to her side and watched them depart.

'I'm glad they're on our side.'

So am I.

The voice was satisfied. It came through the encrypted phone call that was bounced from server to server, across the world, before it came to Merritt's phone.

'Your men did well. The Feds will be wondering what exactly is going down.'

He asked about the boy's condition. Merritt told him. It was still the same. The doctor had arrived, had suggested warm food, good lighting, and a comfortable room. He would start sessions the next day.

There wasn't anything more they could do. He would emerge from his fugue when his mind and body determined to do so.

The voice hung up and Merritt tossed the phone on the bed and lay down.

None of those taken alive know what's happening. They were recruited for a specific task. They executed it. It doesn't matter if they lived or died.

He smiled.

I will give the FBI a few days to think it's all over.

And then, I will throw them another red herring.

Chapter 11

The boy lay shivering in his bed. It was warm and comfortable and he had a freshly laundered blanket over him, but deep sleep wouldn't come.

Events of the day roused him whenever he was sliding into slumber. He thought of his friend in the next room.

All they wanted to do was enjoy a day out, away from the Secret Service. They had planned for the day, and then orchestrated an elaborate ruse on the protection detail, which had proved successful.

His friend knew how to give them the slip. He had done so several times. This escape was no different.

They were enjoying their food when the gunmen burst in and then the nightmare had begun.

He drew the blanket tighter around him. He tried hard, but he couldn't even remember the day in detail. All that he remembered were flashes.

Gunmen firing in the air. Shooting people randomly. Separating men and women. Taking their details.

He knew they were after the two of them when the gunmen paused when he mentioned their names. He had felt terror then. Fright that he had seen reflected in his friend's eyes.

The rest of the day was a blur as he and his friend had prayed like they never had before.

The FBI. The Secret Service. Someone would come to their rescue. The White House was just minutes away.

No rescue team came and when the gunmen fired in the air and explosions sounded, he had moaned, thinking they would die.

In the stampede that followed, he and his friend had tried to thrust themselves deep in the crowd, hoping to evade detection.

Rough hands had grabbed them, guns had been pointed, and they had been herded swiftly away.

They hadn't even considered resistance. Shock and panic had rendered them helpless.

Once they were outside, a handgun had dug deep in his side. The warning, 'If you open your mouth, you'll die here,' had been unnecessary.

He couldn't speak even if he tried to, his throat was so dry.

His eyes tried to adjust to the rapid pace of events and the activity outside the hotel. He could see cops and FBI agents everywhere. None of them came close to him and his friend.

It was only later, when they were bundled in the police vehicle that he noticed the uniforms on their kidnappers. They were outfitted in police and FBI clothing.

He and his friend were gagged and masked and driven for what felt like hours and brought to the house.

It was when they were inside the house, that he noticed his friend's behavior. His friend had no knowledge of who he was. He had no recollection of their day out, their elaborate planning.

He had no idea who his parents were. His eyes showed no recognition when they rested on his friend.

It was as if his memory had been wiped clean.

The boy's heart had sunk. He knew it had happened once before. It was a closely guarded secret that his friend had let slip one day.

His friend had gone into a fugue.

His friend had once explained to him at length, what it meant and what caused it. He didn't remember now.

All he recalled was that it was a temporary phase, during which, his friend didn't remember anything. His body continued functioning. His mind was aware of what was going around him, but he was disconnected from his past, from his memory bank.

The man wearing glasses had reacted in anger when he noticed his friend's state. He thought it was an act. He had slapped and punched the two of them. He threatened to kill them both.

The boy tried to explain. He got rained on with slaps and kicks. He had lain on the floor, curled as tightly as possible, taking the blows to his body. His friend lay passive, moaning and crying, offering no resistance to the beating.

The man with glasses finally hauled him upright and snarled in his face. What was wrong with his friend?

He explained rapidly, stuttering in his fear, and shrank from the cold anger in the man's eyes.

The man had taken his friend to a room and then the screaming began. The boy tried to shut his ears. He closed his eyes.

He couldn't escape his friend's voice, his pleading. He

wouldn't forget the raw pain in his friend till the day he died.

Maybe that's not far off.

He tried to bolster his courage.

Someone will rescue us. Our dads will not rest. The whole world will be looking for us.

The thought didn't offer any comfort as he lay on the bed.

He had begged and pleaded with his captors. Had said they should contact their families and arrange a ransom. He had flung himself at their feet, all the while aware that a single bullet could kill him.

The captors were unmoved. They didn't even look at him, let alone talk. One of them had lashed out with his leg when he had fallen at their knees.

He and his friend were escorted to their rooms and left alone.

His room was bare of furniture but for a bed. A window that looked out into a backyard. A hedge. No other house in sight.

The window was securely fastened. It was armed with an alarm, his captors told him. They would know if he tried to escape.

The door locked from outside.

There was a bathroom in the hallway outside the room, that they would be escorted to.

Tears came as he lay there.

Let us come out alive, he prayed.

The prayers finally stopped when sleep claimed him.

The other boy's mind was in a whirl. He knew he and another boy had been kidnapped. The other boy seemed to be his friend. He had no recollection of that.

He didn't recollect anything.

His mind was a blank when he tried to remember. The only memory he had was of surfacing in this house, surrounded by gunmen and this other boy, his age, for company.

One gunman, a guy with spectacles, had buried his knife in his thigh.

He had screamed once and had then passed out.

The knife was still in his thigh when he had come to.

The gunman kept asking him questions. Strange questions. He had no answers to them. The gunman said his dad was very famous. Very powerful.

The boy didn't recollect anything like that. He didn't know who his parents were.

He didn't know anything.

The torture continued, for what felt like hours. He had passed out again, and when he had come to, he found himself in his room.

His wounds seemed to have been bathed and his thigh was bandaged. The room had nothing in it, other than a window.

He lay exhausted in the bed. Too tired, too weary to rise and inspect the room. The fear mushroomed inside him.

Who am I? Why am I here? What do they want? Will I live?

A doctor was there when he had woken up. A psychiatrist. He smiled kindly at the boy and said they would start sessions soon.

The man with the voice, the paymaster, spent several hours later in the morning, reading the newspapers.

Every newspaper in the country carried large headlines about the hostage incident and the Barlow and Fairman kidnapping.

Newspapers across the world had similar headlines. One French newspaper called it the most significant political attack since the Kennedy assassination.

A British newspaper called it as horrific as 9/11.

The man was pleased. Merritt told him he had aggressively questioned the boy. He didn't remember anything.

The fugue was a complication. However, now that the boys were in captivity, events were in control.

He mentally congratulated Merritt on a well-executed operation.

Merritt could have grabbed the boy any place. Security surrounding him was not insurmountable.

However the man had been explicit in his instructions.

The kidnapping had to be spectacular. It had to grab the world's attention. It had to convey a message to a few select people.

Kidnapping the boy alone, would have grabbed world headlines. When Merritt had told him of the window of opportunity to grab both the boys, he had clenched his fist in elation and had given Merritt the green light.

Boys kidnapped despite Secret Service protection, screamed a headline. The man was confident the message was received.

He turned on the TV just in time to see the vice president make a statement. He had aged a decade in less than twenty-four hours. His wife, beside him, couldn't stop crying.

The president patted him on the shoulder and stood aside for the Veep to read out his words.

The second pair of parents came on and read a similar statement.

The man muted the TV. The words were the usual phrases that were made by thousands of such parents and ended in a plea. A request to the kidnappers to return the boys.

A knock on the door of his study sounded. The man called out.

A butler came in, bearing his coffee.

The butler was an English import. No fakes for the paymaster.

He thanked the butler graciously, sipped at his coffee that was at the exact temperature he liked and followed the rest of the news. The Baltimore gunfight, the attack on Sarah Burke's building.

Director Pat Murphy came on TV and mouthed strong words.

The man snorted. It was obvious Murphy knew nothing. No one did.

The man rose, went to a bronzed mirror in his study and patted his patrician hair in place.

He was proud of his fine features and despite being in his sixties, still looked youthful.

He could trace his ancestry back to the Mayflower. Power and prestige radiated from him.

And so it should.

His butler announced that his car was waiting.

He made his way outside his mansion in Virginia, admired the fountains in the enormous front garden for a moment, and seated himself in the Lincoln Town Car.

He had a Rolls Royce Phantom, but for this meeting, the Town Car was most appropriate.

They met in a downtown hotel in Washington D.C.

There were six of them, all white, all male, all in their sixties. They all had full heads of hair and their faces were young and belied their years. Some of the finest plastic surgeons had worked on them.

They called each other by their first names, a familiarity bred of friendship and shared interests.

They shook hands, helped themselves to the beverages in the conference room and when the man called the meeting to order, they settled down.

The man was their leader. It wasn't a formal title, but due to his experience in such matters, the mantle had fallen on him. He took a look around the table.

The six of them were wealthy, extremely so, and had long stopped counting their money. They owned businesses all over the world; oil companies, mines, retail chains, real estate developments, technology businesses.

'You must have watched the news?' the paymaster asked them.

They never communicated by phone or email. If there was a message to be conveyed or dealings to be discussed, they met in person.

Meeting in person was old fashioned, but it was extremely secure. No one would question their meetings. They were friends, business partners, and in a couple of cases, related by marriage.

The one who went by Paul, snorted. 'Hard to miss the headlines. It looks like the operation went well.'

Darrell, the paymaster, smiled. 'Very well. We have the boys.'

Mitch, at the far end of the table, raised an eyebrow. 'What happened in Baltimore and Alexandria?'

Darrell explained about the false trails. His partners nodded.

Paul took a deep breath and asked the question uppermost on their minds. 'Has the boy talked?'

The rest of them leaned forward in anticipation.

'No. We have a complication. He has gone into a fugue.' He explained about the doctor and the steps Merritt was taking.

Their faces turned expressionless. He knew how they were feeling. If the boy had talked, then matters would have progressed in a particular direction, to benefit them all enormously.

Now, they had to wait for an uncertain period. They had to wait, not knowing.

Waiting wasn't a problem. They had patience. It helped enormously that the boys were in their control. That reduced risks. Waiting was still a significant inconvenience, but they accepted that there wasn't much they could do.

Not knowing was a different issue. The boys posed a risk to all of them, to their way of life, to their very existence. They had to be taken out, however, the six men had to know what the boys knew, and who else knew it.

Now with one of the boys not able to speak, the not-knowing phase grew longer.

Darrell read their thoughts. 'Merritt has the boys in separate rooms, under video and audio surveillance. We'll know if the boy lets anything slip.'

'We have hacked into their friends' phones, email accounts, and social media pages. We have even bugged their phones. Boys that age have their phones with them, always. We will know if anyone knows anything. We can take preventive action.'

He answered more questions and then turned to another man, Mark. 'You'll get all the inside intel you can get.' It wasn't a question.

Mark nodded. He had contacts at the highest level in all the law enforcement agencies. He dined regularly with the Director of National Intelligence, could call the Director of the FBI at will, and had many other such friends.

'Roy, your newspapers and TV stations will run their campaigns?'

Roy smiled. 'You should read today's front page on my papers.'

Roy owned several highly reputable national newspapers and TV stations. They would continually cover the hunt for the missing boys and keep it very much on top of the news agenda; not that there was a risk of it slipping down.

The media outlets would also heap pressure on the law enforcement agencies and scorn their incompetence.

It was yet another red herring; part of Merritt's plan.

Brian, the quietest man in their group, spoke up. 'What about the others?'

Silence fell over the group. They knew who he was referring to.

He's the most nervous. He has to be watched.

Darrell smiled his most reassuring smile. 'As I have said several times before, Brian, the others don't pose a problem anymore. The kidnapping was a message to them. In any case, we are monitoring them. We will take care of them, if they prove to be a nuisance.'

Brian didn't look convinced. It was a question he asked at every meeting and Darrell gave him the same answer.

'Don't be a coward, Brian,' Paul swung round angrily. 'We all knew what the risks were when we started this. We enjoy what we are doing. Darrell said he has taken care of the others. That's good enough for me.'

The rest of them nodded their heads in agreement.

'Do you think we would be sitting here if they hadn't toed our line?' Mark this time, throwing his weight behind Darrell.

Brian bowed his head in agreement, finally.

I bet he's still not convinced. He should be moved onto Merritt's list as a problem to be taken care of, sometime.

They discussed other business matters and when Darrell called a close to the meeting, departed singly, to their chauffeured rides.

They all lived within an hour of Washington D.C. They all wielded power. D.C. was the home of power.

The boy woke, disoriented for a few seconds, and when the events flooded back, collapsed on his bed.

The fear returned. It became a constant, throbbing present. He needed to visit the bathroom. He tried to control it and remained on the bed. He tried to hear any sounds or movements outside his room.

The house was silent.

His friend's room was next to his. In the movies, prisoners tapped out messages on walls.

This isn't a movie, he thought despairingly and hot tears coursed down his face.

He brushed them away angrily and sat up when his door opened.

Glasses entered the room, a gunman behind him.

The boy's heart thudded loudly. If Glasses heard it, he didn't make any comment.

He stood staring at the boy, bent suddenly, grabbed the boy's leg and dragged him across the bed.

He plunged a knife in the boy's thigh without any warning.

The boy screamed and when he paused to draw a tortured breath, Glasses spoke.

'What do you know?'

Chapter 12

'Barlow's and Fairman's phones must have been hacked. So must their email accounts.'

Later in the day, Burke was addressing her investigative team which had swelled to a hundred.

She could draw on more manpower and resources, if she wished. A floor in the Hoover building had been evacuated for her agents and had been equipped with secure comms and all the tech gear they would need.

She broke her task force into smaller teams of fives and tens and assigned tasks.

Randy, the tech whiz in her team would work with counterparts in the NSA and other agencies and attempt to unpack the hackers. They would look into the hacked phones and email accounts. The boys' social media interaction would be unpacked. They would run face recognition programs on the images they had.

A ten-person team was looking into the getaway vehicles. They surmised that the vehicle would be a police cruiser or a SUV, or some kind of law enforcement or medical vehicle.

That particular team was also looking into camera and video footage of suspect vehicles.

Another team would run a software program that would look at all traffic to and from the hotel, before and after the take-down.

Yet another team called intelligence agencies around the world to check if they had heard of anyone recruiting for such an operation.

Three agents went to the boys' school, a private school in Maryland. It was possible that the kidnappers had checked out the school. Someone from the school could have spotted them.

Several teams interviewed the boys' families, friends, and wider social circle.

In a rare moment of cooperation, inter-agency turf wars and ego tussles had been stowed away, to be brought out for lesser missions.

Four interrogation teams would question the gunmen in custody. There were seven surviving hostiles, three from the hotel, three from Baltimore, and one from Burke's building.

So far, all gunmen from the hotel and Baltimore were singing from the same hymn book.

That they had been contacted on the darknet, a year back, and had been promised a significant bounty.

They didn't know who their paymaster was.

The men from the hotel mentioned Glasses, but they had met him only twice and he had never revealed his real name. They knew Glasses as Bob, no last name.

All of them were American, criminals who were into heists, kidnapping, and violent assault. Two of them had killed. They had never been arrested. Not even once.

They boasted about the jobs they had done, proud that they had slipped the law enforcement radar.

They didn't know if Bob was Muslim. They weren't. Money was their religion.

The Feds expressed skepticism at their lack of names and the lack of detail.

The gunmen swore that was how it was. They had participated in drills with the other gunmen, but in their world, real names and details were never shared.

They came together for a job, executed it, and got paid.

They had worked for various private security outfits and had long crossed the divide to execute illegal jobs.

They mentioned how they were contacted by Bob. It was yet another board in the darknet. They gave them the name, their login details.

The board was like a job site.

People like the gunmen listed their availability, specialities, and rates. Those like Bob, posted jobs.

Once they went through a verification process, which included references, Bob met them and introduced them to the rest of his crew.

All went by single names. They hadn't met any of them before.

They all stayed in the same motels, in single rooms, and didn't fraternize with one another.

Bob gave them only parts of the overall plan. Only four men close to him knew what the overall plan was.

The interrogators didn't believe them.

One gunman laughed. 'You can polygraph us, dude. You can waterboard us, or rendition us and let someone else work on us. You won't get a different answer. That dude compartmentalized everything. We only knew about our own part of the job we were to execute. We didn't know anything else.'

One of the agents bunched his fists at the insolent answer; the other calmed him down with a hand on his shoulder.

That Borra dude Bwana interrogated, said the same thing, Broker recalled, as he sat in on the interrogation. His ears pricked at the mention of drills.

'Where did you practice these drills?'

'Several places,' one gunman replied. They trained to take over different kinds of buildings and deal with different security set-ups.

Houses, hotels, offices, warehouses, they trained for all eventualities.

One month back, they focused on taking over a hotel.

Bob found one in Boston that looked vaguely similar to the Presidential View. They trained for two weeks, on that structure.

The gunman gave them dates.

'How did you know about the security set-up at the hotel?'

The prisoners shrugged. Bob had those details. Dealing with the security was the job of the four dudes Bob was close to.

Those five guys, alone, knew everything about the job.

'We came several times, as guests, stayed in the Presidential View and checked it out,' one gunman added. He gave dates.

Broker leaned back in his chair.

'You know Bob killed many of your men. He probably would have killed you, if he had the opportunity. As it is, he left you behind.'

It made no difference to the prisoners. They were alive. So what if the others were dead?

Broker tried another approach.

'Do you now know what you were involved in? Who you guys kidnapped?'

'Like anyone told us? You see a TV here?' Still the insolence.

'You guys helped kidnap the vice president's son.'

He watched the men's faces go blank for a moment and the color drain from each one of them.

This was beyond polygraphs, waterboarding, and rendition.

The Colombian and the South African snipers knew each other. They had worked with Glasses on a previous job in Indonesia, two years back.

Glasses and his four men bombed a nightclub. The snipers' job was to shoot the escapees.

Glasses and his four men. Broker pursued that comment.

'Yeah, those five were tight,' the South African answered in this guttural accent.

'His name? He told us to call him Bob.'

'How did he recruit you?'

The Colombian shrugged. In their world, there were job boards where requirements were posted and applications were made. Then followed up with verification and references. That's how kill teams were put together.

He mentioned a name for the website that had got him together with Bob the first time.

It was different from the one that the hotel gunmen had named.

The South African mentioned the same name and the same process.

They both thought Bob was American. No, they didn't know if he was a Muslim. Religion was never discussed during their time together.

They too confirmed they only knew part of the overall plan.

Their job was to rain down fire on any cop or anyone else who approached the target house. They were not to fire inside the house, or the neighboring one.

'You didn't ask why?'

'Bob didn't like questions.'

'You know how many cops you killed?'

They didn't answer. They didn't care.

'What was your escape plan?' Broker asked curiously.

The Colombian answered after a pause. There was a getaway vehicle, disguised as an ambulance, in an alley in the neighborhood. A change of clothes in it, would disguise him as a medic.

He was to drive to BWI airport, catch a train to Washington D.C. and from there, hire a car, drive to New York, and catch a flight to Colombia.

The South African had a similar escape plan.

They gave details, the FBI agents recorded them. The details would be checked later.

'Which other jobs did you execute for Bob?'

'Just the Indonesian one, and now this,' the South African answered. He yawned lustily and didn't bother covering up.

The interrogators moved an inch back. His stale breath would have woken the dead.

'Which other kills were you responsible for?' Broker persisted.

His eyebrows shot up when he heard the names. Politicians in various countries, businessmen, a high profile socialite on the west coast.

'Why did you kill these people?'

One sniper shrugged. 'We were paid.'

The sole surviving Muslim extremist from Baltimore, Taufeeq Aziz, had nothing more to reveal. His dreams of a jihad were shattered.

His sobbing grew louder when he was told that other than him and his dead friends, no one else seemed to be a religious extremist.

That seemed to be the ultimate betrayal to him; that his willingness to be a martyr had been exploited by someone.

Someone whose ambition seemed to be to kill only a few cops.

Aziz had no connections to ISIS.

He and his friends had wanted to wage their own war, unconnected to any existing terrorist group. They wanted to be known as the American Islamists, a formal name they had coined for their group.

They wanted to teach fellow Americans that they could never be safe.

'Aren't you American yourself?' Broker asked.

The sobbing stopped for a second.

'Not like you,' Aziz spat.

The investigative team spent hours with him but got only the addresses of his dead friends, the mosques they used to go to, the neighborhoods they had grown up in.

The FBI would rip apart their lives, go through all their contacts, their friends, their social media pages, but Broker knew they wouldn't find a lot.

They were amateurs who were prodded into this act. They knew the least.

The gunman from the building was American, from Wyoming.

He, and the others who had been killed, belonged to a right wing militia group that had been on the FBI's radar.

They had been commissioned to carry out the job a week back, using a secure go-between in Chicago.

He and his fellow gunmen had scouted the building, had worked out approaches and had followed Burke a few times, to get her routine right.

The go had come from the go-between, a few hours after the hotel take-down.

He didn't know about Glasses.

The go-between handled everything for them, the job, the bounty, the details.

He didn't know their attack was connected to the Barlow kidnapping.

If it was, his black teeth flashed, it was a blow against the Federal government.

'At the least, we can shut down this gang,' Kowalski murmured when Burke ordered a team to look into the go-between.

No one responded.

Lunch came, people picked at their food, Burke worked without a break, speaking, outlining, briefing, and debriefing.

The energy levels spiked for a moment when a call came to the toll-free number about a sighting

Two male youths had been spotted in the back of a speeding Tahoe in Maryland. The caller said the youths were bound and gagged and a man wearing glasses was behind the wheel.

The local P.D. gave chase and cornered the vehicle.

It turned out to be a domestic kidnapping.

Evening came and with it, Burke called a break.

Everyone filed out of the room but for Burke, Zeb, and his

crew.

She didn't acknowledge their presence and stood staring at a window through which, if she craned her head, she could see the green surrounding the White House.

A couple of hours back she had briefed the press and had been the recipient of savage criticism. The toll-free number had started receiving a high proportion of calls that just vented rage at the FBI's ineptness.

A wall-mounted TV played silently and after the news briefing, a channel organized a phone-in.

Most callers were critical of the FBI and of Sarah Burke.

They said she was too young. Her inexperience showed. They demanded more action. They wanted results, now. They wanted the boys to be rescued. They were appalled at the violence in the capital.

Various news channels reported attacks against Muslims. Some convenience stores refused to serve them.

The White House made a statement condemning the attacks. It said links to extremist organizations were still being investigated, but were so far unproven.

In the cacophony, a caller rang the TV channel that organized the phone-in.

The caller identified himself as Pike, from a small village in New Hampshire. He spoke glowingly of Sarah Burke and the FBI. But for them, he said, their village would have been overrun by gangsters.

'They are right. I am too inexperienced. I have never handled an investigation of this scale. I will stand down.' She spoke without looking at them.

Beth made to speak, but her sister motioned her to silence.

Let her vent.

Burke turned around and faced them, the sunlight shadowing her face. 'The last time, you folks were responsible for my success. You are involved again.' She laughed bitterly, looking in Zeb's direction. 'You should lead this investigation. I bet you will get results, faster.'

'There's just one problem with that, ma'am,' Roger crossed his legs. It had been a long day and yet his white shirt and blue jeans were unwrinkled.

'We folks, we are a blunt instrument. We are a hammer, to be used where there's a nail. We are not investigators. Heck, we wouldn't have a clue how to go about hunting these gunmen.'

He laid a hand on Bwana's shoulder. 'This dude here, he took a Barrett to a pistol fight! We wouldn't know where to start an investigation.'

Zeb let him speak. His crew wasn't just the best deep black operatives in the country, they were also ace investigators. Bear and Bwana were members of Mensa. Roger could debate philosophy while Chloe was a speaker at several scientific conferences.

His crew weren't just hammers. They were much more. However, if anyone in his team could lift Burke's spirits, it was Roger, the soft-speaking Texan.

Burke let Roger's words wash over her and a ghost of a smile flitted on her lips.

'I can see why you are successful with women, Roger.' Her eyes rested briefly on Broker and then moved to Chloe who was sitting next to Bear, dwarfed by his size.

'You see any of us leaving this room?'

Burke frowned, not getting her.

Chloe waited and smiled when the light dawned in Burke's eyes.

'We believe in you.'

Chapter 13

Dinner came and went, but still the task force was at it, chasing down different lines of investigation.

Folding beds and mattresses had sprung up on the floor for those who wished to stay in the office.

At nine p.m. Zeb rose. Abruptly for him, but to an onlooker, he was sitting one moment, the next, he was upright.

He spoke to Burke and she nodded.

He looked at his crew and they joined him and filed silently past the agents and went to the elevator.

The car wasn't empty. Director Murphy was in it, going down.

They joined him.

'You're leaving?'

'To our hotel,' Zeb answered.

Murphy nodded. No more explanations were necessary.

Zeb and his team didn't have any official standing in the investigation. They would end up hampering the task force.

They would be more effective from the *outside.*

Zeb turned to Bear and Chloe when they were on the sidewalk. 'You got enough sleep?'

'Yeah, why?'

'It might be worth keeping an eye on Burke's house.'

Burke would be residing in Georgetown, in a safe house that the FBI owned. Zeb knew this time there would be agents watching her, but none of them were in the same league as Bear and Chloe.

The couple peeled off, after high-fiving the rest and went to a dark SUV.

'You got your gear set up?' he addressed Broker and the twins, this time.

'Got everything in place. Let's do some real investigating.' Meghan flexed her fingers and led the way to their hotel.

'You think we'll find them?'

Bear and Chloe were in their SUV, hunched down, invisible in the night and in the darkness of their vehicle.

It was parked in a line of residents' vehicles, wedged between a Durango and an Explorer.

The FBI's surveillance vehicle was obvious. It was parked

right outside Burke's door, two agents lounging in it.

Burke's temporary residence was a two-story townhouse with a gated entrance, steps to the front door, a light glowing on its porch.

Bear was in the driver seat, Chloe curled beside him, his arm over her shoulders.

He knew what she meant. *Will we find them alive?*

'If anyone can, it's us.'

He didn't know the FBI, but he had immense faith in his team.

Chloe snuggled closer and peered up at him. They had gotten close in Afghanistan, long before they had met Zeb.

Zeb had never once commented on their relationship. He had accepted it and supported it, just like the others had. The twins ribbed her affectionately about it once in a while.

It was all good.

They had chosen a life in the shadows. It was one they wanted and enjoyed. However, she also knew, it could end one day, violently. So long as Bear was with her, the end didn't matter. Every day was a beginning.

Burke arrived at eleven p.m., dropped off by a FBI vehicle. She bent her head down, spoke to the agents in the surveillance vehicle, laughed, and disappeared inside the house.

The lights came on and turned off an hour later.

A couple more hours passed.

Cruisers drifted past the entrance of the alley occasionally. One of the FBI agents got out and stretched his legs. A dog walker came back, glanced curiously at the agents, and went inside his house.

Chloe was asleep on Bear's shoulder. It itched, but he didn't move. He would happily sit uncomfortably for hours if it meant she could sleep undisturbed.

He kept scanning the front and the back of their vehicles, his eyes moving in practiced sweeps. The rear of the house didn't need surveillance. It backed up against more houses. There was no entrance at the rear.

The first man entered the alley just as the clock moved past two a.m.

He stood, weaving unsteadily, bottle in hand.

He approached Burke's house.

An agent stepped out and spoke softly to him. The drunk

turned.

The drunk whirled, spinning swiftly, the bottle coming up in a hard arc.

The agent was prepared. He ducked, slammed the drunk down, and removed his gun.

More men poured in. Five.

Moving swiftly, silently.

The agent shouted something to the one inside.

The second agent fumbled with his comms, flung his door open.

It crashed back on him, caught him on the chin. He sagged back and lost his gun.

Two men surrounded the single agent and attacked him with bottles and knives. They disarmed him easily and kept him at bay.

Three others leapt over the gate.

They were pulled back like a giant vacuum.

Bear and Chloe had moved when the second lot of men had appeared.

Bear skirted the left of the FBI vehicle, snapped a swift glance at the fallen agent and grabbed the first man who was leaping over the gate.

His other hand clawed at the loose shirt of the second man, then rocking back on his heels, he pulled.

The two men stopped in mid-air, crashed into the third, and the three of them fell back.

One of them landed lithely, whirled around, snarling, and produced a knife.

It went skittering away, when Bear, almost lazily, slapped his hand. A second lazy hand slammed into the assailant's face and floored him.

Bear took a step back when the two remaining men turned on him.

No weapons, but for knives and bottles. They stink. These guys look like drunks.

The two men charged at the same time, their fists flailing, their mouths wide in anticipation.

Bear let one fist sail past him. The second man attacked. A leg aimed at his groin.

Bear twisted, grabbed the leg, and spun the man around.

The second man collided into the spinning man. He went

flying when Bear used his momentum to heave him over his shoulder.

The knife man clawed at his ankles. Bear stomped him and when the man squealed, silenced him with a kick.

He watched the men for a moment. They were groaning on the sidewalk and would offer no further resistance.

He looked over the roof of the vehicle at Chloe.

She gave him a thumbs-up.

He had caught flashes of her twisting, ducking, and punching.

Zeb had taken Chloe and the twins under his fold and had taught them his style of unarmed combat. It didn't belong to any one school.

It was a collection of techniques from across the world that he had adapted and improvised for himself. There was karate and judo in it, but there was also savate, ju-jitsu, kalaripattayu, silat, muay lao and several others that Bear didn't recognize.

Zeb had spent years traveling the world after the horrific event involving his wife and son.

During his travels, he had lived with men so old, time was a meaningless concept to them. They had taught him about life, but also about death. They had taught him things about his body that no medical school taught.

They had also taught him different forms of combat.

Bwana had once demanded that they be taught too, along with Chloe and the twins.

Zeb had given him the look. 'The women will be picked on, due to their size. You,' he had sized Bwana with a small smile, 'are rather bigger.'

Bear had seen the difference in Chloe and the twins. Taught by someone like Zeb, honed to a very high proficiency level, they now had something different on top of their inner confidence.

They were burnished steel.

He checked on the fallen agent. He was sporting a shiner. He raised a hand in thanks and continued speaking into his headset.

Bear went round the vehicle. The second agent was checking the sprawled men, patting their pockets.

He raised his head when Bear approached.

'Thank you. We would have been in trouble if you two hadn't shown up. Where were you guys parked? We saw you pass earlier, but thought you had disappeared.'

Bear grinned. 'That was the point.'

Chloe picked a knife by its blade, with her thumb and forefinger. 'These men don't seem to be your usual hitmen. They look like drunks. Guys who sleep on the street.'

'Yeah.'

The first cruiser rolled in silently, its lights flashing, before he could answer.

Two more followed and the alley filled with cops and FBI agents.

The attackers were hauled away after a brief discussion with the agents on watch, leaving the four of them in the alley. A cruiser stayed back, two cops in it.

'How did they know?' Chloe asked the agents.

They shrugged. 'Something Burke will think about, no doubt.'

Four pairs of eyes swiveled to Burke's house.

It was still dark. She had slept through the attack and the ensuing commotion.

One of the cops approached them and grimaced. 'These guys sleep on the street. A couple of them are regulars near the Metro entrance at McPherson Square. Way their story goes is, they were approached at ten, by a man, who threw bills at them.'

'They were told there would be money, food, and an unoccupied house. Maybe a guard or two, outside,' Chloe completed for him.

'Yes, ma'am. Something like that. They didn't know anything about a woman inside. They were to break in, and if successful, there would be a reward. They could keep the money they found.'

'Obviously, the man was wearing a hoodie. They wouldn't recognize him.'

'You got that right, ma'am.'

The cruiser wheeled away after a promise to increase the frequency of patrol. The FBI agents turned down the offer of a stationed police vehicle. They would look after their own.

One of the FBI agents brought out a coffee flask when the cops had left and handed it around.

'You both staying?'

Chloe swallowed a mouthful of beverage and nodded. 'Yeah. Till it lightens up. I figure this was just to throw a scare.'

Bear knew she thought it was more than that.

It's a message. They know about us.

But why send a message?

'You have a leak,' Zeb said bluntly.

Burke was on a video call with them the next day. She in her office, they in Zeb's room in their hotel.

Thirty-six hours had passed since the abduction. No progress had been made. Zeb had already lost count of the press conferences Burke had sat in on.

Her face grew pinched at his words. She shot a glance behind her, even though she was alone, in a closed, sound-proof office.

'It could be a random troublemaker. Someone from my past cases. I have a long list of folks wanting to do me harm.'

Zeb didn't reply. Threats and hate mail came with the territory Burke operated in. The attack though, was too coincidental.

He could see it in her face; she too agreed with him.

'I have a hundred agents checking out stuff. The Metropolitan cops are involved. Virginia State Police are in the investigation, as is the Maryland State P.D. NSA, Homeland Security, a truckload of other agencies are involved. There's a clearing house for sharing info with everyone. The mole, if there is one, could be anyone, anywhere.'

She blew hair out of her eyes in frustration. 'I can't double check on everyone. Well I could get our internal affairs, or even another agency, to look into us but that would be a nightmare. Such an investigation cannot be contained. Everyone would be looking at one another in suspicion.'

She paused and something entered her eyes. A plea. 'What should I do?'

His reply surprised her. 'Nothing different. You are pursuing lines of inquiry that our mastermind will expect. Assign your most trusted agents to those lines that look promising. We could use this mole to our advantage at some point.'

She pondered his suggestion and liked what she heard. They discussed her stay. The FBI's safe house was no longer safe.

Broker could create aliases for her and move her around different hotels every night. Bear and Chloe would stand watch at night.

She protested. Zeb overrode her. He had already spoken to Murphy. The Director had agreed.

She tried thanking them again. She had started the call with thanks, had cut it short when Meghan murmured, sotto voce, 'Move on, babe.'

Zeb ignored her and ended the call. He looked around at the eldest person in the room.

'Broker? What are you doing?'

'We're working. Some of us have to.' Meghan answered instead of him. She, her sister, and Broker were hunched over computers, typing furiously.

He walked over and watched over their shoulders. They were sending commands to Werner, their proprietary artificial intelligence algorithm that resided in a supercomputer in their office in New York.

Werner had been developed by a pair of Stanford graduates and had attracted the attention of the NSA and the DIA. Zeb and Broker had outbid the two agencies and after acquiring the software, Broker and the twins had enhanced it substantially.

Werner talked to numerous highly classified databases in the country and several internationally.

Werner was better than anything any law enforcement agency in the country had, Broker was fond of saying. Zeb had no reason to doubt him. The NSA had a standing offer for Werner and upped its price every year. That was proof enough.

'What are you asking Werner to do?'

'Run facial recognition programs, search for patterns and anomalies in the boys' phone and social media correspondence, run a check on abandoned hotels in Boston, check camera images there,' Beth answered , shortly.

'Won't the FBI do that?'

'They don't have Werner.'

Broker waved an imperious hand and cut short any further questions.

Go away. We are working.

Zeb went to Bwana and Roger. They were sprawled on the bed, watching him. Bear and Chloe were curled on a settee. They too were watching him.

'What are you guys working on?'

Chloe tossed aside the magazine she was flicking through. 'We're watching you work.'

Bwana snorted. 'Doesn't look like work to me.'

A rare smile crossed Zeb's face. 'I've been figuring things out.'

'And?' Bwana propped himself on an elbow and looked expectantly.

'This guy knows us too well.'

The sounds of typing stopped. Chairs squeaked as the twins and Broker turned. Roger sat up on the bed.

'He could be one of us.'

Chapter 14

'Us?' Beth asked in confusion. 'There are only eight of us. Nine, if you include Clare. How could he be one of us?'

'He doesn't mean us as in *us*, dumbo,' Her sister replied disparagingly. 'He means as in special ops, or deep black agents.'

'Meghan's right. The planning, the audacity, the way these guys have just disappeared. These aren't your rent-a-mob guys.'

'They aren't even ISIS or any terrorist group. No demands have been made. No videos of the boys being beheaded have emerged. No group has come forward claiming responsibility.'

Zeb paced, letting his thoughts flow into words. 'Those Muslim guys in Baltimore, they were a false trail. They have led us down false trails everywhere.'

'On top of that, remember that equipment he sent out to the extremists in Baltimore?'

Zeb watched them digest his words, watched ideas take shape, acceptance set in.

'Assuming you're right, how does that help us?' Bear stroked his beard and saw the face Chloe made.

He shrugged silently. *I haven't slept in thirty-six hours. When would I find time to trim?*

A chair squeaked. Broker turned around to his laptop. Two more chairs followed. The twins.

'We find out which agents are missing or dead.' Broker threw over his shoulder and the typing resumed.

'Hold up.'

Broker and the twins turned back in unison.

'The getaway vehicle was a cop vehicle or maybe an ambulance. We agreed on that?'

Seven heads nodded in unison. Meghan's voice rose. 'No point in looking at traffic images. The FBI will do that.'

Zeb shook his head to correct her. 'Nope, I am not interested in that. Beth can you bring up a map of the city?'

She did.

'The kidnappers had a window of seven hours. They could have gone anywhere in those seven hours. However, I am betting they didn't get far. They didn't fly, they didn't take buses. There are no ships to board here.'

The rest of his team crowded behind him and watched the flickering screen over his shoulder.

Chloe scrunched her face when Beth worked out probable distances and highlighted a circle around the city.

'Why only seven hours? They escaped around one in the afternoon. They could have traveled the whole night.'

Bear patted her on her shoulder, a gentle pat for him, a thump for her. She stumbled.

He grabbed her and pulled her close. 'The whole country and its dog was extra vigilant that night. Zeb's assuming they wouldn't travel at night.'

'We are wasting time on this,' Meghan faced them, her body quivering with impatience, eager to get back to what they were working on. 'The Feds will have this covered. It isn't new ground.'

'Sis, will you button up and let Zeb finish?' Beth poured sugar and honey in her voice, drawing a grin from her twin, who bowed elaborately.

'The floor's yours, Wise One.'

'We aren't looking for getaway routes in that radius.' Zeb resumed when he had their attention.

'We want homes where a cruiser or an ambulance was parked. Homes from which no 911 calls were made.'

'Of course,' Broker breathed silently and attacked his keyboard without a further word.

'You've got your uses, Wise One,' Meghan threw back over her shoulder, her fingers flying on her computer, her hair dancing on her shoulders.

Three hours later, Zeb was in Eldersburg, Maryland.

It was a small town, fifty miles from the capital, just over an hour's drive.

His team had trawled the internet, analyzed social media posts, thousands of photographs, 911 call records, and had narrowed down fifty homes in the radius.

A cruiser or an ambulance had been often seen in front of those homes in the three months leading to the kidnapping.

Not a single home belonged to a cop or a medic. The homes had no connection to law enforcement or the medical care business.

Bear, Chloe, and the twins were checking out a home

in Annapolis, Maryland. Bwana and Roger had gone to Fredericksburg, Virginia to check yet another house.

The house Zeb was interested in stood on a rise, separated from street level by dirt drive that wended through grass and shrub and ended at the home.

There were no immediate neighbors and the back of the house overlooked fields.

Broker drove down what passed for Main Street, disappeared into a realtor's office and came out with leaflets.

He drove back to the street, parked, took a leaflet and started reading it, while Zeb exited the SUV and walked up the drive.

Perfectly located. Meghan checked the ownership, it's owned by a trading company in New York, who has offices all over. The home is used by staff who visit D.C.

He pulled a leaflet out and made a show of reading it as he approached the house.

It seemed to be empty. It had the unused feel that unoccupied houses had.

The drive opened into a graveled landing in front of the house. A garage was attached to the right of the house.

He went to the left, circled a corner and stopped.

A man in a loose shirt and jeans was eyeing him suspiciously.

Crew cut. Hands close to his body.

'Howdy. This house is for sale, isn't it?' Zeb gave him a wide smile.

The man narrowed his eyes. 'No. This is private property.'

Zeb frowned. 'The realtor in town told us, this was. It looks perfect for my needs. Isolated. You see, I value my privacy.'

He sensed a presence behind him and turned.

Another man, similarly dressed, had approached silently and stood watching him.

'You heard him, buddy. This isn't for sale,' Second man said. 'You got the wrong house.'

No aggression. But those postures, those hands, those eyes. These aren't your ordinary next door neighbors.

'I get it,' Zeb slapped his thigh and laughed. 'You guys are playing hard to get aren't you. I should have guessed. I have done it myself, a time or two.'

'Look,' he spread his hands. 'I am in the market to buy a

house. Why don't you take me around the place, and if I like it, we can discuss numbers?'

The first man lost his politeness. 'Friend, we told you twice. This house isn't for sale. Do us a favor and leave.'

Zeb stood stubbornly, anger and protest showing on his face. He was half turned, both men in his vision.

First man came, his hand reaching out to clasp Zeb's shoulder and turn him around.

Second man took a step back, to fall behind Zeb.

'This is unnecessary. You don't have to force me,' Zeb huffed and turned to leave. 'I'll surely be having words with that realtor.'

A breeze sprang up; dry leaves flew in the air and settled on gravel. The second man's shirt flattened against his body and outlined a shape on his waist.

Handgun.

Second man fell in behind Zeb, to his right. First man was to his left.

Zeb cast a glance at the house through the corners of his eyes. A third man was peering through a window.

'You aren't really looking to buy, are you?' Hardness crept in first man's voice.

The sun was behind them, throwing long shadows; dark shapes that Zeb followed on the ground.

One shadow came closer. First man. A hand reached out.

Zeb whirled, grasped the hand, twisted it, bent the first man around and shoved him against second man.

They crashed into one another, the second man stumbled and fell.

The first man swore, recovered, clawed beneath his shirt and froze when he saw Zeb's Glock trained on him.

A door slammed and the third man came running out, a gun in hand. He came to a stop, crouched and yelled.

'Police. Drop your guns.'

Zeb's Glock didn't move.

'Drop it,' The third man commanded.

A shotgun clicked behind him.

'I never liked Mexican standoffs,' Broker chuckled.

It took an hour to clear things up. The three men were from the DEA, based out of New York, visiting the capital on an investigation.

The house was a safe house they used occasionally.

They demanded Zeb and Broker's identity. They got a number to call in return.

The third man, the lead agent, made the call, his face tightening as he listened. He spoke in monosyllables and grunts and when he ended the call, his game face was on.

'They're friendlies,' he told his men.

String tight nerves loosened.

'We're to share everything regarding this house.'

They didn't have much to share.

They had arrived just that morning, picked the keys from beneath the largest stone in the front yard and were making themselves comfortable when Zeb had showed up.

'When was the house last occupied?' Zeb asked them as he walked around the living room.

Cheap furniture. Bland pictures on the walls. Dining table is bare. No fruit in the bowl.

He opened the refrigerator. It was empty but for a can of milk and a few bottles of water.

The lead agent shrugged and made a call.

'Six months back.'

'What?' he asked, when Zeb's head snapped toward him.

Burke arrived two hours later, Bubba behind her in a SUV bristling with his team. A third vehicle followed and from it spilled three dogs. Search and Rescue animals.

The FBI team disappeared inside the house. Zeb and Broker stayed outside, along with the DEA agents.

'This is connected to the kidnapping?' The lead agent asked after a lengthy silence.

Zeb didn't answer.

His eyes were trained on the door in which Burke stood.

Her eyes were alert. Her face was sharp.

'They were here.'

'They found the first house,' Darrell told Merritt.

The boys were still locked up. The one in the fugue was still in his private universe. The doctor had started his work. He reported no progress.

The second one was still scared. He didn't know anything, despite Merritt's questioning.

He looked up fearfully every time Merritt's man entered, as

if expecting to be shot. Both the hostages were scared.

Killing them is still a possibility, Merritt thought as he wedged the phone between his neck and ear and turned on the TV.

He had taken his time on the second boy, but time hadn't been required. The boy had babbled everything he knew the moment Merritt's knife had pierced his thigh.

They stopped making tough kids a long while back.

He watched absently at rolling coverage of the house in Eldersburg and a brief interview with Sarah Burke.

She had nothing much to say other than they were progressing.

Yeah, but it won't get you anywhere.

He had expected the house to be found.

They had gotten away from D.C. with the hostages and had come to the house. There they made a change of clothes, changed the color of the vehicle, and left.

What surprised him was the speed.

I didn't expect the Feds to turn up so fast. I know how they work, how the other agencies work.

'Can you find out who exactly discovered the house? Was it the FBI or someone else?'

Darrell said he would check and come back.

If it was the FBI, have I underestimated them? He shook his head unconsciously. *No. I know them very well.*

'What's the doctor saying?' Darrell's voice in his ear brought him back to the call.

'The usual. We should give it time. He's trying everything he can, but medicine doesn't have an answer to everything.'

Darrell fell silent. Merritt let it build.

'He's qualified, isn't he?'

'Yeah. He's a psychiatrist. I have worked with him for a while.'

'Are you safe there?' the paymaster asked finally.

'Yeah.'

'There's something you should know. There are some civilians working with the FBI.'

Merritt shrugged silently. 'All the agencies in the country will be working with the Feds. They must have hired a few specialists.'

'These aren't just any other specialists.'

Merritt focused on the voice.

'These are supposed to be some deep black, special ops group no one has heard of.'

'Can you find out more?'

Darrell laughed. 'I can find anything.' He could laugh, now that the boys were in control.

He had been a nervous wreck once the threat had surfaced and had even suggested to Merritt that the entire family be taken out.

'Did you see the parents' interview?'

Both parents had gone on several TV shows and had made appeals to the kidnappers. Shawn Fairman's mother had broken down and said she would gladly take her son's place.

It made for good TV. It heaped more pressure on the investigative agencies.

It didn't elicit a drop of sympathy from Darrell.

The boy could hear faint conversation from somewhere in the house. His leg throbbed, his body ached, his mind was in a constant state of fear.

Glasses had inflicted such pain on him that he had fainted a few times. Glasses had started again when he came to. He now knew what his friend had faced.

The boy didn't know anything. He told Glasses repeatedly, but the gunman had continued, until he had finally believed the boy and had stopped.

A doctor had then rushed in and had attended to the boy.

He should have killed me, the boy thought dully.

He couldn't cry anymore. He was cried out. He didn't even know what day it was. It was just a rolling state of grey routine.

He woke, was escorted to the bathroom, returned to his room, and lay there all day. Meals were brought to him.

No one spoke to him. He had tried once, and had been hit several times.

He saw his friend's room when he visited the bathroom. He knew the doctor was attending to him. He could hear faint conversation from the neighboring room, every now and then.

Does my friend know something? Was it why we were captured? Did he see something?

Or did they capture us because of our ability?

He always had that ability. He hadn't given it any special attention when he was young, thinking everyone was like that.

As he grew older, he realized what he had was quite unique. He got bullied several times when he was at school when flashes of his ability were noticed by other kids.

He didn't report those incidents to his teachers. Neither did he mention them to his parents. He didn't want a fuss to be made. He didn't tell them of his ability either.

Why did I hide it from them?

He didn't know. Hiding that capability had become second nature to him. He had perfected the disguise.

Maybe I didn't want anyone to treat me like a museum exhibit.

He and his friend had jelled quickly when they had met. They followed the same football team, had similar tastes in movies and books.

It was one day at school that he had noticed his friend disguise his answer to a question. His friend was bright, sharp, smart, similar to him.

There was no need for him to disguise his answer.

Something leapt in him.

He started observing his friend's habits closely. He found that his friend adopted the same tactics that he did, whenever something historical was asked. Something that needed reciting.

Maybe he has it too?

One day, when they were alone, playing with a baseball bat and ball, he had narrated a piece of poetry he had seen a while ago.

His friend had stopped. The ball had smacked him in his chest. He had ignored it. His friend narrated the rest of the poem.

From then on, the boys became closer. They became like twins. They shared their stories and experiences.

His friend, too, had hidden his ability from his folks and teachers. In his case, the urge to be normal was greater. He too had been bullied. He too didn't want to be seen as an object of interest.

They both knew they would have to reveal their abilities at some point. They had decided to wait for a year or two more.

A month back, his friend had sent him a text. He wanted to discuss something. He had messaged back, suggesting they meet.

Meetings in their circumstances were always elaborate. The families had to be told. The security detail had to be informed. Last minute changes were a nightmare.

They both had always wanted to evade the constant security. Be normal. Like normal kids.

This could be the opportunity to give them the slip.

He had suggested a breakfast meeting. His friend had snorted in laughter. Like adults?

The idea had appeal though. He told his friend how they could escape unnoticed.

They planned and when the day came, the plan worked perfectly.

Look where it got us.

Chapter 15

'How can a safe house have police vehicles in front of it?' Broker asked quietly.

They had known of the house when a random onlooker had snapped a picture of a cruiser in front of the house and uploaded it on the internet. That photograph was more than two years old.

However, that wasn't the only one. A couple more had surfaced. Police vehicles in a quiet neighborhood attracted attention.

Attention was easy to record and post online in the day of camera phones and superfast WiFi networks.

Those photographs had enabled Beth to pinpoint the house, make confirmation calls that the house wasn't law enforcement property and neither had any distress call been ever made from it.

Zeb didn't answer. The question had struck him too and he made a note to ask Burke.

They were in their SUV, a short distance away from the house, and were watching the comings and goings from behind darkened windows.

They had moved the moment news vans had arrived and after Burke had briefed them.

The briefing was short. The dogs had detected the presence of the boys. No other evidence had been found thus far.

Teams were canvassing the neighborhood, to check if anyone had seen any traffic at the house.

They watched for some more time, saw Burke emerge and scan the street. Zeb called her.

'We're down the street.'

Burke swiveled, her eyes searching, till they landed on their vehicle.

'There you are. Nothing much to report.' Her voice had lost its initial burst of excitement. 'Neighbors, who are pretty far away, didn't spot anything.'

'They used it as a staging house. Change of clothes. Change of vehicles. Maybe even change of drivers.'

A thought struck him. 'Did anyone check the garage? Any paint in there? Paint guns?'

Her head moved. She shouted at someone. Kowalski came running, listened and went away.

He returned moments later, nodding his head.

Burke came back on. 'Yeah. Several cans of black paint. The fumes are still hanging in the air.'

Broker pumped his fist in silent triumph and leaned forward. 'Burke, check the trash cans for any strips of pills or syringes or cotton. It's possible they drugged the kids while they were repainting the getaway vehicles.'

'Will do.' She lifted a hand in a wave and disappeared inside the house.

The bounce had returned to her step.

The call from Pieter van Zyl, the Director-General of the South African State Security Agency, came when they were returning back to the capital.

'I guess there's no point asking how you are, my friend,' Pieter's voice boomed out of the speakers fitted in the vehicle. His voice was deep and had only a trace of an accent. 'The TV stations and newspapers here have nothing else to cover.'

He laughed and a speaker trembled. 'Our local politicians are unhappy. Everyone has forgotten them.'

The laugh disappeared, seriousness set in. 'I guess you are involved?'

'Just watching,' Broker replied laconically.

'Hello, Broker. I know what your *watching* means.'

They heard papers rustle. 'Right, let's get down to business. I have shared these details with your FBI too, but there's some stuff here which is for you alone. You can pass it on, if you wish.'

'The two snipers from Baltimore, Botha and Alletta, both were contractors to our Defense Intelligence Division. They were used occasionally, when the DID didn't have or didn't want to use internal resources.'

He cleared his throat. 'They were also used when special messages needed to be conveyed.'

Broker looked at Zeb. They knew what those messages could be. There was a time in the country's history when violence and brutality was adopted by the state to quell domestic or foreign enemies.

'Botha is the live one, isn't he?'

'Yeah,' Zeb replied.

'Is he singing?'

'He has, but he hasn't revealed anything much,' Broker didn't hide his disgust.

'We want him here. There's an outstanding warrant for him for several unsanctioned kills.'

Broker chuckled. 'You're joking aren't you, Pieter? There's no way you're getting Botha. He will be tried and sentenced here.'

Zeb held a hand up to silence Broker. 'Pieter, what is it?'

'We kept tabs on Botha and Alletta and many others like him. There are rumors that they both worked with Russian agencies and Russian mobs.'

A cup clinked on a saucer. They heard him take a sip, van Zyl loved his tea.

'I made some calls like you asked.'

Zeb had called the intelligence heads of clandestine agencies all over the world. Many of those agencies owed him favors. Many of those heads knew him personally and considered him their friend.

Most of them had come back with scant information. The kidnappers or the Baltimore operators were unknown to them.

'I spoke to Andropov,' van Zyl paused for Zeb to make the connection.

Grigor Andropov ran an agency in Russia that was similar to Zeb's Agency. Andropov was Clare's equivalent, a man who lived in the shadows and whose existence very few people knew of.

'Andropov said you should meet him. He said he called you several times.'

Zeb looked at Broker, who turned and fumbled in the rear and returned with Zeb's satphone.

Zeb pressed his thumb to the screen and unlocked it. Broker scrolled through the logs and swore softly.

There were three missed calls from the Russian.

'Did he say why?'

The booming laugh rang out again. 'You know how he is. Even his shadow doesn't know who cast it. All he said was that it was important.'

Zeb dialed Andropov as soon as the South African had hung up. The phone rang several times. The Russian didn't believe in voicemail.

He called Burke. She said they hadn't heard anything from the Russians.

'Why?'

'Just asking,' Zeb told her. He didn't want to raise her hopes unnecessarily.

It was late evening by the time they reached their hotel, a different one.

Broker parked the vehicle while Zeb went to his room to change and hit the pavement for a run.

Running gave him space, freedom. It was when he did his best thinking.

He didn't want to go to Moscow. There were too many leads to be chased down and Murphy wanted him to be around.

Hope Andropov can reveal whatever he has in a call.

He ran several laps on the National Mall, paused for a moment to take in the tall, white, obelisk in the distance and the soaring monument opposite it, an ode to the sixteenth president of the country.

He turned back to the hotel, dodging pedestrians and office goers, cutting through space and crowd, his mind in its grey space, thinking, figuring, calculating.

He neared the hotel, approached a patch of sidewalk that wasn't lit, had no foot traffic, and didn't pay attention to the solitary car.

'Mr. Carter.'

Move. Turn. Draw.

He was on the ground, on his right shoulder.

His right hand stretched out, ending in his Glock.

His eye on its sight. The sight on the figure in front of him.

All this even before his brain had computed that the voice was an older man's.

That his radar hadn't pinged. That the beast hadn't stirred.

He waited for the man to emerge from darkness and stand under a lamp.

Zeb rose and holstered his handgun.

The man was in his sixties, balding, dressed as if he was returning from his workday. White shirt, dark trousers, dark jacket.

He came closer to Zeb and the hollows under his eyes, the

lines on his face, became clearer.

He held his hands up in apology.

'I'm sorry. They told me not to approach you from behind.'

Who's they?

Zeb recognized the man in front of him. It was Larry Fairman, father of Shawn Fairman.

Larry Fairman was a lobbyist with a well-known firm inside the Beltway. Larry Fairman was well known himself, having acquired a reputation for getting things done in the Beltway.

Good rep. Good income. Could afford to send his son to private school, which was where Shawn Fairman met and became friends with James Barlow.

'Can I have a minute of your time, Mr. Carter?'

'I'm here, sir.'

How does he know my name?

Larry Fairman nodded, acknowledging the irrelevance of his question. He searched for words and then spoke carefully.

'I'm told you are helping find the two boys, Mr. Carter.'

'No, sir. You heard wrong. I am a security consultant, visiting the city on business.'

A ghost of a smile came on Fairman's lips.

'She told me you would say this. She seemed amused.'

'Who's she, sir?'

'Clare. She didn't give a last name. Neither did the prince.'

Why would Clare speak to him, let alone say that?

He read the expression on his face. 'Mr. Carter, I helped the Royal Family of Saud on several matters. The prince reached out to me when--'

He broke off, looked away, composed himself and began again. 'We spoke when the boys were kidnapped. It was a long call. He said he knew what it felt like. His daughter had been kidnapped once. He said she was rescued by some Americans.'

'He backtracked when he realized what he had said, but I pinned him down, took advantage of our friendship. He said he could not reveal who the Americans were, but he gave me Clare's number?'

'Clare took your call?'

'She did, Mr. Carter. When she heard who I was. I spoke. She listened. Like I said, she was amused when she gave me your name and where you would be.'

'She said it wouldn't do anyone good if I let slip where you stayed to anyone. Or revealed her number. She wasn't amused then.'

Sounds like Clare. Broker will have to get her another secure number.

'I asked your friend. A big man, African-American. He said it was probably best to wait for you here, when you returned from your run.'

'Do you know what I do, sir?'

'I can guess, Mr. Carter.' He raised his hands reassuringly. 'I am not here to spill any secrets of yours, Mr. Carter.'

'Why are you here, sir?'

Larry Fairman didn't answer. He half turned as a door thumped and a figure rose from the car and emerged.

It was an elderly woman, as old as Larry Fairman, her white hair framing her eyes which were tired.

She came forward slowly and gripped Larry Fairman's arm.

'Madeleine, my wife, Mr. Carter.'

'We had our son late, Mr. Carter, as you might have guessed.' Her voice was low, soft, and exhausted.

She patted her husband's arm. 'This was my doing, Mr. Carter. You have to forgive Larry. I forced him to drive up, park here, meet your friends, and wait for you.'

'We met Sarah Burke. She's a good woman. Director Murphy, he's a good man too. We met several other people. All earnest people. All working hard.'

'They are all working to get the missing boys back.'

'I wanted to see you, too. Larry told me you are not part of the investigation, but I am a mother, Mr. Carter. A mother, in such times, does not act rationally.'

'I told Larry, I want to see Mr. Carter. Even if he is not involved. I just want to see him. We don't want anything from you, Mr. Carter. I just wanted to see you, see what manner of man you are.'

She stopped. Zeb didn't speak. The city didn't speak.

'You are a good man, Mr. Carter. I can see it in your eyes.'

She waved a hand helplessly. 'I am sure all this sounds weird to you, Mr. Carter. However, I am the mother of a son the world seems to have forgotten.'

'I just wanted to see you for myself.'

Larry Fairman patted her hand. 'We are sorry for bothering you, Mr. Carter. Have a good evening. God Bless You.'

He led her back to their car and drove away.

Zebadiah Carter flew to Moscow that night.

Chapter 16

Zeb met Grigor Andropov in a quiet hotel in the Basmanny District of Moscow.

It was the same hotel he had met him in, during a previous mission. Even the couches seemed to be the same. The lack of traffic in that corner of the hotel was the same.

It was a busy hotel. It was tourist season. But not a single tourist or hotel staff walked through that corner.

Cleared by his men.

Andropov was an inch taller than Zeb, had green eyes and short hair that had started to grey. He hugged Zeb close, held him for a long time and patted him on his back.

Zeb had saved his life in Iraq. The secretive Russian had never acknowledged it. He hadn't forgotten, either.

He laughed when Zeb's eyes flicked to his hair. 'I am getting old, brat.' Brother. 'But I am still of use to my country.'

Russia and the United States were at a low point in diplomatic relations. However, the intelligence agencies of the two countries still spoke to each other via back channels, when it suited both the countries' interests.

The kidnapping of the Veep's son and his friend had thawed relations and there was a higher amount of traffic between the agencies.

'You are looking good, Grigor.'

Grigor flicked the compliment away. He *was* looking good, but appearances were merely a tool to be used in his business.

The spymaster looked behind Zeb and seconds later a waiter came rushing with a silver tray, flask, and two cups. Zeb was sure the service wasn't available to other patrons.

His agency probably owns the hotel.

Grigor poured for the two of them, handed a cup to Zeb, moved to the couch to sit alongside Zeb.

It was a message. He would help Zeb to any length he could. Zeb took a sip of the bitter tea, let it race down his body and faced the spymaster.

'The South Africans and the South Americans were recruited on the darknet, yes?'

'Yeah. That site has disappeared.'

'It was taken down. Not long ago, just a few months back.'

Zeb paused, his cup near his mouth, and stared at Grigor.

'We took it down.'

Zeb placed the cup down carefully.

Grigor smiled and the years fell away from his face and he became the agent Zeb had met in Iraq.

'It's not like that, brat. We know who created that website. We asked him to take it down, politely. He agreed.'

'This man is still alive?' *Not lying at the bottom of Moskva with a hole in his head?*

The smile grew at Zeb's unsaid words.

'Of course. We don't do that anymore. These days it's about computers and drones and phone hacking.'

'You questioned him?'

'Nyet. You can ask him anything.'

'Who is he?'

The smile dropped. 'You have heard of Vitali Belov?'

Zeb ran the name through his mind. He shook his head.

'Not many people have. Fewer have seen him. He is the most powerful organized crime boss in Russia.'

'You let him live?'

Grigor flexed his hands. 'He's more powerful than I am.'

Zeb sat silently, digesting the spymaster's words.

That can't be possible. Andropov can make things happen in this country that mortals can't even imagine.

'He launders money for the top politicians,' Grigor said simply.

He nodded when understanding dawned in Zeb's eyes. 'All the way to the top. He does deals for them, acts as their front for their investments. He's their bank manager, their accountant, their treasurer. He knows more about their wealth, than they do.'

'He owes me some favors and has agreed to meet you. Beyond that, I can't guarantee anything. He might tell you all that he knows. He might not.' He shrugged.

'When?'

'Tomorrow. Someone will pick you up.'

They talked about past and present friends. Of missions and men. It was late when Grigor rose and stretched. He hugged Zeb one last time.

'He's not normal. Be prepared for anything,' he warned one

last time and walked away without looking back.

A stretch limo was awaiting Zeb the next day. A black monster, standing in solitary splendor in the hotel's drive. No other vehicles were allowed to come near it.

The doorman ushered Zeb to the vehicle, deferentially, and opened the door for him.

Zeb slid inside and seated himself on warm leather.

Leather, fur, cushions, were his first impressions.

Opposite him was a bar, but the man on the far end of the seat caught his attention.

He was craggy faced, with slicked black hair, dark eyes, and clean shaven. He was powerfully built, dressed in a spotless white shirt over dark trousers.

The dark eyes bored holes into Zeb as the man crossed his legs, which were adorned with spit polished shoes.

'You are Carter.'

No accent. Andropov said his English was flawless.

'And you are Belov?'

Belov inclined his head.

A bodyguard opposite them made to search Zeb.

Belov waved him off regally and the limo set off.

It drove past the Kremlin, past stately buildings, past dark, forbidding structures which hid years of history and bloodshed behind their closed walls, and wound through narrow streets before coming to a halt.

Zeb looked through the dark window. It was the entrance to a gym.

'Come,' Belov beckoned.

Zeb followed him, falling behind his protection detail. Two massively built men at the front, cleared the way for Below.

One of the hulks opened the door with a hand the size of a shovel.

The aroma of sweat and grunts and loud music assaulted them as they entered the gym.

The music died when Belov went deeper.

Evidently a person of some importance.

Belov went to a boxing ring and watched two men fight.

One, a lean, lithe man with a narrow face, was dressed in red. Red shorts, red gloves, red shoes. No headgear.

His opponent was shorter, broader and dressed in blue. He

too wasn't wearing headgear.

The lean man attacked. Flowing from dancing to attack in a split second.

The blue man ducked, evaded, and counter punched.

The man in red danced back, languidly smiling.

He waved a hand at Belov without turning.

Blue took the opportunity to attack. A flurry of kicks and blows, aimed at the head, the chest, the groin.

Red parried easily, went on the back foot, turned defense into offense as he suddenly leapt in the air and felled Blue with a swinging kick.

A watching crowd gasped and murmured in awe. No one had seen that coming. Not even Blue. The fallen man lay still.

Red leaned over him, lay a hand over his neck, and shrugged.

Two men came rushing and hauled Blue off on a stretcher.

Muay Thai, Savate, many different styles. Red is good. Very good. And not just an amateur fighter, either, going by the scars on his chest. This is someone who has faced deadly combat.

Belov slapped hands with Red, laughed and joked and turned to Zeb. 'Sergei Lagutov,' he introduced Red. 'You heard of him?'

The name rang a bell. Zeb thought for a while and then Broker's voice flashed in his mind. Broker showing him an article on a screen.

'Moscow MMA champion?'

Belov nodded vigorously. 'For five years. Now he'll fight the world champion next year.'

The mobster's eyes turned sly. 'He's like you. He's ex-Spetsnaz.'

Lagutov eyed Zeb. 'You are Seal?'

Zeb shook his head.

'Marine? Special Forces?'

'I was just a soldier. Now a businessman.'

Lagutov looked at him carefully. 'You fight.' He gestured and a trainer came running with gloves and shoes and a pair of shorts.

Zeb declined. 'Not for me.'

Lagutov's lips curled. 'You scared?'

'Yeah, who wouldn't be? You are very good.'

'Better than you?'

'Light years ahead.'

Belov roared with laughter, slapped his thigh and led Zeb away.

Zeb turned once and saw the fighter watching him, the way a panther watched its prey.

'Who is he?' Zeb asked Belov once they were back in the limo.

Belov looked at him surprised. 'He's my bodyguard. Most dangerous man on earth.'

Belov dropped him back at the hotel. 'Tomorrow, we talk.'

Zeb watched bemused as the limo whispered away.

That must have been some kind of test.

He checked with Broker. The facial recognition programs hadn't yielded anything.

Zeb was expecting that. The kidnappers wouldn't have gone unmasked if they were in the system.

Camera images in Boston hadn't turned up anything. There were no cameras around the abandoned hotel.

The FBI was tracing the paint found in Eldersburg. It was a common variety found in hundreds of stores. They weren't hopeful.

He briefed them on his day.

Meghan chuckled in the speaker phone. 'Let me get this right. You met a spymaster and a mobster. You went for a ride in a fancy limo. You then met a champion MMA fighter. That was your day?'

'That sounds like it.'

Zeb woke, making the transition from sleep to awake, without any change in his breathing.

It was late night. His room was dark. The street outside was dark. He lay motionless, thinking about what had woken him.

It hadn't been any noise outside. Not any sound in his room.

His gun lay within hand's reach. He was dressed in a faded T-shirt and a pair of shorts.

The beast was prowling inside him, his radar was pinging slowly, yet he couldn't detect any danger.

'It's me,' A voice chuckled.

Lagutov! What's he doing here?

The beast flooded through him, amped him to alert in an

instant.

If Lagutov could enter his room without alerting him, he wasn't exceptional. He was of Zeb's caliber.

'I made some inquiries. Spoke to some people. They said there were rumors of an operative who looked like you. An American operative. They said if you were who that man was, you were lethal.'

Lagutov smiled in the dark. 'They said I should keep away from you.'

'Naturally, I was curious. I wanted to see how good you were.'

'Why?'

Lagutov was surprised. 'Why not? I live for fighting.'

Nothing in his voice changed. No shadows in the room moved, and yet Zeb sensed the attack.

He flung himself out of the bed, rolled away from it and rose to his feet.

Don't look for shadows. Feel the energy.

The wrinkled old man, his mentor in Indonesia, had drilled it in him, as he had made Zeb fight in the dark, blindfolded, against multiple opponents.

He felt the force, and then the rush of air as Lagutov approached.

He bent his knees, swayed his body and a strike sailed above him.

He grasped the retreating hand, met air, felt another strike coming, and leapt back and crashed into the wall.

Lagutov laughed. 'You are good, Carter, but I am better.'

Zeb didn't go to the location of his voice.

It'll be a trap.

He moved on the balls of his feet, his breathing low and steady and moved deeper inside the room, to the bed.

Something moved. Sharp and hard. Toward him.

He rolled underneath it. Lagutov's leg, in a spinning kick.

Another something moved. This time faster.

It slammed into his chest like a pile-driver and flung him on the bed.

The beast roared. He rolled. It scanned his body.

He was fine. A bruise on his chest, but he was fine.

Lagutov followed swiftly with strikes.

Zeb parried and ducked, and danced away.

Silence fell in the room, not even the sound of breathing

broke it.

Something flew.

Zeb ducked.

Something crashed in the wall. A lamp.

A white shape floated.

Zeb squinted.

Fell, when a hammer-like blow struck his temple.

A grunt escaped him.

He rolled.

He couldn't. His hand was trapped by Lagutov's leg.

He sensed the other leg approaching in a kick.

He twisted his free hand, his left, aimed his elbow and made contact with Lagutov's shin.

His left arm jarred at the force of the blow. He heard Lagutov gasp.

His leg loosened. Zeb freed himself.

And launched into attack.

A numbing blow caught Lagutov on his right thigh.

His right hand shaped unconsciously into a sheet of iron and slammed into the Russian's ribs.

The Russian groaned and fell back.

The two men parted and circled in the dark.

Lagutov attacked, a flurry of force and energy.

Zeb leaned *into* the strikes. Took the blows on his neck and chest.

The beast ignored them. It was dark and angry and snarling.

It wasn't like Lagutov. It didn't seek fights. It didn't like being bested, either.

It absorbed a hammer blow, a right fist from the Russian.

The fist lay for a microsecond, high on Zeb's chest.

Zeb twisted it, applied a lock that pinched a nerve on the wrist.

The Russian screamed.

Zeb applied pressure, applied force, bent the arm back, so far back that something cracked.

The Russian groaned, reached behind with his left hand, struck hard.

Zeb absorbed that too, didn't let up on the pressure.

Till he suddenly released and the Russian stumbled.

Swirl around. Catch. Spin.

Zeb floated around the falling Russian.

One arm around the man's waist, like a lover's.

One arm on his back.

One leg kicking out Lagutov's feet.

He spun on his feet.

He hurled.

Lagutov crashed through the window and disappeared into the night.

Chapter 17

Grigor Andropov was the first on the scene.

He had arrived within fifteen minutes of Zeb's call, dressed in a wool jacket, dark shirt and dark trousers, his shoes immaculately polished.

It was late at night, not much moved on Moscow's streets, but that wasn't a reason for an old spymaster to lower his standards.

He didn't look at the body initially.

He held Zeb by the shoulders and looked him up and down. 'You're okay?'

Zeb nodded.

He was jacketed and holstered. There was no telling how Belov would react.

'What happened?'

Zeb told him, briefly.

Andropov raised an eyebrow when he had finished. 'Lagutov was a rising star. He was widely predicted to be world champion. He was also a hothead. He picked fights for no reason. In bars. Night clubs.'

He circled the body once and then surprised Zeb by kicking it.

'He raped teenage girls. Several of them. It was never proven, it never became public, but we knew it. He was protected by Belov. We asked Belov to drop him, but he didn't listen.'

Zeb looked down the narrow street at the side of the hotel.

Where are the cops?

'They won't come.' Andropov smiled, reading his searching glances.

Juice. He's got as much juice as Clare has.

Belov made them wait for an hour.

In that time not a single hotel employee or guest had stepped into the street. No traffic had passed, either. Zeb didn't see Andropov's men, but he knew they were present; they had a tight grip on the scene.

Belov's limo purred silently and came to a halt a hundred feet away.

The two large men stepped out. One of them held the door open for the mobster. Two other hoods emerged. They had the hard look of gunmen.

Belov, too, was dressed in an evening suit, an ivory cane in one hand.

Must be a Russian mobster thing. The higher up you go, the more refined your dress and accessories.

Belov and Andropov exchanged hugs.

They aren't forced. Cordial.

Andropov stepped back while Belov approached the dead man.

The four goons curved behind Zeb.

Just in case I decide to hoof it.

Zeb crossed his arms. It gave the perception that he was wary. Defensive.

It also brought the Glock closer to his gun hand.

If it comes to that, I will go down, but so will Belov.

He was sure gunplay wouldn't be involved.

Belov finished his study and came to him.

'What happened?'

It was the first time he had looked Zeb in the eye, ever since they had met.

Zeb repeated the evening's incidents.

Belov didn't speak for several moments and then he sighed. 'What do I do with you?'

'You should thank me.'

Six heads turned in his direction as if he had lost his senses.

'He was a liability to you. He was no longer effective as a bodyguard. All this championship nonsense had gone to his head.'

'You are one of the most powerful men in Russia.'

No harm in stroking his ego.

'That comes with unwanted attention and enemies. With him around, you couldn't have kept a low profile.'

'As long as he was around, the pressure on you to give him up to the police, would have risen.'

Belov's eyes flickered at Zeb's implication. That Zeb knew of Lagutov's criminal activities.

'Did you see the mob outside the gym yesterday? The reporters, the fans? How long do you think it would have taken for his activities to surface?'

Zeb shook his head. 'Lagutov was a liability. I am sure that thought crossed your mind several times.'

'Lagutov is in the past. He will be forgotten soon. My country is going through a tough time. I am sure your help will be appreciated.'

He felt Andropov nod approvingly. It was the right tone to adopt.

Zeb had perused Belov's file that Meghan had sent, earlier in the night. The mobster owned casinos and hotels in the U.S. He was suspected of money laundering, and some of his known offshore accounts were being watched.

Those accounts and properties could be seized if Belov was suspected of withholding vital intel.

Belov got the message. 'What do we tell everyone? How did he die?'

Zeb looked up at the window through which the fighter had fallen. Belov followed his glance.

'He tried to fly.'

Andropov took care of the body and before leaving, hugged Zeb and whispered softly.

'Neatly played, tovarich. Why don't you stay in Moscow for some time and get rid of all gangsters?'

Zeb joined Belov in his limo, declined the offer of a drink and leaned back while the limo sped down empty streets past red lights – what were red lights to the most powerful Russian mobster – and stopped in front of his office.

The office was twenty stories tall, had a mirrored glass and a modernistic feel, and was behind the Kremlin.

'A short distance to run when my masters call,' Belov said when Zeb looked at the domes of the Russian palace.

He smiled knowingly when Zeb understood the oblique reference.

He led the way inside, nodding at guards who sprang to attention.

A private elevator opened into an office half the size of a tennis court, on the fifteenth floor.

The two man-mountains disappeared, presumably to pump some more weights. The hard faced men took their positions on couches and stared at nothing in particular.

Belov picked up an ivory-colored phone, spoke into it softly and then poured two cups of steaming coffee from a silver flask.

A young man entered the office, carrying a laptop. He had long flowing hair, a thick brown beard, and wore a loose Grateful Dead T-shirt.

It was nearing dawn, however, if Belov was awake, so was the rest of his organization.

'Oleg,' Belov introduced him to Zeb. He didn't mention a last name and didn't introduce Zeb in return.

Oleg plugged his laptop, typed furiously in it, looked at Belov for confirmation and when he got a nod, turned the screen toward Zeb.

Zeb leaned forward. It seemed to be a message board. Its name was blanked out.

'That is where the South Africans were hired. Oleg set the website up for people to post jobs, others to respond.'

'I thought it was taken down!'

'It is down,' Belov replied drily. 'What you are seeing is a static page.'

Oleg went into technical details, spoke of Tor, the dark internet, and used other terms that Zeb was sure the twins and Broker would understand. They didn't matter to him.

He was interested in the buyer's identity.

Belov sensed his impatience and cut Oleg off.

'All job posters went through a verification process. They had to prove who they were.'

'How was that done?'

'A video call with Oleg.'

'Those can be faked, can't they?'

'Not if there is a live TV playing in the background, tuned to a specific news channel.'

'They could wear face masks.'

'They could,' Belov acknowledged. 'That is something we have no control over.'

'What if they don't want to reveal themselves?'

'They don't get to post, then. There are hundreds of such sites in the darknet. They can go to those, or use other means of recruitment.'

'Why should they trust you?'

'Because I am Vitali Belov. Those in the darknet knew this board was mine.'

Oleg ran a search and came back with several records. He clicked on one and the screen opened to reveal the job.

Snipers Wanted, ran the headline.

The details were thin. The poster was seeking snipers to carry out a job in Asia. The snipers had to prove their kills and those interested could contact the poster.

The ad was more than two years old.

'That's the one the South Africans and the Colombian responded to,' Belov said simply.

Oleg highlighted a line on the screen.

The job poster's name. *Chameleon8362.*

Oleg went to a directory, scrolled through several files and clicked on one.

It was a video file.

He played it.

A dark room came up, a TV in the corner with a Russian channel playing on it.

Zeb sucked in his breath when a man came into view, wearing a T-shirt and jeans.

It was who the snipers called Bob.

Zeb knew him as Glasses.

Chapter 18

Zeb slept for eight straight hours on his return to D.C.

He had returned with Bob's email address, bank account details and the video file.

He had put a nervous looking Oleg in contact with Broker, the twins, and Yuri. The four of them would extract every available detail from Oleg.

'No one will touch you,' he told Oleg. Oleg looked unconvinced.

'He means it,' Belov told him in Russian.

'Da. Andropov is my reference,' Zeb replied in the same language, with a Muscovite's accent, on top.

Belov and Oleg stared at him in astonishment, and then Belov chuckled slowly and burst into laughter.

'You are a sly one, my friend. Lagutov didn't stand a chance, did he?'

Belov dropped him back to the hotel, signaled for his protectors to leave him, and when he was alone with Zeb, spoke carefully.

'How friendly would your government be if someone of my position, was to give up all secrets?'

Zeb settled back in the limo and considered Belov. 'You have power. You have unlimited wealth. You are untouchable. Why would you give all that up? You will be a hunted man, if you cross the line. Remember Litivenko?'

Belov nodded. The former FSB officer's poisoning by radioactive material and subsequent death, while living in London under asylum, was well known in intelligence circles.

'I have a daughter who asks me why we don't have a normal life. I tell her, this is normal. However, she is eleven years old. She knows what normal is.'

Belov will be a treasure trove of intel. Any intelligence agency in the world will scoop him up.

'I will talk to the right people.'

Belov recited a phone number and smiled in thanks when Zeb memorized it instead of writing it down.

'It's secure. No one else has access to it.'

He stopped Zeb when he was exiting. 'We never had this

conversation.'

Zeb shook his hand. That was a given.

Andropov was silent for several minutes when Zeb told him of Belov. They were in the spymaster's car, on their way to the Domodedovo airport for Zeb to catch his flight.

'Politics in Russia will never be the same again, if he crosses over.'

Zeb stared at him. 'You want it to happen, don't you?'

Andropov grinned. 'Of course. Life will be interesting. Every politician will be jumping around like that cat saying you have.'

'My country will become cleaner,' he added softly.

That's the real reason.

Broker had rented several rooms in the hotel and had outfitted them as temporary offices, in the two days that Zeb had been absent.

He found the twins and the older man huddled around a conference phone, after he had freshened up.

'Yuri,' Beth mouthed silently at his inquiring look.

'We heard you turned down the opportunity to be Moscow's MMA champion.' Meghan smirked when the call had finished.

Beth swung around, her flying hair almost knocking off a paper cup. 'Oh, yeah, tell us about that. How did you wriggle out of that?'

Zeb glossed over the details but told them about Belov's offer.

Bwana's eyes widened. 'He wants to defect? That still happens?'

'More than you imagine. A lot of it happens at the low level or is unreported. Ever since Litivenko was killed, no one wants to create more targets.'

Bear gingerly took a sip of whatever was in the paper cup. Chloe had started him on some new age drinks which he consumed stoically. The things one did for love.

'I read,' he said defensively when all eyes turned toward him at this explanation.

Zeb brought them back to the investigation. 'Any clues in that video or in the login details?'

'The Feds are running down the voice print and comparing it with everything that the NSA and other agencies have.'

Broker crossed his legs, which were adorned in some kind of high-end brand of jeans that Zeb didn't recognize.

He recognized the shoes though. They were Louboutin and Broker wore them when he was feeling positive.

Over the years the NSA had sucked phone calls, email messages, text messages, any kind of internet communication, from the ether and had created a huge database against which any voiceprint could be compared.

The NSA wasn't the only agency at it. Several other national and international agencies had their own databases. All those databases were now made available to the FBI.

'Werner is running those prints too. In addition we are looking at where else *Chameleon8362* popped up on the darknet and the IP address of the job posting.'

'You can access the darknet?' Zeb asked as he watched the mute replay of the video call.

Broker didn't deign to answer. Zeb was tech savvy. However, he had a habit of asking inane questions which were beneath Broker's dignity.

Zeb's eyes narrowed as he took in the video again, ignoring the wash of voices. He dimly heard threat vectors and IP masking and tunneling and other terms being discussed.

He leaned closer to the video, over Meghan's head, a wisp of her hair tickling his cheek.

She squeaked, startled, and moved away. He didn't pay attention.

He watched Bob – it was easier to call him that, than Glasses – talk briefly and then the video ended. He played it again, unaware that the others had fallen silent, watching him.

He played the video twice more and then straightened and let the world enter his bubble.

'You saw something?' Chloe's voice sharpened as she leaned forward too, trying to spot what he had.

'That TV behind him,' Zeb explained.

'What of it?' she demanded. 'It's a Japanese model. We thought of tracing down its purchase, but it would be impossible.'

'Not the TV itself.' Zeb waited, giving them time to figure it out.

They crowded around Meghan who played the video, brought up another program that ran the segment in slow-mo.

The TV ran silently.

Bob entered the room.

Bob turned toward the TV and pointed at it.

He turned back to the camera and spoke into it.

'Ignore him,' Zeb told his people.

They focused on the channel, a news channel. Headlines floated at the bottom of the screen, in Russian.

They were all fluent in Russian.

The weather came on.

Meghan sucked in her breath. Other exclamations followed.

'It's a regional channel. A local Moscow channel.'

'There's something else.'

They turned back to the video.

Beth screamed a moment later.

'It has the cable operator's logo.'

'No one knows who they are. Murphy knows, but he isn't saying.'

Darrell's refined voice spoke over the speakerphone in the center of the dining table in the house in Lighthollow.

Merritt was having his breakfast, alone. His team had theirs. The routine was unchanged. Two men guarded the boys. Two others patrolled the house and its front and backyard. From the inside.

No one stepped outside, other than Merritt.

Merritt had cameras all over the house, pressure sensors, infrared beams, motion detectors, all the electronic equipment that he needed was deployed.

Monitors were all over the house and his room held the central command.

'There seems to be eight of them. Three women, five men. A lot of FBI agents, remember them since two of the women are twins in their late twenties. That kind of detail tends to stick.'

Merritt spooned cereal into his mouth, crunched quietly and didn't speak. He hadn't come across the eight. He would have remembered twins.

'They are the ones who found the house?' he asked finally.

'Yes.' Darrell never used the informal *yeah*. Formality was in his breeding.

'Two of them. A guy called Zebadiah Carter and another

one named Broker. That kind of name stays in the memory.'

'The FBI shared all this with you?'

'They know me,' Darrell replied with quiet pride. He didn't mention that Mark had contributed too.

'Where are they holed up?'

'No one knows. They aren't with the Feds any longer. I am told they are the ones who thwarted the hoodlums you set on Burke.'

Merritt stopped stirring his spoon. 'I thought it was the two FBI agents outside her house.'

'That was made public. Two of Carter's agents were stationed there too.'

Okay. So what? He shrugged and another spoonful went inside him.

'There's something more.' Darrell's voice became taut.

Merritt eyed the phone as if he could see the patrician face.

'I overheard something when I was in the restroom. This isn't anything I could verify.'

'Carter and his people were in the hotel.'

Carter was his usual impassive self, Broker was smiling slightly, the two large men were looking bored, but the women, especially the twins, seemed to be bouncing as if on springs.

Burke had received a call from Broker, a request to meet, half an hour back. He hadn't disclosed the reason.

She knew they were pursuing the investigation, their way. She hoped they would share whatever they found.

Of course, they would, Burke. He shared the video. Besides, remember Eldersburg?

Kowalski and Randy flanked her, followed by several other agents, as Carter's team took seats.

Carter and the two large men with him – she always forgot their names – leaned against a wall.

'Got anywhere with the voice prints?' Broker asked, a hint of amusement underlying his words.

'Come on, Broker, it's not even a day since you sent that across to us.' Burke clicked her tongue impatiently.

Randy went into an explanation of petabytes and exabytes of data. Broker waved him off.

He removed a USB stick from his pocket. 'Can we plug and

play this?'

An agent took it from his hand, plugged it into a laptop, fiddled with a remote, and a screen appeared.

'We have seen this. Several times. We have analyzed it to pieces. Nothing new to be seen,' Kowalski declared when Bob's video came up.

'Describe what you see,' Broker steepled his fingers and asked in a bored voice.

Kowalski looked at Burke. She shrugged. *Go ahead.*

Kowalski broke down the video, frame by frame, and when he had finished, waited expectantly.

Broker chuckled. 'We suspected you wouldn't spot it. None of us did either, except for Zeb.'

'Spot what?' Burke asked in mounting irritation.

'Why, the cable provider, on the TV.'

A split second of silence, then Kowalski and Randy dived for the remote. Randy got to it first. He thumbed it, fast-forwarded it and paused when the TV came on.

He cursed when his eyes narrowed on the tiny red symbol on the bottom right of the TV screen.

'You got a name?' he asked Broker, his eyes frozen on the TV.

Broker gave him the name.

Randy, Kowalski and the rest of the agents rushed out before Burke tasked them.

'You'll talk to the cable operator's people, they sure as hell won't roll over at the initial request. You'll go to the FSB and they'll drag their feet.'

She looked at Carter in silent acknowledgement of the truth in his words. 'You got a better way?'

'Is this room recorded?'

She hesitated, remembering a time when Carter had confessed to a killing in an unrecorded room.

'Yes.'

Carter waited.

She sighed. 'I'll get it turned off.'

She went out of the room and when she returned in ten minutes, Carter hadn't moved from his position.

'He's into all that Zen stuff. Motionless. Lighter than air,' Beth snarked when Burke frowned in his direction.

'All clear. Your secrets won't be recorded by us evil people,' she said sarcastically.

Carter came to the sole table in the room, pulled a phone out of his pocket, dialed a number and put it on speaker.

It rang three times and then a voice came on.

'Da?'

Burke stared dumbfounded as Carter and the man at the other end conversed in a language she hadn't heard before.

She could recognize most of the world's leading languages. She could speak passably in Spanish, French, and German. She could understand a few phrases in Russian.

Carter was speaking in none of those.

The conversation was short, mostly silence at the other end.

It ended with a *Da, okay*.

'We should get a list of all their subscribers in the next half hour.'

The bearded large man, Bear, stirred. 'Current list won't –'

'Going back ten years.'

'Who was that? Which language was that? You started and ended in Russian, but the in-between was alien.' Burke tried hard to keep the accusatory tone out of her voice, but she knew she failed.

This dude drives me nuts!

'No one you know. Not a language you'll have heard of.' There was no trace of irony on Carter's face as he pocketed his phone and rose to leave.

'He still does that to us, even after all these years,' Meghan lingered behind when the others had followed Carter out. 'How's the rest of the investigation coming along?'

Burke turned her attention from the now empty doorway and focused on the twin in front of her.

'You folks ever given him a good kicking?'

Meghan laughed. 'And more. However, he won't change. He's Zeb.'

'I'm learning. The investigation? That video is the first proper lead we have. Thanks to Carter,' Burke responded drily.

Merritt was going through videos at his end too. Camera footage from their time in the hotel that one of his men had copied to a hard drive.

He had gone through the residents. Carter and his seven companions weren't staying in the hotel.

He went through the conference rooms. No bunch of eight people. No twins.

He finally turned to the restaurant and went through the several tables one at a time, front to back.

He spotted the twins first. They were hard to miss. Brown hair, green eyes, ready smiles, chatting away to those seated around them.

One was a large man, bearded. Another was an equally large man, black. No fat on them.

The security cameras were one of those high definition ones. Not cheap. The hotel catered to the wealthy. It could afford high end security.

The muscle definition on the large men was apparent.

Yet another man, an older one, seated beside an older woman.

Another woman

And then a man.

Merritt focused on him and even though he had never seen Zebadiah Carter before and heard of him only that day, he was sure, that man was Carter.

Carter didn't speak much in the few seconds of footage.

He looked once directly at the camera.

He seemed to be mocking Merritt.

Chapter 19

Merritt went through the rest of the footage on the hard drive. There was more, from cameras at different angles, in different parts of the hotel.

He frowned at one time.

The group of nine had thinned to five.

He called his four men and pointed out the group to them.

A couple of them said they recognized the twins. The other men weren't sure. It was a large hotel, they had their assigned tasks.

An idea struck Merritt.

He pulled up the footage from the parking lot and after searching, found the vehicle Carter had arrived in, along with the two large men and the good looking man.

His hand stilled on the mouse when he saw the same vehicle exiting the basement, a few minutes before the takedown began.

He left the hotel. The others remained. Yet Darrell was insistent Carter was there.

Unless….

A cold feeling gripped his belly. He shouted at one of the men, Pico, the one who was the tech whiz.

Pico came running.

Merritt pointed to the image of the vehicle exiting the parking lot.

'Can you figure out if that footage is fake? '

Andropov delivered in two hours.

I can go back twenty years, if you wish, he said helpfully in the anonymous email that came to Zeb and Burke.

He rarely used emails and phones to deliver intel, but this was one exception.

'Twenty years of subscriber details? Which universe do these guys live in?' Kowalski mumbled as he ran his eyes down though the sheets of paper.

There were names, addresses, photographs, bank account details, credit card numbers, the cable package they had subscribed to. There were special symbols to mark if a subscriber had bought on-demand content.

'It's called Russia,' Roger countered. He leaned back with

the satisfied air of someone who had put in a hard day's work and was enjoying his beer.

There was no beer. Just the eight of them, along with Burke, Kowalski, Randy, and a few other agents in a closed room in the Hoover building.

They had been in the room all day and the room should have stunk of perspiration and stale pizza.

It didn't. Modern air conditioning had come a long way since its invention.

Chloe rose to raise the shades on the darkened windows and orange rays of the setting sun bathed the room.

Strips of light and dark shadowed her face when she turned to Roger. 'Been a long day, Rog.'

Roger shrugged off the sarcasm with a grin. Texans had the thickest skin on the planet. 'Yeah. Motivating you guys, providing inspiration, making sure Burke doesn't deck Zeb. It can drain a man.'

A reluctant smile broke on Burke's face. She went over to Randy and peered over his shoulder at a program he was running that compared the photo-IDs of the subscribers with Bob's.

Fifteen minutes later, they had a name.

Alejandro Peres. A Mexican citizen who had hired an apartment in Moscow for a year, three years back, and had signed up to the cable TV network.

Pico worked on his computer silently, his fingers flying, his eyes still on the screen, occasionally dropping to his keyboard.

Pico was their comms guy. He ensured their gear was encrypted, set up security perimeters for them, erased their electronic footprints. In addition to his many skills, he was also an ace hacker and could go into any commercial network and wreak his brand of destruction. He was also good with guns and knives.

He had entered the hotel's security, had disabled all alarms and had taken control of it, the moment Merritt given him the green signal.

Pico worked with the Medellin cartel in Mexico. He was their lead comms dude. Merritt had tracked him down and had made him an offer.

More money. Job security, and more importantly, life

security.

In the grey world of drug cartels, even if that cartel was the largest in the world, Merritt's offer had been tempting, and Pico had grabbed it.

He and Merritt had been working together for a long time, along with the three others. Avram, Carlos, and Fiske.

They referred to each other only by single names, never the full name.

All of them went under the knife every five years and came out with a new nose, new ears and new hair styling.

Merritt had considered surgery after every mission, but there was a limit to how often identities and faces could be changed. Too much change could lead to errors in remembering.

Merritt didn't pace impatiently, he didn't crack his knuckles, while Pico worked. He had patience.

Pico raised his head finally after more than an hour.

'Someone inserted a loop.'

'When?'

Pico typed some more. 'About half an hour before we unloaded with our guns.'

Half an hour. Did they suspect something? If they did, why didn't they raise an alarm?

'Can you detect any intrusion in the system?'

Pico shook his head. 'I would need access to the hotel's network for that. However, I am sure there wasn't any, other than our own.'

Merritt nodded absently. The fact that Pico hadn't, didn't mean much. There could be better hackers than Pico, out there.

'Get everything you can on one Zebadiah Carter.'

He left to make a call to Darrell. It was time to apply more pressure on the FBI.

Zebadiah Carter was going through another printout, a single sheet of paper, on which were names and ages.

It was a list of missing agents in the last fifteen years; a list that Broker had cajoled from various covert agencies and in some cases, he had just hacked into.

Broker had a very liberal interpretation of *classified.*

Burke noticed the crowding around Zeb and drifted over. She had returned from another media briefing and her pale face said it hadn't gone well.

It was nearly a week since the kidnapping and the killings. The FBI had no meat to throw at the media. They were hungry. They were angry. So were the three hundred million people in the country.

'Got something else?' she asked, her eyes on the single sheet.

Zeb turned it over when she tried to read it upside down and got a frown. 'Something we are looking into. We'll tell you if it has teeth.'

She doesn't like it. However, Broker's methods will compromise her. She doesn't need to know right away.

'Way to make friends, Zeb,' Bear chuckled when she marched away, her back stiff in annoyance.

Zeb ignored him and resumed scrolling through the list.

'Why fifteen years? Why not ten or twenty?'

'His age.' Meghan replied promptly. 'Bob looked like someone in his early forties. An agent gone missing fifteen years back would have ample time to build a new legend, take on assignments and make a name for himself.'

Smart. But then, that's why we took them on.

'We have a problem don't we?' he mused.

Broker nodded. 'We'll need files on those men. Burke won't be able to get them. I can, but it'll take time.'

Zeb rose, his crew rose with him.

'Leaving?' Burke called out.

'Yeah.' He turned back to her. 'Alejandro Peres. Can Randy run face altering programs against his image and then run facial recog?'

The altering programs would throw up different likenesses of Peres to take into account cosmetic surgery. Those likenesses could then be searched for in various databases, such as airport arrivals, port terminals, wherever such databases were maintained.

Burke gave him a scornful look. 'Grandma. Eggs,' she retorted and shut the door behind them.

Clare listened silently, her face giving nothing away when Broker told her about the list.

They were in her office, fifteen minutes away from the FBI's. It was plain and bare. A wooden desk, a laptop, a phone, a few chairs, and nothing else.

There were no awards or certificates on the wall. No photographs of her with presidents or politicians.

She reached out to the phone and made a call when Broker had finished. She didn't ask any questions.

Her laptop was tuned to a news channel which was replaying Burke's media interview.

They needed results.

She spoke softly, her eyes seeing but not seeing, the men and women in front of her.

Bwana and Bear made her office seem small. They leaned against the wall, their arms crossed, listening impassively.

She put the phone down. 'You'll have them, in four hours. If you don't, call me.'

Zeb turned to leave, halted, and patted his pocket when his phone buzzed.

It was Burke.

He glanced at Clare, she nodded. *Take it.*

Her voice rang in the office even though it wasn't on speaker.

'They have made contact.'

Chapter 20

'Call me Bob.'

The voice on the speakerphone in the FBI's office was hollow and metallic sounding.

Zeb and the rest were back in the Hoover building, Clare along with them. The conference room was packed with Federal agents and personnel from other agencies.

Murphy and Pierce were present, their eyes on the speaker as if they could see Bob.

Burke was playing back Bob's call that had come to the toll free number. The call was genuine.

Not a single person outside the room knew that Bob was how the snipers and the hotel gunmen had identified the ringleader.

'Now that I have your attention, here's what will happen. I will call you in precisely half an hour. That'll give Special Agent in Charge Sarah Burke time to gather everyone in the investigation. It'll save her briefing all you folks over and over again.'

Bob hung up.

Murphy turned off the speakerphone with a stubby finger and glanced at the clock.

Ten more minutes.

No one moved. No one spoke.

Bob called precisely after ten minutes.

'Burke, are you there?'

'Yes, who are you? What do you want?'

'We'll get to that second part. As to the first, I am Bob. That's enough for you. I am sure your agents are running down every Bob in the country. A word of advice. Don't. You'll waste your time. You'll do it in any case, since you need to be doing something.'

There was utter silence when he stopped speaking.

He resumed. 'I am also sure you'll try to trace this call. Good luck with that.'

'Burke, I liked your press conference. A brave face in front of the wolves. You should get a commendation just for that.'

He laughed. The sound rang in the room.

Burke leaned forward. 'Bob, are the boys alive? Are they

in good shape?'

'Of course they are alive. What good would they be to me if they were dead?' A chuckle.

Zeb saw Burke raise her eyes to three men. They shook their heads defeatedly.

Linguistic experts would be my guess. Bob's voice is coming through a filter. That will kill any accent.

'How are James and Shawn doing, Bob? I bet they're scared,' a white-shirted man, seated opposite Murphy, spoke. His voice was pleasant, warm, designed to relax listeners.

Bob went silent again. It lasted for a second.

'Who's that? Burke, I bet it's one of those fancy negotiators you folks have. Get him off the line. Right now or else I'll end this call and you'll never hear from me again.'

Murphy waved a hand in resignation. The man left. Five others followed him.

Negotiating team, Beth mouthed at Zeb. He nodded.

'They've gone, Bob,' Burke told him.

'Great. That's what I liked about you from your press conferences, Burke. You answered promptly, never ducked a question. Of course you spun tall tales, but you were there.'

'Is Murphy there?'

'I am here,' the director replied.

'Hey, Murphy, the prez called for your resignation yet?' The laugh came on again.

Murphy didn't reply.

Bob let it pass. 'Let's get down to business. You asked what I wanted. I want five million dollars by tomorrow evening, deposited into my account.'

He recited a number. No one took it down. The call was being recorded. Note taking wasn't needed.

'Call it a safety deposit. A gesture of goodwill, although I'll admit, the goodwill will be fake.'

Bob was on a roll. He was laughing and chuckling, knowing that his audience was in no position to argue.

'That's a lot of money, Bob. The parents will have to be notified, they will have to make arrangements. Tomorrow is too early to get that sum together. On top of that, we need proof of life.' Burke, this time, waving away another white-shirted man. Another negotiator.

'The Veep is a rich man. Larry Fairman is not exactly on the dole, is he? I'm sure the two together can put together that sum. It's five mil. Not fifty mil.'

His tone hardened. 'As to proof of life, how about Fairman's pinky finger? I'll send that across. The boys have twenty fingers and twenty toes between them. I will send one digit each day. Not to you, but to a TV channel. Each digit to a different channel.'

Pierce lunged forward. 'You can't get away with this, you monster. The whole country is hunting you. You'll be found sooner or later.'

'Who's that? The least you folks could do is be courteous and identify yourself. I quite like your description though.'

Zeb felt eyes on him. The twins, Broker, all his team were looking at him.

He read their thoughts. *He's toying with us.*

Murphy silenced Pierce with a gesture. 'That was Deputy Director Pierce. He's right you know, Bob. How do you expect to get away with it?'

'Enough talking. Five million tomorrow into my account.'

'Oh, and before you folks go back to analyzing my voice and all that fancy stuff you do, the money will be transferred by one man, from a coffee shop, in McPherson Square.'

'Just one man. He will enter the café at five p.m. He will carry a distinctive laptop. Let me think.' He paused. 'A red-colored laptop. That's distinctive enough, wouldn't you folks agree?'

No one disagreed.

'He will log onto the free WiFi and make the transfer.'

'That's simple isn't it? Even you folks shouldn't be able to goof that up.'

'Before I forget, it's not any random man. I want Carter to make that transfer. Then we'll talk.'

He chuckled one last time and hung up.

There was a restless stirring in the room while Burke, Pierce, and Murphy conferred. Four other agency heads joined them. Many agents looked at one another.

'That was the weirdest call I've ever heard. That dude was windy,' One agent whispered.

Several heads nodded.

'Who is Carter? Do we have a Carter?' 'Probably. It's not an uncommon name.'

'Why him?'

Shoulders shrugged.

Burke straightened and addressed the room. 'Voice analyses. Location tracking, you know the drill. I want one team to check this café out. That entire neighborhood. Look into short term and long term tenants. Especially those with a view into the café.'

Agents drifted out, the room thinned.

Zeb remained. Clare stood next to him. His crew joined him.

Murphy looked at him. 'He wants us to know.'

'Yes, sir. He's found out I was there. Maybe he knows about the others too.'

'You think we have a mole, don't you?'

'Yes, sir. However, the mole's not our problem.'

Burke watched Carter. He was calm. Nothing changed on his face. The nation's intelligence heads were questioning him. He wasn't fazed.

Not questioning. They are listening. None of the heads are asking who he is. They either know or Murphy has asked them not to question.

One of the intelligence heads, the director of a covert agency raised his eyebrows. 'A mole's not a problem?'

'No, sir. He didn't have to let on that he knew. He knows an internal investigation will consume resources, might stall the investigation. Every agent, every agency, will regard the other with suspicion. It's not a healthy situation.'

'It need not be a mole,' The Director of National Intelligence countered. 'There has been enough TV coverage for someone to have spotted you.'

They know he's Carter. Do they know what he really does? I would like to know that, for sure!

'That's possible, sir. However I have reason to believe there's a mole. The snitch need not be an agent. He could be anyone who is privy to intel.'

'Burke has the mole aspect under control, sir.'

She flushed when all eyes turned on her. 'I have compartmentalized the investigation --'

'Yes, she has it under control. We have other measures too,' Murphy interrupted her and returned to Carter.

'You think there's something else going on?'

'He's moving too slowly, sir. If this was a ransom situation, he should have made contact earlier. If he has other motives, so far he's not revealed them. He knows the whole country is looking for him. He's in a high risk situation.'

'Then there's the ransom, sir.'

'What about it,' another covert agency director demanded, as he paced the room.

'It's too small.'

The director whirled on him, mouth agape.

'Five million is small change for you?'

'Yes, sir. The Veep could easily raise that money. I have no idea about the extent of Mr. Fairman's wealth, but I believe he too has considerable assets to his name.'

'There's something else at play,' Murphy said slowly.

'Yes, sir. However till we know what that is, we play his game.'

'So you'll go?'

'Of course, sir.' Carter replied, surprised.

Burke cornered him when the directors had left. 'He wants eyes on you.'

'That thought had crossed my mind,' came the expressionless reply.

Darrell listened while Merritt outlined the developments. He had heard most of them through Mark, but Merritt had more.

He rubbed his temple and crossed his feet on a footstool. It was silk cushioned, the silk imported from one of the oldest weaver-merchants in China. Darrell didn't shop at discount stores.

'Why haven't they gone public with details of your call?'

'They don't want to turn McPherson Square into a circus. They might think I'll be there.'

'How are the boys?'

'No change. The one with the fugue is still a zombie. The other seems to be getting his courage back. Maybe he's getting some hope, since we haven't popped him yet.'

'Does he know anything?'

'No. We asked.'

Merritt detected the return of fear in Darrell's voice. Right before the grab, after he had given the go, he had worried about the hammer falling.

Once the boys were in custody, the threat of the hammer was in control, but it hadn't disappeared.

The boy still hadn't spoken.

'The psychiatrist –'

'Is doing everything possible. Nature has to take its course.'

'Can't you administer some truth serum or any other fancy stuff?'

'We've discussed that. The doctor says we run the risk of playing with his memory. He might never remember what you want.'

'Relax. We have the boys' lives in our hands. We know they haven't revealed anything to anyone else. We have discussed this.'

Darrell's breathing slowed, became steady. 'Till then you'll keep the Feds busy?'

Merritt smiled. It wasn't a pleasant one. 'I sure will.'

'You'll take this Carter out?'

The smile became feral.

'I won't have to.'

Chapter 21

Zeb had just returned from his run that night, when he got the call from Marvin Tempers.

Tempers had done time for killing his wife and her lover with a baseball bat.

He had reformed, during his lengthy stint in prison, and now worked as a construction foreman in Brooklyn.

He also worked with inner city youth, mentoring them, guiding them, using his life experiences to steer them clear of crime.

Zeb had come across the Jamaican when he was pursuing a serial killer in New York. Tempers had treated him suspiciously, initially, taking him to be yet another white man who judged the West Indian based on his past.

The suspicion had turned to grudging admiration, and then warmth which turned to friendship when he found the white dude was unlike any other he had known.

'Why,' he had asked a long time later, once they had become friends.

Zeb had looked at his teardrop tats and knew what he was asking. *Why did you trust me?*

'I have a shadow in my life too.' Tempers hadn't understood then. It was only when he had heard Zeb's back story, a year later, that the cryptic reply made sense.

'There's someone gunning for you,' Tempers said, when they had exchanged pleasantries. His West Indian accent was warm and soothing and brought to mind images of crashing surf and coconut trees.

Tempers was a changed man, but he still had an active underground network and passed information to Zeb.

'You have some friends in Chicago. They have been told you're in D.C. A squad is coming. Watch your back, buddy.'

Zeb thanked him and stood for a long while in darkness. Rivera's in Chicago. No one else in that city has a beef with me.

Louie Rivera headed a gang in Chicago.

At one time, it had been the largest one in the city and ruled criminal enterprises with an iron hand.

Zeb had cut the gang down, destroyed large parts of its business and had publicly humiliated the gang boss.

He'll never learn. Criminals never do, which is why they have a short shelf life.

He found his crew waiting outside his bedroom the next morning.

'We're coming with you,' Meghan said fiercely.

'To breakfast?' he asked nonplussed. 'Sure.'

She rolled her eyes. 'To the coffee shop.'

'Nope. We don't even know if I'll be going. There's the money to be arranged, formalities to be done, the Feds have to agree.'

'You're behind the curve, Zeb. Burke called. She said you weren't picking up your phone. You're going.'

'You're still not coming.'

They argued with him. They threatened. They cajoled and pleaded. He didn't change his mind.

'Look, Bob isn't going to try anything there.'

No need for them to know of Tempers' call.

'Burke will have the place surrounded. There will be snipers, covert agents, undercover police. She'll have hacked into the system. She'll have bugs. The baristas will be Fed agents. Not even a speck of dust will escape notice. It's the safest place to be.'

'He'll come after you.'

'He won't. With this amount of heat, he will not come out of hiding.'

They kept up trying to convince him till he held a hand up. 'Look, he won't try anything today. It's too soon for him.'

Broker surprisingly supported him. 'Zeb's right. Any attack will come later. Today is about making the FBI dance to his tune, and getting a look at Zeb.'

Meghan rounded on him angrily. 'That's an assumption we all are making. We could be wrong.'

'We aren't.' Zeb climbed into the SUV, powered it to life, and drove toward Burke's office.

They found organized chaos at the Federal building.

Burke whisked him to a room where he was fitted with a pinhole camera and a bone phone. The device used bone conduction technology and was invisible even to close surveillance.

'So, it's a go?' Zeb asked Burke as she watched him being outfitted, her arms crossed. She could have passed for a FBI recruitment poster, but for the shadows under her eyes.

'Did you doubt it?' She laughed without humor.

He hadn't. They didn't have a choice.

Randy came up with a laptop, its lid bright red, and explained what he had to do. He had to open an encrypted funds transfer application that would move funds from one account to Bob's.

'Whose money is this?'

Randy shrugged and looked at Burke. She made a face in a *don't ask* gesture.

Federal money, to bait Bob.

There were still a few hours to go. Burke disappeared with her team. Broker huddled with the rest of his crew and went over dead agent files that Clare had sent.

They would look at the back stories, look at their photographs, whittle the list down to the most probable ones and then dig deeper.

Zeb rose, feeling uncharacteristically restless.

We are missing something.

It didn't come to him.

The job of watching Zebadiah Carter came to Marty Solano.

He called himself a professional watcher. He usually hung out in Dulles airport and photographed VIP guests and sold those pictures to media outlets.

He also worked with criminal gangs who asked him to look out for their targets.

Marty didn't know who Carter was nor did he care. He didn't even know the target's name. He got a message from a familiar criminal network. It ordered him to station himself in the café and capture a man with a red laptop in glorious high definition.

Marty didn't know that Merritt, the most wanted man in the country, was behind the request.

Merritt had made use of Marty through various cutouts in the past. One such cutout had made contact with the watcher.

Marty dressed in a suit, an American flag pin on his lapel, a burnished leather briefcase in his hand, and strode inside the store at three p.m.

He grabbed an empty table, opened a laptop, plugged in an earpiece, pulled out his phone and began a lengthy call.

He rose occasionally, paced, ordered drinks, all the while lobbying for a farm bill with a nonexistent person.

Those who overheard his conversation took him to be a senator's staffer. He looked the part. He spoke the lingo.

At four thirty, a brown-haired man entered the small café, went to the counter and ordered a drink.

He was carrying a slim laptop in his hand. Red colored.

Marty's heart leapt.

This would be easy.

The man took his drink, searched for a table, waited for one to empty and seated himself.

He took a sip, and opened his laptop.

His fingers moved. Marty rose.

'Can I count on your support, sir?' Marty spoke, and paced while waiting for an imaginary reply.

'No, sir. The senator won't negotiate anymore. He's already watered down the bill so much that it will become a puddle on the floor of Congress.'

He laughed at his own joke.

Click. Click. Click.

'Hold on, sir. I have another call coming in.'

Marty looked at the photographs. They came out well, from different angles. Now for some video.

'Sorry, sir. That was the senator. He needs to know you're onboard.'

The man shut his laptop and rose at five fifteen p.m. He went to the bin and trashed his paper cup.

Marty brushed his shoulder, mouthed an apology and pointed to his headset. Bills had to be passed, laws had to be made, the country had to be governed. It was important stuff.

The man nodded in acceptance and walked out of the café.

Marty hung around for another hour, maintaining his act and finally wrapped up his phone call.

'The senator will be most grateful, sir. Thank you for your support.'

Marty left the café and fired off a message with the photographs and video.

Two days passed with no contact from Bob.

The investigative team didn't reach their breaking point. Burke rotated agents, sent many off to get sleep. The replacements chased down leads, which were getting thinner.

The FBI got nothing from the café. Burke agreed with Zeb's theory that Bob had not gone in for electronic surveillance. He probably had a watcher stationed inside or outside the café.

The FBI had checked out the patrons in the café. All of their identities held.

They were looking into pedestrians and onlookers outside the café.

The facial recog on Alejandro Peres didn't get them anywhere. It had been a good call on Zeb's part, but Peres or Bob or whatever his real identity was, hadn't turned up on any database.

Meanwhile, both pairs of parents went on TV and made another plea. Director Murphy faced the media for the umpteenth time.

All he could say was that the investigation was progressing.

The five million disappeared into the offshore account and a team was liaising with the bank, using threats and persuasion. The bank revealed a shell company. It was owned by yet another shell company. Boxes within boxes.

The money stayed in the offshore account.

Zeb went for his run late in the evening on the third day. He went from a slow jog to a rapid pace that he could maintain for miles if he had to. He had occasion to, several times in the past.

His blood pumped in exhilaration, his feet floated as if on air. He ran through darkened streets and passed solitary street lamps. He circled parks and ran down the mall.

He turned back to the hotel and entered the stretch of darkness where he had met Larry Fairman.

A few cars were parked, dark and silent.

In. Out. In. Out. His breathing was steady, his eyes were constantly moving.

He passed the first car.

His left foot landed.

Then he was flying, over the empty street, his body inclined in a tight narrow line.

The Glock appeared in his hand.

The front doors of a car flung open. Tubular shapes burst through its windows.

Trigger break.

A window burst. A barrel disappeared.

His gun's report was drowned in the barrage of firing that emerged from behind the car doors. Rounds flew and punched holes in the air where he had been.

Zeb landed, rolled and ducked behind an empty vehicle on the other side of the street.

He fell to the ground and aimed at shadows beneath the doors of the car. The shadows were the feet of the shooters.

A one, two burst, found one pair of feet.

A gunman yelled. His body sagged. Other shooters grabbed him and bundled him inside the car.

Barrels turned in Zeb's direction. The roar of shooting became thunderous.

Zeb ducked and frowned.

He snatched a quick glance under his vehicle.

More shadows were on the street.

Behind and ahead of the vehicle.

All of them were firing into the gunmen's car.

The roar reduced and then stopped.

A voice shouted. 'Stay inside your homes. Don't come out on the streets.'

Zeb recognized the voice.

He rose from behind the vehicle, the Glock casually held, yet alert.

Bwana turned his head, his teeth gleaming white in the darkness.

'You're not the only friend Marv has.'

The cleaning up took hours.

The street to the side of the hotel was closed down by cops and they began their investigation.

They questioned Zeb and his people. They tried to take their guns, but Burke stopped them. They argued with her, calls were made, and finally they acquiesced.

Yellow tape was strung out and half a mile of street became a no-go area.

No shooters survived. There were five of them. Two behind each door, and one who had shot from inside the car.

Two of them were black men, a couple looked white and the fifth looked Hispanic. They sported gang tats on their bodies.

Zeb recognized the ink.

Rivera's gang.

Burke came and stood next to him and watched the forensic team photograph the scene.

'You know the shooters?'

'Nope. I know which gang they belong to. Rivera's in Chicago.'

Her head swung to stare at him. 'The same Rivera?'

'Yeah.'

Burke knew of Rivera. She knew of his trimming down the gang.

Footsteps sounded behind them.

The twins, along with Chloe, approached. The men were behind them.

Beth looked at him searchingly.

Zeb wore armor beneath his sweat shirt.

On his face was ceramic cloth. It was Broker's latest gadget. The cloth was a malleable paste that could be applied on the human body. It molded to the surface when dry, hardened and provided a defensive layer.

The idea was bullets would bounce off it, due to its smooth, curved shape.

It had never been tested on live humans. Zeb was the first to wear it. Luckily, his face hadn't been shot at.

The twins helped him remove the ceramic layer and then Beth punched him hard in his bicep.

'Whoa,' Burke stepped in between to stop her.

Beth stood down, breathing furiously. 'You knew they would attack today. We got the same message from Marvin. Yet you had to be the hero and go on your run.'

She let fly with her fist.

Zeb caught it easily, gentled his grip and held her hand. 'I knew that you folks knew.'

He smiled and let go of her hand and held her wrist till she calmed down.

Roger came to him and followed his eyes to the gunmen's car.

'How did you know?'

How did you know which car they were in?

'That was the only car facing me. Street light was behind

it. It was dim, but even in that light, I could see the shapes inside.'

'They could have been a couple, necking,' Burke laughed.

'I would have been left looking foolish then. Wouldn't be the first time.'

Burke watched him as he wiped his face with a towel Bwana handed. His hands were steady. Not a tremor. His voice was even.

I bet his pulse will be slow.

She thought she should be angry that Carter hadn't put her in the loop, but she wasn't.

She understood his reasoning. He had explained at length when she had reached him.

This was strictly a side show organized by Bob. If the shooters were lucky, they would have got Carter. Nothing changed for Bob, if they weren't.

Besides there was the mole to be thought of. The fewer who knew of what Carter had planned, the better.

She was happy for the cops to investigate the shooting.

The media came, their vans and choppers lighting the street. Carter moved away into the shadows and stood watching, a dark shape against a brick wall.

'I have never seen him scared.'

She didn't know she had spoken aloud till she felt Roger's eyes on her.

'You know his backstory?'

She shook her head.

She waited.

The Texan didn't say anything for a long while.

When he spoke, his voice was soft and affectionate.

'He used to be. A very long time back.'

Chapter 22

Merritt was joined by the doctor as he watched the news coverage in the lounge.

The psychiatrist had a belly that strained against his shirt, and wore glasses, and had a perpetual sheen of sweat on his large forehead. He was staying with them till the boy recovered.

He wouldn't return, but there was no reason for him to know that.

'Your doing?' The doctor pointed his drink at the TV.

'Nope,' Merritt replied. He could lie straight faced. He could lie with a polygraph strapped to him. Telling a lie to the psychiatrist was effortless.

The psychiatrist used to work in a respected hospital in Boston.

Long hours and a weak spirit drove him to a drug addiction. The addiction got him sacked, ruined his marriage, and led him to move to another state. He joined another hospital in Virginia and also had a private practice.

He was already on the slippery slope down, when Merritt found him and started using him.

Merritt watched for some more time and then left the TV to the doctor.

He had more pressing concerns.

They know about the Moscow video. That was a mistake on my part.

His contacts in the Moscow underworld had alerted him to the development. His snitch didn't know who from the Feds had gone to Russia. Just that someone had been there and the video had been shown.

He stripped down his 9mm, and brought out a Hoppe's cleaning kit and started his elaborate routine. The mechanical activity and the smell of gun oil helped him think.

They can analyze the video all they want. They won't get anywhere. Dale Johnson didn't look like Alejandro Peres.

He went through the entire operation and tried to pick holes in it.

He could have lain low after grabbing the boys. The diversion tactics weren't required.

They help in consuming the FBI's resources, heaping pressure on them. Never a good place to be in, for an investigation.

He liked diversions. It appealed to the darkness inside him. The cold professional in him approved, so long as the diversions didn't jeopardize the plan.

We're good. Even if, by a leap of faith, they stumble on Dale Johnson – that will lead them to a dead end too.

He put the gun back together and racked the slide.

Dead ends and deaths, everywhere.

Marty was feeling pleased. Pleased was an understatement. He was floating on air. Those giant airliners at Dulles had nothing on the way he felt.

A cool hundred and fifty thousand dollars lay in his bank account, for just walking around in a café and snapping pictures and videos.

It was the day after the café surveillance. The day was bright. Gleaming aircraft took off, outside, mocking earth's gravity. Smaller aircraft floated gracefully and landed.

In the distance, he could see the White House. Marty was on top of the world.

Marty, my boy, this was the best career choice you made.

He allowed himself a self-congratulatory smile and hurried to his usual spot in Dulles, from where he could watch the arrivals.

A congressman had been caught doing stuff with his girlfriend while his wife was away. A tabloid newspaper wanted Marty to confirm his presence in the city so that they could ambush him.

Marty snapped a newspaper open in front of him, adjusted the pinhole camera on his hat, checked its feed on his phone, and waited.

He felt a presence next to him. He moved.

The presence moved with him.

Marty shifted some more, his eyes not leaving the trickle of people coming out.

The person bumped his shoulder.

Marty bit back an oath.

Tourists!

'Watch out, buddy,' he warned without looking sideways.

'This job isn't healthy for you, Marty.' The person next to

him, spoke.

Marty froze. In all his years as an information gatherer – that's what he called himself – not one person knew his name. Not even his clients. He had a false one for them.

He turned his head slowly.

The laptop man!

Laptop Man removed Marty's hat, examined it and separated the camera from the lining.

Marty didn't stop him. His heart was thudding. His mouth was dry.

Laptop Man held his hand out silently.

Marty didn't move.

He raised his eyes and looked into Laptop Man's eyes.

They were brown. Cold. So cold that he shivered.

He handed over his phone, his fingers trembling.

Laptop Man pocketed it without glancing at it.

'So long, Marty.'

Rivera was negotiating a drug deal.

His city needed powder. His supplies were running low.

Like any civic minded gangster, he was making arrangements to ensure the city would not run dry. It would not do for his retail consumers to go without their fix.

Rivera would fix that.

The suppliers were East European. They had powder. Loads of it. High quality. Their price was high too.

Rivera was haggling with them in the supplier's warehouse, a large structure that once used to be a meat packing factory.

The East European's hoods ranged behind their gang bosses, their hands on AKs and Uzis, their eyes never leaving Rivera's men.

Rivera's men were behind him. They too carried guns.

Gunplay wouldn't be involved. This was about business. Still, it never hurt to have guns around.

Rivera was driving the price down, successfully he thought, when a phone rang.

He carried on. It wasn't his gang's phone. They knew better than to let phones ring when Rivera did important stuff.

The phone rang again.

He felt the East Europeans' eyes on him.

My phone?

His phone rarely rang. He made other folks' phones ring.

He patted his pocket, pulled the device out and stared stupidly at the ringing icon.

There was no number on it.

It continued to ring, relentlessly.

Rivera thumbed the call, reluctantly.

'Hello?'

'You never learn, do you?'

The voice made Rivera go weak. His knew his face had paled and averted it from the suppliers.

It won't do to show weakness, he thought dimly.

'I could have killed you. I let you live, thinking you were too stupid to make a move against me.'

'You proved me wrong.'

'Here's a lesson. Walk away from that deal you are negotiating. Your offshore account hasn't the funds to cover it.'

The call ended.

Rivera kept looking at the phone. He felt blood pounding in his ears in anger and humiliation. He had no reason to doubt the caller.

Carter always made good on his statements.

He walked away from the deal.

Zeb joined his crew in their office.

Bwana and Roger were going through dossiers sent by the NSA. Broker was reading another lot of files. The twins attacked another pile.

They had narrowed the list of missing or dead agents to twenty. All twenty were dead.

The faces of those twenty had a few features similar to Bob's.

Cosmetic surgery could work wonders on a person's face.

It couldn't do anything about some characteristics that a person was born with. The distance between the eyes. The distance between the ears.

Zeb acknowledged the looks of his people by producing Marty's phone. Chloe took it and handed it to Beth. It hadn't been difficult to identify him once they went over the footage in the café and lengthier calls were made to various politicians.

'Rivera?' She asked.

'He'll live. For now.'

They went back to their folders, Beth to the secrets in the

watcher's phone.

Three hours later they took a break.

Somalia. Iraq. Nigeria. Italy. Afghanistan. China. Pakistan. Serbia. The twenty agents had lost their lives in various parts of the world.

Their deaths were meticulously recorded. The reports were extensive. There were interviews, there were photographs, there was subsequent verification.

There were DNA records in all but seven cases.

They focused on the seven cases.

'Let's talk to their case officers,' Zeb told them.

It would be difficult to organize. The deaths were old. The case officers could have retired or died or they could have moved on.

Clare could cut through the red tape though.

Meghan reached out for a phone, when another one rang.

It was Burke.

Bob would be calling in forty-five minutes.

Chapter 23

Bob called right on time. His dry voice filled the room which was crowded with the same faces.

'Thank you for the five million, Burke. It will be well spent. I hope you didn't have to jump through too many hoops to arrange it.'

'How are the boys, Bob?' She ignored his mocking tone.

'As good as two kids in captivity can be. Which means they are alive. For now.'

Her fingers tightened on the side of the table.

'The parents want to arrange an exchange. They want you to name your price.'

'Who said this was about money, Burke?' Bob acted surprised. 'If it was, wouldn't I have asked for more than a mere five mil?'

'What's it about, then, Bob?' Director Murphy didn't mask his impatience.

'Why, I like to see you guys flapping around. I like to see you folks running in ten directions, clueless.'

'You folks are the most powerful agencies in the world. Look how helpless you are.' Bob gloated.

Burke felt the weight of a stare. She looked around.

Carter. *Let him speak*, he mouthed.

She turned back and held back her words.

Bob spoke for another minute, humiliating the agencies. 'You know, I could record these calls and send a tape to the large TV stations. I wonder how many of you would still have a job, after that.'

He chuckled. Faces blanched and looked at one another.

'Relax. I won't do it. It's not your fault that you have come up against me.'

'Why did you call?' Burke couldn't hold it back any longer.

'Why, Burke, you should have asked me that at the start. It would have saved you my gloating.'

He paused for effect.

'I want the Veep to stop lobbying for the Syria bill.'

A collective gasp sounded in the room.

The Syria bill, if passed into law, would place extreme travel restrictions on visitors from that country and from the neighboring countries in which terrorists resided.

It was a bill that was gathering momentum after the San Bernardino attacks. Public opinion was behind it. The Muslim extremists in Baltimore had fueled more support.

'That's an impossible demand, Bob,' Pierce shouted. 'You know the United States government cannot heed such demands.'

'You looking for a career in politics, Pierce? That line would go down very well in front of cheering supporters.'

'Why don't you talk to the Veep and ask him what's more important? The bill or his son?'

Bob waited for a response and when none came, he spoke. 'I need another five mil. Keeping such high profile hostages in captivity is an expensive proposition. I don't see any reason why you shouldn't pay for their comfort.'

'We don't need to go through the same procedure. I trust you folks.' He chuckled. 'Besides, I know what Carter looks like, now.'

'The Veep isn't going to do that, is he?' Chloe asked Zeb as he drove them back to their hotel. He skirted the horde of reporters and broadcast vans and curious onlookers, squinted against camera flashes and picked up speed.

'Nope. This is another red herring,' Bwana grumbled before Zeb could reply. 'What I don't get is why he's doing this?'

'Yeah, these demands he's making aren't deliverable. He knows that, as well,' Bear agreed.

'It's almost as if he's buying time.'

'For what?' Roger asked in frustration. 'He's in control of the narrative. He had no reason to call, other than to make demands. His monetary demands aren't significant.'

Zeb halted at a light, listening, not saying anything.

There's something. He searched for the wisp of thought that had troubled him for days. It remained elusive.

The light changed. He moved forward.

He fell in behind a SUV. In front of it was a school bus.

Kids' faces peered at them. A young girl stuck her tongue out at them and giggled precociously.

Beth waved at her.

Another vehicle came to their left and kept pace with them.

Zeb glanced sideways.

A mom. Two kids in the rear.

Two boys.

Two.Boys.

Something fell into place. But it was still incomplete.

He slowed to match the mom's speed. He drove automatically, leaving it to the conscious part of his brain to drive safely.

He heard Meghan call out, asking him why he was slowing.

What's it about the boys?

The mom glanced at him and sped away.

Mom.

I am the mother of a son the world seems to have forgotten.

He stopped right in the middle of traffic, the swearing, cursing, and furious honking of other drivers not registering.

Meghan called more urgently. Beth, seated next to him, turned to him. She said something. He didn't hear.

Are the boys alive? Are they in good shape?

'He didn't answer.' He broke his silence.

'What?'

'You are not making sense, Zeb.'

'You need to lie down, Zeb.' The last was from Broker.

Zeb steered the vehicle to the side, stopped illegally and turned to face them.

'Bob didn't answer Burke when she asked about their health.'

They fell silent as they played back the call in their minds.

Roger shrugged. 'So what? He didn't give us his real name either.'

'Where are you going with this, Zeb?' Chloe quietly cut through the chatter and protests.

'We might have been looking in the wrong place.'

Kale School was an exclusive private school in northwest Washington D.C. Its sixty-acre lush green campus was dotted with pristine white buildings, a deer park, football and sports fields, an Olympic-sized indoor swimming pool and gym.

It was the most exclusive school in the Washington metropolitan area. The rich and the powerful sent their kids to the school.

So did the politicians.

James Barlow and Shawn Fairman were two of its students.

Security was tight when Zeb approached the school's gates in his SUV. Meghan sat in the front with him, Beth in the rear.

The rest of his team was chasing down the details of the seven dead agents.

Two armed guards at the gates took their names, checked them against a pad, compared their faces against photographs and then let them through.

The long driveway went past kids playing in a field, past immaculately maintained lawns and gardens, and was designed to impress.

The twins were impressed. Beth whistled when they passed a Grecian fountain.

'Must cost a bundle.'

Meghan referred to her notes. 'It sets parents back by fifty grand. That's just for day schoolers. Boarding is much more.'

The school had been extensively featured in interviews after the kidnapping. Several presidents' children had studied there, as well as celebrity offspring. The school was used to high profile students. It had its own security apparatus.

That apparatus became apparent when three suited, hard-bodied men, directed their SUV to a parking spot.

They were searched, the twins patted down by a female guard.

Zeb's Glock drew attention.

Two men got behind him, while the third questioned him.

'I have explained all this, before.'

'Please humor us, sir. Run us through why you need a handgun in a school.'

Zeb explained. That he had been sent by the FBI to check on a couple of leads. The men were unconvinced.

Zeb didn't look like a FBI agent. Neither did the twins. They didn't carry any official identification. The men positioned themselves for a swift takedown.

The headmaster came hurrying and defused the situation.

He apologized to Zeb and the twins, thanked his men, and led the way inside.

'Those are ex-Secret Service men. They know their business. They go through their own verification, irrespective of who the gate lets in.'

Zeb nodded. It was standard operating procedure in his world.

He didn't think the men would have attacked him, but with the kidnapping, nervous energy was running high.

The headmaster took them on a tour of the school, answered their questions, introduced them to the boys' teachers, all of whom said their behavior was exemplary. They met a few students, who said the boys were great guys to hang out with.

They spent a few hours in the school and returned with nothing that pinged their radar.

'Fairman came to this school five years back, didn't he?' Zeb broke the silence.

'Yeah. The family moved to D.C. five years back from Columbus in Ohio. Larry Fairman was a lobbyist in state politics there. A major D.C. firm headhunted him from there.'

'There's nothing in their backgrounds, Zeb,' Beth said dismissively. 'Those backstories have been gone through over and over again, folks have been interviewed, facts have been cross checked.'

Zeb didn't reply.

'When did Barlow and he become friends?'

'About a year after his enrolling at this school.'

'A lobbyist can afford that school? I don't think Mrs. Fairman works, does she?'

'You got to live in the real world, Wise One.' Beth chuckled. She quoted a figure. 'That's what Larry Fairman earns. He negotiated a company house as part of his package and pays a subsidized rent. Believe me, he can afford it.'

The hum of tires on concrete filled the SUV. An occasional honk interrupted it.

'The boys drink? Any history of drugs? Girlfriends?'

'They're clean. No girlfriends.'

Zeb flashed his turn signal, hung a right and accelerated, closing the gap with the traffic ahead.

The city moved on, even though it was the center of the most intensive manhunt in the country.

The world hasn't moved on for two families.

The Veep had stepped down from official duties for a week, but had now resumed them. Some media channels had asked him if that meant he had given up hope. Thousands of people had condemned the interviewers.

Meghan gave him a sideways glance. 'You aren't convinced?'
'Nope.'
'You got anything to go on?'
I am the mother of a son the world seems to have forgotten.
'Nope.'

Pico called Merritt to his computer and pointed at an image.
It was Carter with two women, the twins in his crew.
'They visited the school today.'
Merritt's face was expressionless, but inwardly he tightened. Carter was everywhere.
Pico had inserted a tunnel in the school's security system and got a constant feed. It was one of the precautions Merritt had insisted on.
He patted Pico's shoulder and praised him warmly. 'Good work, Pico. Keep an eye out on happenings there.'

Merritt went to his room, shut it, and called Darrell.
Darrell listened, agreed, and cautioned. 'It has to look like an accident. Anything, as long as no connection is made.'
'None will be made.'
'You have someone?'
'One of the best.'

Chapter 24

Broker was on a call when they returned to the hotel. He motioned Zeb over and covered the phone.

'General Amin,' he whispered.

The general headed ISI, Pakistan's secret service, and was a good friend to the Agency.

Relations between the ISI and the American intelligence agencies had been strained following the killing of Osama bin Laden. However, Zeb and Clare had maintained their communication and Zeb had helped the ISI in a few missions.

Those missions had enhanced General Amin's reputation and had consolidated his standing in the country's volatile political establishment.

'Al-salaamu alaykum', Zeb greeted the general in Urdu.

'How are you, my friend?' Amin replied. They spent a few seconds catching up while Broker scribbled on a sheet and thrust it at Zeb.

He says the agent's death in Karachi is genuine.

Zeb nodded, dragging his mind away from the school.

Seven dead agents. Maybe one of them faked his death and is Bob. Of those seven agents, one, a CIA operative, died in Karachi.

'You are sure this guy is dead, Syed?' Zeb asked him.

'One hundred percent sure, my brother.'

Amin briefed him on the incident.

The CIA operative had been working with ISI agents to hunt a Taliban leader.

They had cornered the man in a house in Karachi, and had exchanged intense fire. Stray fire had caught the CIA man and a couple of other ISI agents.

'How can you be sure, Syed? The body wasn't found.'

The general became even more voluble as he explained. The body hadn't been found. However, there were enough eyewitnesses.

Zeb's senses sharpened.

Those eyewitness statements weren't part of the secret dossiers the American agencies had.

They wouldn't be, the general explained. Petty politicians had interfered and had made him withhold those statements. The government of his country was still hurting from the

American's brash killing of bin Laden.

'You went on record to say there weren't witnesses.'

The general acknowledged. It was politics again.

Broker scribbled again.

Do you believe him?

Zeb nodded. Amin owed him too much to lie to him. The general also knew what Zeb was capable of.

Beth turned on the news when night fell. They crowded around it and watched another press conference.

This one was more positive. The FBI had raided several houses in Maryland and Virginia on tip-offs.

One house had a large marijuana stash. Another had busted a child porn ring. No trace of the boys had been found.

However, the activity cheered the media. To them activity was progress.

The media had started rating the FBI during and after each press conference. The ratings had been around three in the previous briefings. This time they rose to five.

The assembled reporters went easy on Burke and Murphy.

Burke looked directly at the camera when she finished.

Zeb knew she wasn't going easy on herself.

We still haven't told her about the dead agents' angle. There isn't anything to tell her, for now.

Broker and he left messages for intelligence agencies in Somalia, Iraq, Nigeria, Italy, Afghanistan and Serbia. The dead agents in those countries were the only ones left to be verified.

They had gone through the rest of the agents' files, had spoken to all those involved in the subsequent investigations and were satisfied that the files had everything.

Six agents remain. Let one of them be Bob, or else this investigation is back to zero.

He showered when he returned to his room, something about Shawn Fairman still nagging away in his consciousness.

Sleep wouldn't come. That was unusual. Over the years, he had trained himself to sleep whenever he wanted to.

He rose, restlessly, opened his computer and went through Fairman's file again.

Larry Fairman had worked in Columbus, however, his wife and Shawn had lived in Amherst, a small town of barely fifteen thousand people. Dad spent the working week in the large city and joined his family on the weekends. Sometimes, his family joined him, during school holidays.

He looked up Shawn Fairman's school in Amherst. It was a community school that catered to the neighborhood.

He went to the school's website. It was like hundreds of such schools across the country.

Good, hard working teachers, hard working parents who took pride in their local school.

He looked up the file that the twins had made on the Fairman and the Barlow families. It went deep, looked at every event and incident in their life or in the neighborhood and community they had lived in.

Nope.

Am I relying too much on my gut instinct?

It has never let me down.

He paced, went to the window and looked out. The city was slumbering. It wasn't as active a city as New York, where he had his home.

Yet, D.C. was one of his favorite cities in the country. It was the one city that gave a sense of space and freedom. The absence of high rise towers had a lot to do with it.

A rumble came through the window.

A school bus, passing, presumably to ready itself for the run in the morning.

That reminded him.

He went back to his laptop and looked up the local newspaper in Amherst. He went to its site and started reading editions.

Marriages, deaths, local events, politician visits, school expansions --- he read that one and moved on when he had finished.

He went back to the previous year, and then to the earlier year.

He was about to shut his laptop and hit the bed when the article jumped out at him from a mass of news coverage.

Boy killed in hunting accident.

The boy studied in the same school as Shawn Fairman.

Zeb took the Gulfstream to Cleveland, very early in the morning. He didn't wake his friends up.

Hopefully this won't take much time and I'll be back in a few hours.

He could have called the police in Amherst, or the school. But there was no substitute for talking to people, seeing their faces, gauging their expressions.

The flight took an hour and a half and the car rental at Cleveland Hopkins International Airport took another half hour.

He plugged in the coordinates to the school and started a drive that ran parallel to the bottom shore of Lake Erie.

He reached Amherst just as school buses were rolling in the small city. He slowed to let a bus go ahead, waited at a junction and stopped at the first diner on North Main Street.

On the outside it was aluminum sheets, giving it a box-like feel. Inside, it was warm cream and dark leather – genuine leather – couches around red tables with strips of white table napkins.

He stopped and a passing waitress chuckled. 'That's the reaction we want. Seat yourself anywhere, sir. I'll come to take your order shortly.'

The "Sir" made a difference. Zeb tipped generously whenever Sir or Ma'am was used.

He seated at a table that looked outside, helped himself to coffee, and opened his laptop.

I'll go to the school first, ask about Shawn Fairman, and then inquire about the dead student.

Geraldo Storms was based in Columbus, two and a half hour drive from Amherst.

Storms had received a package from Merritt the previous night. He didn't know it was *Merritt*. It was his cutout, sending him the package.

It was a job. He had to take out a teacher in Amherst.

Such jobs paid for his living.

Storms was a freelance killer and now that the economy was growing, so was his business.

During the recession, he had to make do by taking on smaller jobs. Blackmail. Threats. Violence. An occasional robbery.

Those jobs shamed him, for Storms considered himself to be a killer of the finest kind. One who left no trace behind and made the deaths look accidental.

He could have had a flourishing career on the east or the west coast. He *had* lived on the west coast, in Los Angeles, and had worked with different gangs.

The gang culture didn't sit well with him, however. All that posturing and gun toting and random shooting.

Killing was an art. Killing without leaving a trace and making it look natural, was its highest form.

He had tried explaining it to a gangbanger once. The hood had stared at him as if he were from another planet. 'What good is that, man? No one will know you killed!'

He had called his buddies over and they had a laugh at Storms's expense.

Storms left the city in a week and made Columbus his base.

It was close enough to the largest cities, and large enough to give him business in the surrounding states.

Storms checked the package; it was an urgent job. He normally didn't take such jobs since they had a higher risk attached.

However, this job seemed straightforward. The teacher was in her fifties, lived alone in a house near her school. She had no relatives, no pets, had a few friends who she met over the weekend.

She came home every day during lunch break.

The package had her home address, her school address, and all other details that Storms would need. He looked up her home in a maps program, checked out various views and angles and told his cut-out that he would take the job.

He would set out in the morning, reach the woman's house at lunch time, kill her, and head back home in time to catch the ballgame on his sixty-inch TV.

He stretched and yawned and packed a small bag with the tools of his trade – a handgun, suppressor, magazines, knife, ropes and ties and various other accoutrements and went to bed.

The day dawned and after a healthy breakfast, he set out in a Corolla, a common enough make, with local plates which were false.

I should get more such jobs. Old woman. Single. Lives alone.

I could kill her in my sleep.

Chapter 25

Zeb headed to the school, parked his vehicle in the visitors' lot, ignored curious looks and entered the building.

It was a busy school, one of the largest in the city, and he dodged students and teachers and after a few inquiries, headed to the principal's office.

The principal, Gary Busman, stopped in his tracks when he mentioned he was from the FBI.

He presented his credentials that Burke had provided them.

'We have had several visits from you folks. We have had state cops, the FBI, newspaper reporters, TV crews… just about everyone, visit us and interview us. I don't have anything new to tell you.'

He wasn't rude, though his tone was short.

A teacher bobbed her head in, he waved at her, and she went away.

Zeb looked at him and then at the wall behind him. Numerous awards and certificates adorned the principal's office. He had won best teacher, best principal, at state level, for several years.

There were photographs of him with students, with parents. There didn't seem to be any photographs of him with any politicians.

Time to take a leap of faith.

He rose, shut the door and returned. Busman put a file down and looked down at him questioningly.

'Our investigation is going nowhere,' Zeb told him bluntly. 'We are no closer to finding the boys than we were on the first day.'

'I follow the news,' Busman responded with a small smile. 'You might say, we have a vested interest in making sure the boys are found.'

Progress.

'How did Nathan Cowart die?'

Busman blinked. 'Cowart? What has he got to do with the investigation? He died two years before Fairman transferred from here. An accident.'

'It was investigated thoroughly?'

Busman frowned, puzzled. 'I am sure it was. The police will know more about the case, if you want to know. Is there a connection?'

Zeb shook his head. 'I don't know. I am looking at coincidences, inconsistencies, abnormalities, and the accident jumped out at me. Can you describe Cowart?'

Busman had a skeptical look on his face; however, he rose, went to a filing cabinet, and returned with a folder.

'His dad owned a convenience store in town.'

'Owned?'

Busman corrected himself hastily. 'Still runs it. Cowart had an older sister. She too studied in this school. He was bright. Good grades. Good reports. His teacher will know more about him.'

'Arlene Slayton,' he answered Zeb's look.

He smiled suddenly. 'You are looking for coincidences, aren't you? Here's one for you. Arlene Slayton taught Fairman too. She taught the brightest students in school.'

'What does she teach?'

'English. She's an English teacher.'

Storms stopped just once to fuel and grab a burger. He set off immediately, eating the burger while driving. The road was empty, his tools were beside him, he had an easy job.

Life was good.

He entered the outskirts of Amherst just as it was nearing noon, went to a remote parking lot and stopped.

He moved to the rear seat and changed into dark blue overalls.

Uniforms open doors.

He punched Slayton's house coordinates in his GPS and commenced his drive.

'Can I talk to Arlene Slayton?' Zeb asked the principal. He had asked more questions, but the principal didn't know anything relevant. The teachers were closer to the students.

He kept repeating that Fairman and Cowart were smart. He showed Zeb their report cards.

'We call her Arlene. She will be in class now. She lives nearby, heads home during her lunch hour, and returns for the afternoon classes.'

Busman rose and led Zeb out of his office and to Slayton's

class.

'You met the Fairmans?'

Busman bobbed his head. 'Often, when they lived here. Mrs. Fairman came to school events, parents' events, and was very involved in Shawn's education. Mr. Fairman came less frequently. He worked in Columbus. However, he too took a keen interest in Shawn's schooling.'

They walked past brightly lit corridors which were never empty. Several students greeted the principal. He greeted them back with a smile or a wave. He seemed to be popular.

'Shawn won quiz championships at state level. That boy had a memory like a sponge. He could remember anything.'

Zeb nodded absently and tried to hurry the principal along. It was nearing lunch time. He wanted to speak to Slayton.

Arlene Slayton wasn't in her class. She had a migraine, so she gave her class work to keep them occupied, and had excused herself.

She had gone to inform Busman, but he seemed to have a visitor. She told a few coworkers; that she was going to lie down for a while and would be back after lunch hour.

One of them walked with her to her car. Arlene was a popular teacher. She was in her late fifties and her white hair curled around her face gave her a haloed look.

Her migraines were well known in school. They didn't come often, but when they did, she had to lie down.

Storms drove up the street once and looked at Slayton's house. It looked neat and inviting. It had a concrete drive, a neat lawn, a single garage, and had dark tiles.

A three bedroom house, Storms recalled, from the package he had received.

The street was quiet. The nearest neighbor was hundred feet away and shared the lawn.

Not many cars on the street. A few on the driveway.

Slayton's car was a red Ford Fusion. It wasn't in the driveway.

He drove on. He would circle the neighborhood and return.

Arlene Slayton wasn't in her class. Busman asked her students, they said she had gone home early.

'The usual problem, sir,' one girl grinned.

'Migraine,' Busman explained. 'She has them occasionally.'

He paused uncertainly. 'Maybe you should wait in my office till she returns. She isn't very conversational when she has these attacks.'

Arlene Slayton mopped the perspiration on her forehead with an arm and peered ahead.

Her home was barely a ten-minute drive, but on such days, felt like it was hours away.

Thankfully, this time of the day, the roads were empty.

She sighed gratefully when her home appeared in view, and turned on her flasher even though there wasn't any vehicle behind her.

She turned in her driveway, exited, and leaned against her car for a moment for the blackness to recede.

She opened the door and hurried inside to the bathroom

She ran the tap and bathed her face in cold water, held her fingers to her temple, wiped her face with a towel and headed out.

A bite and a brief rest in a dark room and I will be good as new.

She walked slowly to the kitchen, poured herself a glass of water, started to drink it, stopping when the doorbell rang.

Storms gripped his bag in his left hand, and rang the doorbell with a knuckle.

He put on a smile when an eye appeared in the peephole.

Arlene Slayton opened the door.

'Ms. Arlene Slayton?' Storms smiled wider. 'I am from the water company, ma'am. There are some reports of a leakage on this street. I need to run a few tests.'

The teacher looked him up and down, and behind him. 'How long will it take?'

'Not more than fifteen minutes, ma'am.'

He shifted his feet to convey his impatience. The longer he stood outside, the greater the risk of being spotted by someone.

'Where's your van?'

Storms bit back an oath. 'Don't need one for such tests, ma'am.' He drew out a card and gave it to her.

'You can call my office and verify, ma'am, but it'll be quicker if I run these tests. I will be out of here in no time.'

The teacher stood uncertainly and then opened the door wider.

Jackpot.

He stepped in behind her, slipped on thin gloves and shut the door behind him.

One arm went around her throat, one hand cupped her mouth.

'This really won't take much time, ma'am.'

Zeb sat in a chair in a corner and detached his mind. He ignored the occasional glances from the principal.

Cowart and Fairman were smart. Barlow was also smart. All three had good grades, good report cards.

What of it? Millions of kids are smart.

He chased the thoughts around and after a while, rose. 'I'll drive around the neighborhood. I'll be back just before she returns.'

The principal, who was with a teacher, lifted a hand in acknowledgement.

Clean, wide, streets. Large playgrounds. Good community. Most of the residents worked locally or within an hour's commute.

A random thought struck Zeb. *How did Fairman and Barlow become close? They go to the same school, but live in different social circles.*

He made a note to get the twins to investigate.

He circled the neighborhood and drove down Arlene Slayton's street.

Her car was in the driveway. There was another car on the street driving slowly, approaching him.

He caught a glimpse of the driver, a man in something blue. The driver waved. Zeb nodded in return.

He went down other streets, killing time, and when the lunch hour was ending, he headed back to the school.

The parking lot was crowded.

Didn't see that many vehicles, earlier.

He entered the school and immediately felt the tension.

Something's up?

He headed to Busman's office, crossed groups of teachers

and students who were whispering. Gone was the noise. Gone was the laughter.

Busman was with several teachers.

He looked at Zeb, over their heads.

'Arlene Slayton is dead.'

Chapter 26

'Dead?' Zeb repeated, trying to gather his thoughts.

'She died of a heart attack. A teacher called her to query her on a student. She didn't answer. Arlene is normally very prompt in answering calls. The teacher then set out to her home, knowing Arlene had a migraine.'

'She found her on the floor, in her kitchen.' Busman's fingers shook as he spoke. He clasped his hands when he felt Zeb's gaze on them.

The group of teachers had turned around to look at Zeb; one of them started sobbing softly, another hugged her.

Zeb excused himself, ran to the parking lot and drove to Slayton's house.

It had an ambulance and police cruisers in the driveway. Cops and medics bustled about.

Neighbors stood on the pavement and watched. Cameras and mobile phones clicked.

So it's true.

Why wouldn't it be?

The way Busman described it, felt unreal.

Zeb parked his vehicle several houses away and walked to the dead teacher's home.

A police officer stopped him and asked him, politely, to stay back.

Zeb tried to explain. The police officer was unimpressed. He drew out his credentials, the cop shrugged. He was joined by a burly officer.

'What's up, Flores?'

'Nothing, Chief. I was asking this man to stay back.'

'Stay back, sir. This is police business.'

The Police Chief turned back.

'I'm with the FBI,' Zeb spoke to his retreating back.

The Chief stopped.

Zeb's crew was eliminating the possibles from the dead agents list. Six of them remained. Bwana and Roger took Somalia and Nigeria. Bear and Chloe went after Italy and Serbia. Broker and the twins took Afghanistan and Iraq.

Bwana spoke several African languages fluently. He spoke

to the Nigerian National Intelligence Agency's chief. Isaac Ogdun listened without interrupting and promised to get back. He recollected the incident well. A dead American agent, however covert, always made a splash.

Italy was quickly ruled out. The killing of the agent had been extensively covered, and an eyewitness was still alive. An eyewitness who hadn't been listed in the files with the American agencies. The witness had come forward subsequently, by then the agent's file was closed.

The day dragged on. They knew Zeb had left for Ohio. He had left a message for them.

They took a short break, exchanged notes with Burke, and went back to their calls.

By the end of the day, their throats were hoarse from speaking, explaining.

Somalia had been ruled out. So had been Nigeria, and Serbia.

Afghanistan and Iraq remained.

Those were still active combat zones. Those were proving the hardest to verify.

'Has Zeb called?' Meghan asked, stifling a yawn.

'Nope,' her sister replied.

They bent back to their headsets.

Police Chief Bill Sizemore hadn't believed Zeb initially. He was brusque and dismissive.

Arlene Slayton's death was murder? Her death could be connected to the disappearance of the Veep's son?

The chief was irritated. He hadn't heard such nonsense in his life before. He asked Flores to escort Zeb back to the perimeter and to make sure he didn't breach it.

Flores grabbed Zeb's arm when Sizemore's phone rang.

He listened, a series of *yes sirs*, coming out from him. He motioned for Flores to release Zeb, put his phone away, and jerked his head to the house.

Zeb followed him.

'You have connections, buddy,' Sizemore spoke, just the once.

'Wayne, Mr. Carter, here, is with the FBI. He says there's a possibility Mrs. Slayton could have been murdered.'

Wayne, a white coated, man with a handle-bar moustache,

rose, turned, and stared. Several cops and medics looked at the police chief and the man behind him.

Zeb explained. The disbelieving looks didn't disappear. However, when the cops turned back to their jobs, there was a difference.

They treated the house as a crime scene.

Flores and other cops were dispatched to interview neighbors.

'Ask them if they know of or saw a white Toyota, a man dressed in blue, inside.'

Sizemore squinted at him. 'How do you know this, friend?'

Zeb explained again.

Sizemore sized him up, rubbed his chin thoughtfully, and nodded at Flores, who left with several other cops.

The house had no markings. There was a smudge on the doorbell, but it wasn't identifiable.

There were no strange prints, no fibers that didn't belong. The house was sterile.

'Slayton's body had no markings,' Wayne said. He went into medical terms.

Zeb tuned him out.

He gestured at the body. '*May I*?'

'*Go head*,' Wayne gestured back.

Zeb turned the body on its face and examined the neck. He then examined its back. He asked if Wayne had light filters.

Wayne had them.

Zeb had the kitchen's shades pulled and when the room darkened, lighted the flashlight and screwed on a filter.

He examined the body again, turned it over, and examined the legs, knees, and calves.

The body had been found just inside the kitchen door. To its left, at eye height, was a cabinet in which were neatly arranged glasses and plates.

Zeb rose and studied them.

The glasses were stacked on top of one another. One was askew.

He looked around the kitchen again. Everything was in its place, except for another glass, half full of water, on the sink.

Neat freak, he recalled Busman describing Slayton.

'You got something for us, friend?' Sizemore asked.

'You had a killer in town.' Zeb replied.

Storms reached his home in time to catch the ballgame. He messaged the cutout that the job was done. The message reached Merritt, who conveyed it to Darrell.

'Great. Anything from the boy?'

'Nothing.'

Merritt scanned the local news in Ohio. There was just one line about the death of a teacher in Amherst. Heart attack. The teacher was deeply loved by her students, and several of them gave short interviews.

Storms is good.

The killer was good. I haven't seen such a clean kill in a long while.

Zeb was alone in Slayton's house. It was dark outside; a cruiser was stationed out front, in which were two cops.

Sizemore, Wayne, and the rest had long left. No one else had seen the Toyota. No one owned such a vehicle.

Zeb had explained the method of killing to Sizemore, whose eyes had bulged at the possibility.

Wayne had examined the barely visible marks on the body, again, and had agreed it was a possibility. Such marks were easily explained away in most cases.

The clincher was the skewed glass. Everyone swore that Slayton would have straightened it.

Zeb explained how it would have gone down.

Slayton drinking water.

The doorbell ringing.

Placing her half full glass on the sink.

Opening the door.

The attack.

He demonstrated the move on Wayne.

Her elbow flying out, hitting the cabinet, partly dislodging the glass from its position.

The cops digested his explanation in silence until Sizemore had finally burst out.

'Why?'

Why was troubling Zeb too, as he stood alone in her house. It had been searched thoroughly.

No clue had been found. Sizemore promised to look into

her finances the next day.

The twins had already looked, after Zeb had messaged them.

Slayton had lived a simple life. There was nothing untoward in her finances. She had an older sister who suffered from Alzheimer's and was in a nursing home in Columbus. The sister's care was paid for by selling *her* home.

The two sisters had no other family.

Zeb went to Slayton's bedroom and looked around.

It had been neat. It was less so, now, after the cops' search.

He fingered a diary on a bedside table. There were random entries, relating to school. The jottings were sporadic and the diary had been started several years back.

Before Fairman moved to D.C. Before Cowart's death.

He pulled open a drawer on the table, and removed a Bible.

He opened it. Passages were marked, some had check marks.

She was religious and often read aloud in the local church.

He flipped through the Bible, saw nothing incriminating in it.

He closed it and placed it inside the table when the light caught a page in the open diary.

The page had deep indentations.

He looked at the dates. One page was missing. A year after Cowart's death, before Fairman's move.

He angled the diary to read the indentations. He couldn't.

He went out and asked the cops if they had filters and a flashlight.

They had, luckily.

He shone filtered light on the page and the scribbling leaped out.

A monster has entered my life.

Chapter 27

Afghanistan was ruled out by the time he joined his team in D.C. the next day.

It had been relatively easy to confirm the agent's death. Unbeknownst to the American agencies, a British surveillance aircraft had video evidence of the insurgent attack that had killed the American agent.

That left Iraq.

Zeb said he would look into it and asked the rest to dig into the teacher's life.

'Also Cowart's and what connects his to Barlow's and Fairman's.'

Meghan saluted him silently. Beth winked at him.

There was something to go on, now.

It might be nothing.

He pushed the negative thought away and called General Yasin Abdallah, head of Mukhabarat, the Iraqi Intelligence Service. Yasin was a close friend, whose career had been greatly enhanced by Zeb's help.

The general yelled in delight when he heard Zeb's voice. 'How are you, my friend? Are you ready to marry my daughter?'

It was an old joke. The first time Zeb had saved Yasin's life from a mortar attack, the general had offered his eldest daughter's hand in marriage, in gratitude.

His team turned as one and stared at Zeb when they heard the general's comment.

Zeb frowned when the twins tried hard to stifle their laughter. He turned back to the call.

He cut through the pleasantries and fingered the file in front of him.

'I want confirmation of Dale Johnson's death, my good friend.' He switched to Arabic, not wanting to give more opportunities to his crew to rib him.

How'll that help? They all speak Arabic.

There was a silence from the general's end as he tried to place the name. 'Wasn't that a long time ago, Zeb?' he queried.

'Yeah. We are looking into it again.'

'Is this--?'

'Yes, it is.'

Zeb heard him shout an order and heard papers rustling. 'I've got the file.'

He went quiet as he read through Johnson's file; the Mukhabarat had investigated Johnson's death, along with the deep black agency, and maintained its own records.

'He died, Zeb. It was conclusive. One of your agents walked away and gave an account.'

'He's dead now. He was interviewed several times and his story stacked up. He died of cancer some years back. The other bodies weren't identifiable.'

'They wouldn't be, when you have an intense fire sweep through a camp.'

Zeb didn't reply.

'You want me to investigate, again?'

'No. That will take too much time. Assuming he's alive, what would you look for?'

A lighter clicked and a puff sounded. The general loved his cigars.

'Another missing body.'

The staffer in the general's office had been around for more than a decade. He had survived political purges and mass assassinations. He had seen the overthrow of despots and the invasion of Western forces. He had followed the rise of terrorists and insurgents.

He had seen it all. No one saw him. He was as good as invisible. He was in his sixties and had started working in the Mukhabarat as a clerk. He had cleared the rigorous security checks and had slowly moved up the ladder.

Head clerk. Aide to a colonel. Record keeper for a secret assassination unit.

In the last years of his working life, he was now aide to General Abdallah. He had been courted by Western forces, by Russian Intelligence, Chinese and North Korean spies. He had turned all of them down.

It was too dangerous. He liked that his head was attached to his body.

However, the text message that appeared one day on his personal account was something he hadn't been able to turn down.

It said there would be ten thousand dollars waiting for him in a plastic bag, buried in the sand, near a milestone on a highway.

There was.

The text message disappeared of its own volition. It had come from a blocked number.

There was no more contact for two years and then another message. This time with a request.

Would the staffer be kind enough to message a number if anyone asked about the Dale Johnson file? There was another five thousand dollars, this time buried under goat dung.

The staffer liked this form of business. He could keep his head. He could keep the money. There was a risk that the demands would escalate, but he could cross that bridge later. He was a survivor after all.

He had brought the Johnson file to the general and had hung around for a few seconds.

Without bidding, he had brought the general his black coffee, exactly the way he liked it. Strong. Hot. Bitter.

The general had smiled absently in thanks and had waved him out, but not before the staffer heard the man at the other end.

Someone called Carter.

He messaged the number he had stored in his memory and as he went back to his job, he mused.

Intelligence agencies could build the most secure systems. They could have all kinds of fancy software to prevent leakage.

They could be laid low by simple, human, avarice.

'Nathan Cowart had a phenomenal memory,' Busman was on the phone to Zeb.

He was still shaken by the teacher's murder. It told in his voice and in his delivery. The confidence was gone. He spoke slower.

'He could recollect passages from months and even years back. He could remember stuff that had happened when he was young. Stuff that others wouldn't remember.'

'He was bullied for it. This was before my time. Treated like a freak. You know how it is, especially in a small town. Arlene took him under her wing, spent lot of time with him and his parents, and gradually Nat came out of his shell. Then the tragedy happened.'

Zeb listened, aware of Meghan and Beth sitting next to

him. One twin rolling a pencil, idly, another inspecting her nails. They too were listening.

Memory. Smart.

Something loosened and fell into place in his mind. There was no thunk. No light bulb lit.

He leaned forward. 'Were they friends?'

'Cowart and Fairman?' The principal asked. 'Let me check with other teachers.'

They heard his muffled voice. A chorus of replies came.

'Yes. The boys were close. So were the parents.'

Busman hung up after a few more minutes. Zeb reached for the phone. Meghan beat him to it.

She punched a number. It rang twice and a gruff voice came on.

'Sizemore.'

'Chief, this is Zeb. A question for you.'

Sizemore's reserve had vanished once Zeb had shown how Slayton was killed. He was friendly and cooperative.

Beth had a cynical explanation. 'He sees the opportunities. FBI is involved. So are the media and every other agency.'

'Anything,' Sizemore answered.

'Nathan Cowart's death -- You are confident it was an accident?'

If Sizemore was offended by the question, he didn't show it. His reply was immediate. 'No doubt about it. He and his dad were out hunting. Another hunter mistook them for a deer and let loose. The boy was shot in the lungs and died in the hospital.'

'The hunterserved his sentence for involuntary manslaughter and is home now.'

'He was checked?'

'Yeah. Double and triple checked. He is a farmer, not far from Amherst. This related to everything else?'

'Not now. Not if it was an accident.'

'It was.'

Zeb rose and stared blindly out of the hotel window. The media's presence was still strong, even though it was two weeks since the kidnapping.

Police presence was thick and visible. Perversely, tourist traffic had risen sharply and there was a constant crowd of onlookers outside the hotel, which had re-opened.

A mug of coffee appeared in front of him.

'What are you thinking, Wise One?' Meghan teased.

I am not yet ready. I have a germ of an idea, but it needs to be tested.

'Bob hasn't called. That's unusual.'

Bob was busy.

Merritt had received the message from Baghdad with equanimity.

I have prepared for that eventuality too.

He called his men together.

Carlos and Fiske were on guard. They secured the boys' rooms and came to the room where Merritt, Pico, and Avram were seated.

Merritt briefed them on developments. On Carter. On Baghdad. On his calls to the FBI.

'We need to get more men. Some of them will come here; the others will go to the other two locations.'

'Things will come to a head now.'

'The countdown has already started.'

No one questioned him. None of them was perturbed. They had worked together for a long time. They had full faith in Merritt's abilities.

Carlos and Fiske went back to guard duty. Avram and Pico made calls to the select men Merritt had identified.

The boy heard movement outside his room, heard a lock shoot home. The movement faded.

He had lost weight. He had hollows under his eyes. He couldn't sleep well.

He didn't know how his friend was doing. He knew the doctor spoke to his friend regularly.

Did he get his memory back? Is he okay?

He bent double as panic and fear stabbed him suddenly. He opened his mouth and drew gasping breaths till his pulse slowed and the piercing agony lessened.

He thought of his folks, and his friend's.

We are still alive. Please don't give up on us.

Chapter 28

Bob called.

This time there were fewer people in the room. Murphy was there, but the other agency heads were missing.

It was as if people were already distancing themselves from failure.

'Missed me, didn't you, Burke? You must be a wreck, wondering whether I had disappeared, if the boys were still alive.' Bob chuckled.

Burke grimaced but kept silent. The Veep hadn't stopped lobbying for the Syria bill. She hoped Bob wouldn't bring it up.

He didn't.

'No response? That's iron self-control, Burke. Congrats. You have potential.'

'How *are* the boys? When can we speak to them?' she asked.

An agent gave her a thumbs up at her composure. She had started receiving surprising support from her fellow agents and from other agencies. Even the media had congratulated her on not flagging, on keeping the hunt alive.

Phone-ins were flooded with praise for her briefings. She didn't have much progress to report, but people admired her courage for saying so.

All that's good. But Bob's still at large, out there. Fairman and Barlow are still missing.

'The boys are missing their families. That should be obvious, I hope. They are wondering why the cavalry hasn't arrived, the front door busted in and why I haven't been riddled with holes.'

Bob broke off in a loud peal of laughter that no one else joined in on.

'How's that coming along, Burke? The investigation, I mean. Any closer to breaking down a door? You know, I was thinking of calling one of those talk shows and introducing myself.'

'It would make for great TV. However, it would also increase my risk. I am not stupid. You will agree on that, won't you?'

Burke didn't reply. Murphy rubbed his eyes slowly, his hands knuckled into fists.

Bob sighed theatrically. 'You folks aren't much fun to talk to. How's a guy to have a conversation. All right, I will give what you want.'

Burke raised her head. Murphy stopped rubbing.

'You folks remember Kellie McCoy?'

Burke raced through her memory, drew a blank. Her fellow agents, the director, gave her similar looks.

'Who's she?'

'I *knew* that was the response I would get. I *knew* you would forget Kellie!' Bob's voice rose in rage.

He's angry, a voice analyst looked up from his machine and whispered at Burke.

That's obvious.

'I'll give a hint. A baby.'

He fell silent, giving them some time to think.

An agent snapped his finger, came forward, and scribbled on a paper.

Veep. Affair. Son. Campaign.

Burke stared at the words as distant memories came back

'She claimed to have an affair with the vice president?'

'She didn't claim. She *did* have an affair with him when he was a senator!' Bob raged.

'She had a child by him. It came out when he joined the president's campaign trail. He denied everything. That's what politicians do, don't they?'

'The paternity test failed, Bob. He wasn't the father.' Burke read out what the agent wrote.

'Of course it would fail, stupid. He rigged the test. He had enough clout and enough money to buy out a country. A paternity test was nothing to him,' Bob thundered.

He slammed his fist on something. It sounded like a gunshot. An agent flinched.

'I am sure the vice president will disagree with you.' *Keep calm, Burke. Let him lose it. You keep it together.*

'What has Kellie McCoy got to do with your kidnapping?'

'Everything,' Bob screamed. 'She lost that child when he was five years old. Did the media report that? No. They were sucking up to the vice president. Did Barlow know his child died in poverty? That Kellie McCoy had to resort to doing tricks to feed his son?'

'I bet he didn't. He was lapping up his win.'

Bob's voice dropped to a whisper. 'You wanted to know

what the connection was, didn't you, Burke?'

'I am Kellie McCoy's brother. Find me if you can.'

'He puts up a great show,' Chloe commented once they were alone with Burke, after her task force had dispersed to verify Bob's story. He had made another demand for five million, which the two families were making arrangements for.

'At this rate, he'll drip feed them into bankruptcy,' Bear said grimly after Burke's strained call with the two mothers.

'What do you think? Could this be personal? The stuff that he told us about McCoy, all that's true.'

She rushed on before Meghan and Beth protested. 'Not about the rigged test, though I think there were enough allegations about that too.'

'It was a dirty campaign,' Broker agreed. The president had won by the narrowest margin possible in an election that had polarized the nation.

'It's possible. I wonder why he waited so long, though.' Zeb wondered.

'Don't forget, Bob has planned this for a long time. Who knows what else he has in store?' Beth reminded him

They waited for Zeb to respond and when he didn't Bwana looked heavenward.

'Lord, you left him out on that conversation gene, didn't you?'

Avram watched as Merritt turned off the phone, wiped his face, and drank a glass of water. Acting was a tiring business.

'You don't think all these calls will increase our risk?'

Merritt swallowed deeply, refilled the glass and emptied it a second time. He wiped his mouth with his hand and turned to the gunman.

'We are already high risk, buddy. If the boy hadn't lost his memory, all this wouldn't have been needed. We would have extracted the info, killed both of them, and we would have disappeared.'

Avram poured himself a glass and the two stood silently watching the TV. Director Murphy was in a briefing, suggesting a new lead. They were investigating it.

'How much of that was true?'

Merritt chuckled. 'All of it, except the paternity. That kid wasn't the Veep's. There *is* a brother. He has been missing, presumably dead, for years. The Feds will chase their own tails once again.'

He patted Avram on the back. 'Relax. I've planned this for a long while. All eventualities will be taken care of.'

'What do we do with the doc?' They could hear the faint sound of the doctor snoring, even though a story separated them.

Merritt's smile wasn't pleasant. 'He will die here.'

He peered out of the front window for a moment and then turned to his fellow gunman. 'I'll be going out for a while to prepare those other two locations.'

Avram nodded and shut the door behind him.

Merritt went to the garage and started the white truck and backed it out slowly. The rack on top had a boat, which was securely fastened by tie down straps to the rails.

Merritt repaired small boats. The garage was converted into a large workshop, fully stocked with tools. Boats lay on the floor or stood against the wall, in various states of repair.

Lighthollow was three hours away from the coast, and a few eyebrows were raised when he started his business.

'Less competition,' he countered. The flow of boats to and from his garage had quelled any further doubts.

The cover was good. It gave him all the excuse he needed to move out of the house at will, to create a racket inside the garage, to have people – customers, move in and out of the house.

He had built the cover over two years and had gotten to know the neighbors well. One of them, Greg, a baker, waved at him from his garden. Merritt returned the greeting.

Merrit was a good neighbor. So what if he was a killer?

He drove for an hour and reached Chantilly in Virginia, and after rolling down largely empty streets, he turned into the driveway of a four-bedroom house.

The house was very similar to their hide, except that it was empty.

Merritt jumped out of the truck, unlocked the house, turned on the lights and turned on the most important device in the house.

An internet router.

He logged onto a laptop and sent a few random emails to a

dummy account, making sure the emails had keywords.

Kidnap. Boys. Vice president's son.

He created several other messages and timed them for scheduled delivery.

He left the house, went to the next house in Winchester and repeated the actions.

It was evening when he reached his hide. Greg was watering his lawn this time. Merritt slowed, commented on Greg's neat garden, shared a few laughs and wondered silently if he would have to kill his neighbor.

Zeb and the twins were back at Kale, and were being seen to by Fairman and Barlow's teacher.

Rudy Peele knew every one of his students well and described the boys at length when Zeb asked him to.

'Do you have any video recordings of the boys?' Zeb asked him when Rudy had finished his glowing praise.

'Sure,' the teacher rose and went to a laptop and attached it to a projector. 'We'll have several, I am sure. We record all performances or recitals of the students and play it back to them, for them to improve.'

He scanned several files and brought one up. It was a play.

'Not a play. Something like a debating competition, or a quiz?'

Peele went back to his files. Zeb ignored the sideways looks from the twins.

The teacher brought a quiz first in which Barlow had participated. It was a twenty -minute clip that they watched silently.

'James aced it,' Peele said with quiet pride.

Great memory. What about Fairman?

Fairman showed a similar sharpness in the clips Peele played.

'Anything special about these two boys?' Zeb asked the teacher when he had put away his equipment.

'They were outstanding students, great friends.' Peele looked at Zeb as if to confirm that's what his visitor wanted to hear.

Zeb nodded, thanked the teacher, and left.

Behind him he heard the twins praise the teacher effusively and follow him.

'What was that about?' Meghan narrowed her eyes at him

when they were in the SUV.

He didn't reply.

How easy is it for young kids to conceal their abilities? For fear of being bullied or being mocked at?

Horses surged beneath the hood when he turned the key.

Not difficult at all.

'Aren't we going after Kellie's brother?' Beth asked when Zeb maintained his silence.

'Zeb's probably shot him already,' her twin replied drolly and drew a smile from Zeb.

'Not quite. The Feds will throw enough manpower after him. Besides, I have a feeling it will be another red herring.'

It was dark when Merritt stepped outside again, in the backyard of their hide in Virginia.

The sky was clear and peppered with tiny white dots. Another man would have contemplated the vastness above and reflected on the smallness of man.

Merritt didn't. He wasn't small. He regarded himself as a giant of a man in the world he lived in.

The night was still, broken only by normal night sounds. Vehicles in the distance, a cruiser's wail falling and rising then fading away.

He walked the length of the backyard and reached the thick hedge at the rear.

The hedge was seven feet tall, four feet wide and was a dense barrier that separated his backyard from the one behind. It ran the length of the backyards on the street and was bookended by cul-de-sacs at either end.

Merritt went to the center of the hedge, pressed a section and a door opened.

It was a wooden door that swung silently on oiled hinges. Its outer surface was lined with foliage and was impossible to detect unless one knew where and what to look for.

He went inside the hedge and closed the door behind him.

Over the eighteen months, he had spent considerable time on the hedge. He had worked nights and had hollowed the hedge out to make a narrow passage, a foot and a half wide that ran from his backyard to the cul-de-sac at one end.

In that dead end, a getaway vehicle stood, keys hidden in one wheel well, fueled and ready. Merritt kept the vehicle stocked, fueled and with the right papers.

No one questioned its presence. *Leave something in a place for long enough, it becomes furniture.*

However that wasn't the only trick Merritt had up his sleeve.

In the middle of the hedge, another door opened and led to a backyard of another house. This house was five backyards away from his hide.

This house was his too, owned by a phantom business. In its drive was another getaway vehicle.

Merritt walked through the backyard, entered the house and made sure there were no obstructions from the back to the front.

A quick escape might be required.

Chapter 29

'I have some news,' General Abdallah's voice was cautious. His comment drew Zeb's crew around him.

They leaned over his shoulder and peered at the phone on the center of the table.

'One insurgent went missing that night, when Johnson was killed.'

Beth whooped softly, jumped high to high-five Bwana.

Zeb put a hand up. They quietened.

'I need more than that, Yasin. Insurgents, heck civilians, die every day in your country.'

'I am getting there, brother,' the general replied patientlly.

He went through the events of that night which were imprinted in Zeb's memory after repeated reading of the mission files.

Johnson and three other deep black agents were tasked with kidnapping an Al Qaeda terrorist in Mosul. The terrorist was suspected of masterminding a series of domestic terrorism plots in the U.S.

The plan was to abduct and evac, leaving no clue behind. Their covers were perfect. They all had tanned skins and had a Mediterranean look. They were oil traders from Baghdad, in Mosul to arrange supplies from the black-market. Oil was the only commodity that had any value in the war torn city.

The terrorist occupied the second story of a ramshackle house, away from the center of Mosul.

The terrorist came out every night for a cigarette, smoked in silence, with a couple of guards with him, relieved himself against a wall and went inside.

This was a routine he had never broken.

Johnson and the others would grab the terrorist while he was smoking, kill the guards with silenced guns, and drive away, out of the city, in a getaway truck.

The bed of the truck had oil barrels; one of them was empty for the terrorist to be concealed in. Once outside the city, they would exchange the truck for another, which too had oil barrels.

They would drive through the night, to Baghdad, their truck filled with friendlies – tribal men who supported the West.

In Baghdad, an extraction unit was on standby. So was a bird.

They had cash, lots of it, to bribe anyone they met.

It wasn't a foolproof plan. It had holes. But it was the closest thing they had to grab the wanted man.

Johnson and the agents were hunkered down in a stable opposite the terrorist's house. To call it a stable was to glorify it. It was a ramshackle structure that housed goats. It had hay, which the animals munched on, and relieved themselves on.

It stank. It had animal feces all over.

It was the perfect place for them to hide.

No one knew how the fire started. It started small. Two agents tried desperately to put it out, with Johnson helping, but it raged suddenly, as if it was fueled.

The fire drew the attention of the opposite house.

Shouts emerged from it. Shadows tumbled out.

Johnson looked at his men. This was going south, fast.

They looked behind. More people were running toward them.

He fired and jumped into the fire which was now an orange wall. The idea was to go through the fire, then behind it, seeking cover against an extended wall.

They might be spotted, but if they stood their ground, they would die for sure.

Johnson's shot attracted return fire and the other agents were caught in a firefight.

The fire burned intensely, its heat putting off the approach of any terrorists. A couple of men still approached.

One agent clubbed one of terrorists and threw him into the fire. His scream rang out in the stable and then died.

The other gunman opened fire, killed one agent. The gunman himself fell when the two remaining agents caught him in a hail of fire. However, the gunman did damage before he died. One agent was injured fatally.

'Johnson,' the sole surviving agent called out.

The fire roared in reply.

The agent looked out desperately. Shadows were hurrying, shouting. Some stray shots were fired, but the stable wasn't salvageable. No one was coming near it.

He grabbed the dead insurgent, dragged him behind a half-fallen wall, stripped him of his clothes, donned them, and threw his gun away.

He grabbed the dead terrorist, hoisted him on his shoulder and yelled out in Arabic.

'Don't shoot. I'm bringing Ijaz.'

He ran toward the men outside, dropped the dead man on the ground and examined him.

'He's dead,' he shrieked and beat his chest with his fists. He slammed his head on the ground repeatedly till some men pulled him away.

He went with them willingly, his head bowed, praying that no one would know who *Ijaz* – a name he had conjured up – was.

The insurgents waited for the fire to die down and then went inside the stable. They gathered around the bodies and spat on the dead agents.

The surviving agent spat along with them. He was lucky to be alive, lucky that not one insurgent had thought to question him.

He eyed the two charred bodies. They were beyond recognition.

He returned to the scene when it was deserted and the embers had cooled. Johnson's body lay near a collapsed wall at the back of the stable.

The body didn't have any identification, however, none was required. There was no way a strange body could have come into the stable.

The agent took photographs and rendezvoused with his exfil team. The fiasco never came to light. The operation was deep black and there was nothing to report.

They heard the scratch of a match and a contented puff. 'That night ten insurgents died or went missing in that part of Mosul.'

He recited names. 'All of them were accounted for and their bodies were found. All but one. Samir Najaf, an insurgent, was on patrol a couple of buildings away. He was never found.'

Another puff. 'He was similar in build to Johnson.'

'Surely he was searched for?' Chloe questioned.

'He was,' the general confirmed, 'but not for long. The Western forces were pressing hard that night and all able men were required to fight back.'

'Why wasn't this ever reported to the American authorities?'

'It's war here, my friends. A terrorist turning up dead or missing isn't really big news. No one really made the connection between the burned body and Najaf.'

Bear raised his hand as if to signal a question. Chloe rolled her eyes and gestured at him. Go *ahead.*

'How come Najaf's still remembered? This was a long time back.'

They heard a soft tapping sound, the general dislodging ash from his cigar. 'Najaf was the sole son of a goat herder. His father is now in his eighties but has never given up his search for his son. Everyone in Mosul knows him. He goes around with a photograph of his son and asks random strangers if they have seen Najaf.'

'He is regarded as a harmless, old man who has lost his mind. The insurgents see him as a source of entertainment. He was more than eager to tell the story of his son's disappearance when my man spoke to him.'

It's possible, Zeb thought. *But it's still tenuous. We need more*.

Need more, Buster thought as he looked at his fast dwindling stash of powder.

Buster had spent his life on the streets of Manassas. He slept in doorways, under cardboard boxes and during the day, shuffled through the city, rummaging through trash cans for food.

Occasionally he did the odd job; mowing lawns or helping folks move, and made some money.

His burned through his earnings fast, on drinking and on his drug habit. He shot up in lonely alleys and drifted through life in an alcohol and powder induced haze.

His hands trembled as he stared at the last few baggies in his possession.

He needed more.

He stumbled to his feet, knocked down a trash can, didn't bother to set it right, and wandered off in search of his source.

His source was Doctor Beldwin.

Buster had his head buried deep in a trashcan in the parking lot of a big-box store, when he had heard the car drive up.

It was night, the lot was nearly empty and Buster was shrouded in darkness.

He raised his head groggily and looked at the car. Its dome light turned on and the driver turned and searched for something in the rear.

Buster shuffled closer.

The driver was alone in the car, and was wearing one of those white coats. Buster squinted his eyes and saw there was something dangling off his neck.

It was one of those cards that had a person's name on it.

The driver brought out something that Buster immediately recognized.

A syringe.

He went closer. The driver didn't look up.

He was just a couple of feet away from the car when the driver rolled up a sleeve and shot himself up.

Buster's eyes popped out. This dude was getting high right in front of him, like he had no care in the world.

He tapped on the window and showed his teeth when the driver dropped the needle, startled.

He tried the door handle. It was locked.

The driver tried to start the car. It didn't.

Buster grinned wider. He smashed the window with a large fist. He didn't feel pain.

'Open it,' he shouted.

The driver tried his car again. The engine refused to cooperate.

Buster hit the window again. It trembled.

The driver rolled down the glass an inch.

'What do you want?'

Buster pointed a dirty nail at the syringe.

'That.'

That was the moment Buster's life had changed for the better. Doc Beldwin was just like him. So what if he went about treating people. They shared the same addiction.

'I'll report you,' he had told Beldwin, the moment he had read the card around his neck.

Buster knew where the doc worked. Heck, he had spent many a night in the shadows of that hospital.

Beldwin said he wasn't a normal doctor. He was a mind doctor, a psychiatrist.

It didn't make a difference to Buster. A doctor was a doctor.

They came to an arrangement. Doc Beldwin would write prescriptions for Buster. He would pay for those too. Buster would keep quiet about his addiction.

The agreement worked, till the day the doctor disappeared and Buster was left without a supply.

Buster stuffed the remaining baggies in his pocket, along with a syringe, and got to his feet. He walked, his mind whirling, and reached the hospital.

A guard frowned at him but didn't stop him.

He went to the desk and asked for Doc Beldwin. The woman behind it eyed him carefully and asked him to repeat the name.

Buster controlled his impatience and repeated the name.

She clicked on something and told him the doctor was away.

'When would he be back?'

'Sorry, sir, we don't give out that kind of information.'

'Why not?' Buster raged.

People turned to look at him. He didn't notice them.

He thumped a fist on the desk. When would the doctor be back?

The woman's eyes grew large behind her glasses and she looked behind him.

Buster felt arms around him. They tightened and dragged him away.

'I want Doctor Beldwin,' he shouted.

He broke loose and grabbed a vacant chair and threw it against a wall.

A woman screamed.

Footsteps pounded and big men surrounded him and subdued him.

'Doctor Beldwin?' he screamed.

He got no reply.

Chapter 30

Werner tagged the first email that contained the keywords and went after its source. It was from a house in a small city in Virginia. Werner filed it away and took no further action.

Action would be required if it spotted more such messages.

That wait wasn't long.

Another email swam in the internet. It too had the keywords and it too came from Virginia.

Werner looked at it suspiciously, and tracked it back. Another address in a small town.

Two emails with the similar keywords, from two locations.

Werner went *hmmm.* It couldn't of course, but it would have, if it could.

Werner sent a message to his two favorite people in the world. The twins.

It then opened a port and chatted with another supercomputer in Washington D.C.

The two machines chatted about their day, about petabytes and memory and mentioned the two emails.

The other supercomputer had spotted them too and had flagged them. They talked about life in the ether, about their bosses. The other supercomputer was envious of Werner's bosses.

It had a ponytailed guy as boss. He was okay. However, if it had a choice, it would trade the guy for the twins, any day.

No trade, buddy, Werner chuckled. No one else is getting the twins.

Werner closed the port, satisfied and went back to its passive state, waiting for the twins to awake.

What was it with humans and sleep?

The thought came to Zeb when he was sleeping. One moment he was in a dreamless state, the next, the image had inserted itself.

His eyes opened.

Of course. Why didn't I think of it? Maybe Burke has, and checked it out.

It was three a.m. he thought of calling Broker or Burke.

He thought better of it. Both of them would curse before hearing him out. Broker's would be colorful. Burke's would be polite.

It could wait till the morning.

The morning came with a banging on his door.

'We got a house in Chantilly,' Beth started. 'And another, in Winchester,' Meghan completed.

Zeb listened as they broke it down for him. Werner's flagging the emails. The keywords.

'Who's in those houses?'

'Werner's looking into them.'

Meghan was bouncing, her hair flying, her eyes shining. Her sister was in a similar state.

Their war-room, a conference room in the hotel, was buzzing with energy when they entered.

Broker was typing, Bear was on a call, Bwana and Roger were huddled over another phone, Chloe was on another computer.

'I have another idea,' he said when his crew put their phones down.

They looked at him expectantly.

The additional men had arrived. Merritt deployed six of them to the house on Chantilly, another six in Winchester, and took four men in his hide. All fourteen men were hard, well recommended, and used to close-quarters fighting. All knew that they might not survive whatever transpired.

They were generously paid for the risk.

His hideout now had eleven people, including the doctor and the boys.

The four men, reinforcements, came at night, one at a time. Their instructions were clear. They were never to step outside.

He ordered another truck and a rundown boat from an online site. He would have to pick the truck up from a dealer's yard and the boat would arrive in a week.

Merritt was making preparations for exfil, if he had to.

The men in Chantilly and Winchester would be diversions. They would be cannon fodder, not that they knew it.

He and his inner team and the boys would leave in a week's time, to New York state. The boys would be concealed under the boats.

He hoped it wouldn't come to that. That the boy's memory would return, in which case, he would kill all of them except his inner team, and depart.

The boy heard the men arriving. He could feel the house swell with the numbers. He was feeling better, irrationally.

He had seen his friend earlier in the day, when he was escorted to the bathroom. His friend's door had been open a crack and through that narrow space, he had seen him

He had been lying on his bed, staring at the ceiling. He seemed to be intact.

The second thought that gave him hope was the arrival of the men.

That many aren't required to kill the two of us. They're preparing for a showdown.

In the privacy of his bathroom, he prayed for his friend and himself.

He looked at the opaque window.

We are alive, he shouted in his mind.

There was a tape from the nightclub bombing in Indonesia. It showed gunmen entering, shooting in the air, and escaping, before the venue exploded.

The digital tape had been caught by the security cameras and had been stored in servers in an office far away from the venue.

Zeb stopped Meghan as she played the video file.

'Can you rewind? Go back ten minutes.'

She paused and went back, played a few times, rewound a few times, till he was satisfied.

The tape wasn't the best in quality; however, the images were clear enough.

A mass of heaving people. Flashing lights. A viewing platform that ran at the top on which were more people and dining tables.

The DJ's corner in which a figure bobbed and swayed.

The first gunman entered and fired. Meghan turned down the volume at the sound of shots.

More gunmen poured in and surrounded the crowd. A few gunmen disappeared.

The mass of people screamed and broke. They were turned

back by firing and were contained by the ring of guns.

One gunman spoke. His voice was drowned out by the torrent of voices.

The gunmen who had vanished, returned.

More firing in the air, and then the gunmen exited.

The crowd stood uncertainly for several minutes and then a flash of fire.

Zeb made Meghan go back to the scene of the speaking gunman.

'Can you eliminate all the background noise and get his voice?'

A silence in the room while they considered his implication.

Broker swore softly and moved swiftly to his computer.

Meghan looked at him with something in her eyes. Beth bowed low.

'You truly are the Wise One.'

Normally the cops would have just hauled Buster away and locked him up for the night. They knew him well. He would be back to his somnolent state after a good sleep. Buster wasn't worth any paperwork.

However, the hospital wished to file charges. It was insistent. It had a reputation to protect. Buster had assaulted an employee.

The weary police officers heard the hosptial administrator patiently and then corrected him. 'He hurled a chair against a wall. No one got hurt. We know Buster, sir. He's no harm. He'll apologize when he's sober.'

The administrator grew voluble and red faced. The police officers sighed inwardly and started taking statements.

Their computers recorded the statements and the system took over. The hospital issued a press statement assuring the public that its patients were safe.

The incident came to Werner's attention. Addict out of control in a hospital. Seeking a psychiatrist.

Werner couldn't see how it could be remotely connected to the kidnapping and the hunt for Bob. It shrugged. Its role was not to reason why.

Humans were peculiar. Just that morning, Meghan had tasked it to be on the lookout for any random event in the states surrounding Washington D.C.

Werner dutifully logged the incident and went back to reading up on gravitational waves. Now, that was something.

Zeb read the message from Werner and didn't pay it much attention. No one did. They were listening to the twins explain what they had done with the recording from the nightclub.

The twins had run the video file through some fancy software and had erased layers of noise. They went into technical detail and when they saw Zeb's eyes, they stopped.

'You are lucky, you have us,' Beth said witheringly. Meghan muttered something that suspiciously sounded like *Neanderthal,* and played the file.

Nothing had changed except a low level of noise.

'We couldn't strip it out completely,' Meghan explained.

The lack of noise made the crowd's dancing look jerky. Beth skipped ahead to when the first gunman entered.

The shots were loud. The crowd broke and fell back when the other gunmen arrived.

'Stay where you are. We'll shoot anyone who runs.' The speaker's voice was clear enough.

Beth played the line several times, looking at her friends.

'That's too small a segment,' Broker voiced, dubiously.

'Agreed. However, we missed this in the original file since there was lots of surrounding noise.'

She forwarded the file to several minutes and pressed play.

'Don't leave the nightclub for half an hour. Anyone who exits will be shot. I repeat, don't leave the nightclub for half an hour.'

Zeb's crew leaned forward as one.

Meghan held her hand up to stem their voices. Her eyes were shining as she brought up another program, loaded Bob's recording in Moscow, and the nightclub file.

The program analyzed the two voice imprints and came back quickly with a result.

Fifty-five percent match.

Meghan whooped and bumped fists with Bwana and Bear. Beth jumped in the air and screamed a loud 'yeah.' Zeb sat motionless, a small smile playing on his lips.

'Call Burke,' he told the twins when they had calmed down.

Meghan punched the agent's number and when she came on, started to tell her the news.

Zeb cut her off. ‘You need to come here. Just you and whoever you trust.’

He rose and went to a window.

We know who you are. Now, where are you?

Chapter 31

Merritt was briefing the new arrivals in Lighthollow. They gathered in the kitchen, their weapons dangling casually from their shoulders.

Avram had given them a quick tour of the house, not that there was much to be seen, and Pico had walked them through the security setup.

There were cameras, pressure pads, infrared sensors, all kinds of tricks that Pico had set up.

They were told there were two hostages, and were shown the closed doors, but weren't shown the boys.

They were introduced to the psychiatrist and told to leave him alone.

If any of the new arrivals guessed their identities, they didn't mention it. Merritt liked their look. They were tough, competent, and all of them were average looking. Brown or black hair, dark eyes, tanned skin. Nothing that made them stand out.

All four would man the lower floor. Merritt's original crew, alone, had access to the upper floor.

The new arrivals didn't demur. They listened, took their orders, and went silently to their posts.

Merritt spoke to Darrell after the briefing and updated him on the arrivals and the arrangements at the other locations.

'They haven't traced the emails yet. I spoke to some folks I know and the FBI is still chasing red herrings,' Darrell chuckled.

The reinforcements seemed to have bolstered his confidence in some way, since he sounded relaxed.

The boy was still in his private world, but that didn't seem to bother the paymaster.

'They will find those emails, and then those houses. Those messages are timed to go out periodically. Sooner or later, some supercomputer somewhere will spot them.'

They discussed payments and ended the call.

Burke listened silently as Broker explained about the dead agents. Her lips tightened when she heard about the calls made to Iraq, Pakistan, and the other countries.

'Why didn't you tell me?' she interrupted angrily, knowing what the answer would be.

'You have a leak. Besides there wasn't much to tell at that point,' Broker replied, baldy.

Kowalski frowned. 'So you've got something now?'

'We know who he is.'

Burke sucked in her breath sharply and waited. Broker made her wait and resumed the explanation.

He got to Iraq and Mosul and the operation, when Roger, the handsome one, took over.

He ran through the operation. Stalled her questions with a *we checked and double checked with the concerned agency, ma'am.*

They played a snippet of General Abdallah's call.

Burke crossed her arms. She had heard enough. She wanted the name.

'Dale Johnson,' Chloe mentioned the name, softly. She mentioned the agency's name.

It didn't ring any bell.

'It's deep black for a reason,' Bear chuckled.

'How certain are you?'

Carter stirred for the first time and nodded at Meghan.

She played a video. Burke recognized it – it was the nightclub bombing.

She played another video. It was the same one, without the noise, just the one voice. She explained about stripping. Randy nodded his head vigorously.

She played the comparison and when the match percentage came up, she fell silent.

To lay people, fifty-five percent was low probability. To those in Zeb's world, it was an actionable percentage.

'This remains with the three of you,' Carter looked at her.

She agreed. Director Murphy was handling the internal investigation, but he was moving very cautiously. He didn't want to spook the leak.

'The good news doesn't stop there.' Beth's excitement was infectious and Burke couldn't help smiling.

'Hit me with it.'

'We got two locations in Virginia.' Beth brought up the emails.

'Yeah, we know of those,' Burke was puzzled. 'Randy is checking out the residents and the ownership.'

'We've got all that,' came the quick reply. 'Both houses are owned by shell companies and are accommodations for office staff.'

'Get this, though. Both houses were acquired at the same time the gunmen trained on that hotel in Boston.'

Burke felt warmth spread through her. It wasn't much on its own, but it was another thread and the various strands were coming together.

'Good work.' She praised the twins and cocked her head at Broker. 'How come you got those details faster than Randy?'

'There are some advantages to private enterprise, ma'am.' The light in his eyes warmed her further.

She turned back to Carter to hide her confusion. *Why am I feeling like that? Where did that come from?*

'We'll check those houses out.'

'We'll do it, if you don't mind.'

She understood what he was getting at and nodded. She kept her eyes resolutely on him, not looking at the urbane, older man, next to Carter.

Once outside, Randy donned his shades, looked once at the hotel, and led them to their ride.

'We would be chasing our tails, without Carter.'

Neither she nor Kowalski refuted him.

Zeb made a few calls when Burke had left and explained his first idea to his people.

'I'll go,' Beth exclaimed.

'I'm older. I have the maturity,' her twin countered.

'Older by just a few seconds. As for maturity, where's that?' Beth scoffed and made a play of inspecting her sister.

Bwana crossed his arms, thrust his legs out, and closed his eyes. 'Wake me up when they decide who's going.'

The plan was simple. One of the twins would deliver flyers to all the houses in two streets in Chantilly. One of those houses would be the email house.

'Make it four streets, including the one we're interested in,' Zeb announced. Broker agreed. The cover had to be good. More streets, the better.

The flyers advertised a local takeout place whose owner had a friend who knew someone who in turn knew Zeb.

The flyers came with a deal – a contest for which home owners had to consent to in person, their names given, and if they won, they would have free food for a week.

No one turned down the prospect of free food for a week. The owner liked the deal and agreed to do a favor for his friend. As it happened, his flyers hadn't been delivered to those streets. He wouldn't refuse the offer of having them delivered in that neighborhood.

The twins squabbled and turned to Chloe.

'Both of you deliver. One street each. However, Meghan will do the email street.'

Beth protested halfheartedly. No one argued with Chloe when she had that look in her eyes. Not even Bear.

'I bet I'll collect more tips than you,' she told her sister.

'It's delivering flyers, not pizza, dumbass.'

The sisters called a truce and listened to Broker's instructions.

They were simple.

They would be outfitted in the takeout's uniforms. Their hair would be dyed, black in Meghan's case and Beth would go blonde. The older twin would wear grey contacts, while Beth would have her own green eyes.

Broker would be in the takeout's office, manning the phone, as a just-in-case.

Bwana and Roger would be in one vehicle, keeping an eye on Beth. Bear and Chloe would be in another vehicle, watching Meghan.

Zeb would be in a third SUV, parked at the other end of Meghan's street.

Both the sisters would have pinhole cameras that had a record time of two hours. Ample enough to complete their deliveries.

The flyers had to be hand delivered and acknowledged by the residents, not slid under the door.

Beth completed her round with no fuss and came back with twelve orders. The owner beamed when he heard her and offered her a job on the spot. He calmed down when he felt Broker's eyes on him.

Meghan started out on her rounds. At one house, a dog trotted up, barked, and when she looked at it, sat down and wagged its tail. She petted it and took an order from the homeowner.

She delivered the flyer to more houses, spoke to many homeowners. Who wouldn't want to spend a few minutes in the company of an attractive woman?

She came to the email house. It had a wide driveway, a double garage, and its curtains were down, even in the middle of the day.

No dog barked when she rang the bell. Nothing happened for several minutes.

She waited patiently and then rang again. She then felt eyes on her, but kept her head down, fingering the flyers in her hand.

The door opened an inch and a swarthy face showed. She hoped her face gave nothing away. The man looked familiar, but she could be wrong.

She gave him her brightest smile.

'Hey, I'm sorry to disturb you. I am from the takeout around the corner. We have a special offer for the great people of this neighborhood.'

She fell into her practiced spiel, making sure her eyes didn't stray from his face. She swung her body subtly for the camera to get the best angle. She was also wearing a voice recorder that detected the slightest trace of any ambient noise.

She thrust the flyer out at the man, and stood poised pencil and pad in hand.

Short nails. Rough hands. Calloused fingers.

The man read it for a few seconds, jerked his head back when a voice sounded from inside.

Her heart leapt. *At least one more man.*

'The offer applies to all the residents in the house. Shall I make that two? Three? Can I have your name, sir?'

Something changed in the man's eyes. He handed the flyer back.

'Sorry, not interested.'

'Are you sure, sir? There are no strings. We'll deliver food for a week. There's even a menu you can order from.'

The man's lips twisted in a smile. He shook his head. 'No, thanks.'

'Alrighty. You have a great day, sir.'

She felt his eyes on her through the window as she left. She turned right, ignored the two vehicles parked on either side of the street, and went to the next house.

An ambulance was parked in front of one of the houses and medics were helping an elderly woman inside. She gave them a hand, handed all of them flyers and went to the next house.

The twins took a couple of hours more to finish their deliveries and then walked back to the takeout. They gave the owner the filled out forms; he thanked them and gave them several boxes of food.

'The orders have already started coming in,' he couldn't stop smiling.

Broker drove the twins back to the hotel and when they had joined the rest, he spoke. 'A few calls came in to verify the deals were genuine. Two of those were from blocked numbers.' He shrugged his shoulders. 'Couldn't trace their location.'

Meghan described the man, and all that she had seen in the house. Broker removed the camera and recorder, plugged it in his computer, while she narrated.

'Certainly more than one man,' he said after a while. 'Possibly four or even six. There's enough trace noise of bodies moving. Those recorders are so sensitive, they can pick up human breathing. I'll do some more tests and we'll know for sure.'

'I'll run his image through face recog. If we're lucky, he'll be wanted in five countries,' he grinned.

'I've got his prints too,' Meghan waved the flyer triumphantly. Beth snatched it from her hand and bagged it. The flyer would go to Burke as they didn't have forensic equipment.

Meghan described his hands at length, and Broker brought up the images. 'Could be caused by gun action,' Bear said, when the callouses came up.

'Anyone recognize him?' Zeb asked.

'Could be one of the hotel gunmen. Problem is, they all looked more or less the same. Similar heights, hair. This dude is no different.'

'Those ambulance guys have offered me a free ride, anytime.' Meghan laughed when she described the medics' reaction to the deals. The owner had called them and offered them a week's food, no contest needed.

Ambulance.

Zeb remembered the vehicle approaching, turning in the driveway, the woman being helped out.

What was it about the ambulance?

He let his mind go blank, let it roam freely, let the room and his crew disappear.

It came to him after a few minutes.

Werner's message about Buster and Beldwin.

He brushed past Broker and searched for news on the incident. There wasn't much more than what Werner had flagged.

Beldwin's bio was on the hospital website. It was an impressive resume.

He searched the internet for Beldwin and after several random hits, came across another news item.

Psychiatrist sacked!

He read the article from a local newspaper in Boston and when he had finished, became aware of his crew crowded around him.

'Here we are hunting killers and you're looking up psychiatrists?' Roger asked bemusedly, as he leaned over Zeb's shoulder to read the article.

'This's the same dude Werner messaged about?'

'Yeah.'

'What's your interest in him?'

'*Are they in good shape?*'he repeated Burke's question saw frowns appear and disappear when they remembered Bob's call.

'You're reaching,' Bear said finally, but his protest was halfhearted.

They knew Zeb's hunches by now. They were wild, but they were invariably true. In any case, they lost nothing by checking.

Broker and the twins reached out for their devices, to start a new search.

Find Beldwin.

Chapter 32

Burke arrived, with Kowalski and Randy in tow. She listened when Chloe briefed them on Chantilly.

Broker's eyes still had that light. She refused to look at him after the initial greeting.

Steel resolve, Burke. You're on the largest manhunt in the country. Nothing should distract you.

Randy went over to Broker and the two men discussed the technology behind the voice recorder. Broker explained how he had removed the ambient noise and identified the various layers.

'Five or six men,' he agreed with Broker. 'We've got those recorders, too. They are amazingly sensitive.'

Beth handed her the baggie. 'That flyer has his prints. So far our face recog hasn't got us anything.' She handed a storage device which contained the camera's recording.

Burke thanked her with a smile and turned to Carter. 'You'll do a similar run in Winchester?'

'Yeah, but we'll have to use some other ploy. Broker will think of something.'

'It'll have to be soon.'

'Tomorrow.'

'We'll run a drone over the Chantilly house and see if we can get more visual. Kowalski, can we do that tonight?'

'Sure thing.'

'There's one other development.' Chloe's tone caught Burke's attention.

'Anything unusual?' Merritt cradled his phone on his shoulder as he commanded the email servers to send another batch of messages.

'Nope,' one of the men from Chantilly replied. 'It's quieter than a grave here.'

Merritt nodded unconsciously. He had chosen all the neighborhoods for just that.

'Make sure just one of you goes out for the food run.'

'Yeah. There's a takeout nearby. We might go there. A woman came offering deals today.'

Merritt stopped what he was doing. His voice sharpened. 'What time? Describe her?'

His shoulders relaxed when the gunman described a dark-haired, grey-eyed, woman. *Not Carter's women. I know that takeout. It has a few women working in it.*

Carter was on his mind a lot. He was following the news bulletins and Darrell's briefing kept him clued in.

It was apparent to him that the FBI's investigation was going nowhere. They had busted down doors in several states only to come away empty handed. They had arrested several people, only for those to be quietly released.

They made appeals. The parents made appeals. The president made an appeal.

The pressure and anger toward the FBI had started mounting again. However, it was Carter that Merritt considered his real foe.

That man was something else. Darrell had finally gotten a nugget; that Carter probably worked for a no-name agency.

Merritt had thought of that already and it made sense. That was why there was no trace of him on the internet. It was why it was he who had made the connection to Eldersburg.

'You have the takeout's number?'

Merritt's man gave it to him.

It didn't hurt to double check with the takeout.

He ended the call and dialed the number.

Broker had set up a call routing so that all calls to the takeout also got routed to their war room. The calls got answered by the takeout's people and Broker occasionally listened in.

This call came just as Chloe had finished explaining about Beldwin and Burke was digesting it. There was a lull when the phone rang and the voice came on.

The voice was unnaturally loud in the sudden stillness.

'Hey there, you folks have a deal going on, don't you? One of your girls was with us earlier.'

All heads turned as one to the phone.

Beth dove at it and jabbed a button to record the call.

The voice was bland and had a curious quality to it. They were intimately familiar with it. They didn't need to run voice recognition programs.

It was Bob.

The owner answered and ran through the details of the offer.

'You're calling from Chantilly, sir, aren't you? That's where our girls were, today. Did you sign up for the offer? Can I have your name?'

The voice demurred. 'Perhaps I'll come down and have a look and if that red-haired lady greets me, I'll take you up on it.' He ended with a laugh.

'No red-haired women, here, sir. Carol, is dark-haired, and Rosalie, is blonde. It must be one of those two who greeted you.'

'My mistake.' The voice spoke for a few more minutes, promised to visit the takeout and hung up.

'Can you trace that call?' Sarah Burke asked Broker urgently.

'No, ma'am. It's blocked,' he replied regretfully.

She flicked hair back in frustration. 'There must be something we can do.'

'Ma'am, stick to your earlier plan. Run your drones at night. Get visual. We'll take it step by step. We know he's there. We know he's connected to that house. Now we need to make sure.'

He smiled and this time Special Agent in Charge, ace investigator, ice-cool professional, Sarah Burke, couldn't help smiling back.

The Feds would run down Beldwin's details. They would organize surveillance in Chantilly.

Zeb and his crew planned for a run on Winchester. The air was electric now. The twins seemed to be floating on air. Bwana, Roger, and Bear had taken to stripping and cleaning their weapons.

Zeb alone seemed to be unconcerned. He lay on his couch and stared sightlessly, answering in monosyllables.

Bwana looked at him a few times and shook his head in disgust. 'It's always this way. Black man does all the work. White man sleeps on couch.'

He grinned at a chorus of groans and ducked when Chloe threw a cushion at him.

Zeb didn't hear him. He was thinking of Beldwin, of why a psychiatrist might be required.

Why were the boys grabbed in the first place?

It was a question he had asked himself several times. All of them had. Not one person in that room or at the FBI had an answer.

The next day Roger and Chloe rented a pickup truck from a local dealer. They got it painted with a handyman's logo, along with a phone number and then bought used overalls and several pieces of equipment that a handyman would carry.

They reached Winchester just before noon and started knocking on doors on their first street, handing out leaflets to each person that answered.

Broker had printed the leaflets which had the same logo that the truck sported.

Roger and Chloe were the safest choices. Bwana or Bear were too memorable; Broker said he didn't stoop to do such kind of physical work. No one wanted Zeb to present himself.

Chloe did the knocking and the speaking and when homeowners saw that it was an attractive woman in front of them, they opened their doors wider and spent time.

The two took a break, drank water, wolfed down sandwiches, in full view of anyone wishing to watch them.

They moved to the target street, started at the other end of where the house lay, and made their way.

They collected orders.

'You can ditch Bear and start your business. He won't be any use to you. Ladders will break the moment he climbs them.' Roger winked at Chloe.

She slapped the flyers against his shoulder and went to the next house.

Roger fetched a mop and a bucket and joined her when they approached the target house.

As with the house in Chantilly, its curtains were drawn and no movement was visible.

Their cameras picked everything, the recorders heard every noise.

'There's breathing from the living room,' Broker spoke in their ears. 'I can't make out how many people.'

Chloe rang the bell and they waited.

No one opened the door.

She gave it five more minutes and rang again. She turned to Roger as they waited and began a conversation on cleaning schedules and supplies.

'They might be watching us,' she mouthed, with her back

to the house.

There was no response from the house.

Roger pressed a finger against the bell and let it ring longer. He prepared to turn away when the door remained stubbornly shut.

It was Chloe who had the idea.

She pulled him back and directed him to the windows on the left and she took the ones in the living room.

She wetted her mop, adjusted her ball cap over her face and ran the mop down the window.

Top to bottom, bottom to top.

From the corner of her eyes, she saw Roger do the same.

The reaction was instantaneous.

The door was flung open and two men crowded in it. They didn't recognize the men.

'What the hell are you doing?'

'We have been cleaning this house for years, sir,' Chloe smiled disarmingly at him.

Chloe's smile could melt steel; it had no effect on the man. Roger joined her and stood beside her.

'We rang the bell, sir, several times. We figured there wasn't anyone home. It's standard practice for us to wash this house if no one responds.'

The speaker, of Roger's height, blonde hair, closely cut, drew his eyebrows together. 'You start washing without the owner's permission?'

'Like she said, we have the owner's permission, sir,' Roger interjected. 'We have been doing this for years. We'll be happy to email you the contract if you share the details.'

He pretended to peer round the men. 'Isn't he home?'

The second man moved and blocked his view. 'No. The house doesn't need cleaning. Please leave.'

Roger ran an eye on the exterior of the house. 'You're sure, sir? Looks like it could do with a good wash.'

'Yeah, I'm sure,' the first man growled. 'Please leave, now.'

Chloe handed him the flyer. 'We are a call away, if you need us.'

He took it, balled it up, and returned it. 'We won't need you.'

They left.

Beth was tapping her foot in nervous energy when they returned. 'Burke's got print confirmation from yesterday's dude. He's wanted in Argentina for a drug killing,' she burst out the moment they entered their office.

Meghan shushed her. 'Looks like you folks turned tail at the first sight of trouble,' she smirked.

'We got prints,' Roger said defensively and handed the crumpled sheet to Broker. He placed it in a plastic baggie and spoke softly in a phone. To Burke.

'I analyzed the recorder when you were returning. This time there was interference, however there are several bodies in that house.'

'The first man was packing,' Chloe added when she had finished describing the men. 'Maybe the second one was too. He moved fast and cut off Roger's line of sight.'

'They could be having their girlfriends over,' Roger cautioned.

'Nope,' Bear's reply was definitive. 'Another series of mails went out when you were there. This time, Broker managed to crack the recipient's address.'

'The two houses are talking to one another.'

Roger whistled softly when it had sunk in. 'Any phone chatter?'

'None that we can hone in on. It looks like they're using encrypted phones.'

Broker hung up. 'She's coming.'

'What?' he asked when they looked at him as one.

Burke listened quietly, took the baggie from Broker, and when Chloe had finished, turned slightly to have Zeb in her view.

He was lounging against a wall; his arms crossed, and was looking at her with an expression she couldn't read.

'We're mounting surveillance on the two houses tonight. We want to make sure your visits don't spook them.'

She took a breath.

'We are going in tomorrow.'

Chapter 33

Beldwin was jumpy. His Desoxyn supplies were low and while Merritt had procured some more, Beldwin was shooting himself up more often.

Being cooped up in the house all day, with grim faced men as companions, wasn't doing any good to his disposition.

Merritt was the only one who spoke to him. The others just grunted or spoke in single words. The new arrivals had heightened his uneasiness.

He had queried Merritt about them, and had got a casual making *sure we have backup*, in return.

However it was that small item of news that had made him restless.

Beldwin was allowed half an hour of internet time every morning and evening. He wasn't allowed any phone calls; Merritt had confiscated his phone the day he had entered the house.

Even his internet time was monitored. Avram or Pico kept watch on the sites he frequented and if he was using email, they read every message he received or sent.

'Surely you have taken precautions,' the psychiatrist had protested when Merritt had outlined the surveillance.

'I have, however, one can't be too careful.'

The article had caught Beldwin's attention the previous night, just as he was logging off.

It was from the local newspaper in Manassas.

Drunk runs rampant in hospital!

Buster's name had jumped out at him and when he had clicked on the headline, a hand had reached out from behind and had turned off the computer.

'Time's up,' Pico had said.

He couldn't look up the article in the morning. Pico was hovering behind him and the doctor didn't want to read it in front of the gunman.

Did Buster ask for me? What was he doing there?

Beldwin paced nervously and when he felt Fiske's curious glance, he forced himself to relax. He went to the kitchen and brewed some coffee and joined Merritt who was, as usual, watching TV.

'How come they haven't made any progress?' he pointed his mug at Burke's image on the TV.

'Progress requires leads,' Merritt replied with a chuckle.

'How long will we be holed up here? The boy might come out today, or he might take more weeks.'

Merritt nodded in acknowledgement. 'I've been thinking that.'

Beldwin waited, but Merritt didn't elaborate.

He patted the doctor on his shoulder. 'Relax, Beldwin. Everything is in hand.'

He exited the kitchen leaving Beldwin alone.

Not alone. His laptop's here.

Beldwin darted to the door and peered out. He heard murmuring from the living room, but no one was in sight.

He craned his head up. No one was on the stairs.

He hurried to the laptop and pressed a key before it went into sleep mode.

He brought the newspaper's website and read the article.

Buster had yelled and shouted in the hospital. He had thrown a chair. He had been arrested.

However it was one line that made Beldwin clutch his chest.

Buster had asked for Doctor Beldwin.

Beldwin blinked furiously, read through the rest of the article, closed the browser and wiped the keys with a napkin.

He went to the sink and downed two glasses of water in rapid succession. The cool liquid brought a semblance of sanity and his mind started working again.

He had taken a leave of absence from the hospital and all his regular patients were covered. His official emails were diverted and another psychiatrist was taking care of them.

How much has Buster told the cops? Does the hospital know? Have the cops or the hospital tried to make contact?

He hadn't checked his email in a few days. Now, he didn't want to read them with a gunman over his shoulder.

Merritt returned, sat at his laptop and clicked the keys.

Through his rising panic, Beldwin had an idea.

I'll use his computer again the moment he disappears.

Zeb waited. His team waited. They were used to long hours of nothingness. The twins had a hard time getting used to the waits, when they had first joined the crew.

Zeb and the others trained them. Made them think of time as yet another inconsequential object. They had a tough time accepting the concept. Now they were as patient as the rest of them.

They were waiting for developments from Burke's end. That the FBI was going in was confirmed. The second set of prints hadn't yielded any hits. However, several international agencies had yet to confirm.

The search for Beldwin had become a dead end. His residence had been checked out by a couple of agents. No one had seen the doctor for more than a week.

His phone showed no activity.

Broker hacked into his personal email; it showed no recent activity. The past emails were innocuous.

The hospital in Manassas said he was on an extended leave of absence. They had a contact number for him, but he wasn't answering that. They said they used his work email to send him any information.

There was nothing in his work emails to indicate where he had gone. 'It's not unusual,' the hospital said. 'Our staff is obliged to give us only a phone number and an email address, when they are on vacation.'

The hospital was aware of Beldwin's troubled past. It also said the psychiatrist was clean now and was highly respected and they couldn't afford to let him go.

They pored over his sacking in Boston, spoke to the hospital there, and spoke to his ex-wife. They confirmed his addiction to prescription meth.

'Search for prescription meth purchases,' Zeb suggested.

The twins searched. They got a few hits from pharmacies across the state. Burke's people were looking into those.

Zeb called his underground contacts, as did Broker. They left a message. They were interested in a meth addicted doctor.

They waited for calls to be returned, for Burke to make progress.

Beth brought out a pack of cards and they played poker quietly. All of them, but for Zeb.

Zeb was in his usual spot, toying with the usual thought.

What is it about the boys?

Evening came and with it a text from Burke.

Going in hard at one a.m. Doppler and radar drones confirm six bodies in each house. Weapons detected.

The poker game went on. The twins were leading.

Broker's phone rang, as did Zeb's.

Broker rose, picked up his phone and tossed Zeb's to his friend.

Both calls were from their underground contacts. There were several doctors, including a few psychiatrists, who were addicted to meth and who bought from a select few dealers. Not one of them fit Beldwin's description.

Zeb rose and sat at Broker's laptop and brought up a map of Boston. He marked the hospital and the doctor's residence and brought up a list of pharmacies in a five-mile radius. He figured Beldwin could have bought from stores in his former city.

Meghan turned around and looked at his screen.

'Did that. Called them. No purchases for more than a year.'

He entered another search parameter; pharmacies in and around Chantilly and Winchester.

Surely Beldwin wouldn't be so stupid. He wouldn't buy close to his base.

He changed the parameters to search for all pharmacies in Virginia. A long list came up. Chain stores, small independents, the list ran to hundreds.

He would go where there would be minimal records, less cameras.

He ignored the chain store pharmacies, and printed out the independents.

'Did that too,' Meghan smirked from behind

He crumpled the sheet and threw it in a bin.

Who would know Beldwin?

The doctor didn't have a social life. He had lost his friends when his addiction had been exposed. He wasn't in any relationship.

Buster!

'Did you speak to Buster?'

'Nope.'

Chapter 34

Bubba had two teams organized, fifteen people each.

He went over plans with them in detail. Hit hard. Hit quickly. Hit both places simultaneously.

Hit from the front. Penetrate from the rear. Take down a sidewall. Flash bangs, and snipers from choppers.

Shock and surprise.

It didn't matter how good the hostiles would be. His men were better.

Drones had recorded the right number of bodies. A chopper had flown once, high above, but hadn't got anything much. There were plain clothes agents on the streets, none of them reported any movement.

'I don't want a repeat of Baltimore,' he told his men. They nodded. None of them did. They had gone through Baltimore, over and over again and they all agreed they had hurried the entry.

This time, they had ample time and had checked out not just the neighborhood, but several neighborhoods in the immediate vicinity of the houses.

They checked out residents. Agents disguised as health inspectors, utility company servicemen, and in various identities had double checked several houses in the neighborhood. All residents were genuine.

The neighboring houses were scrutinized even more closely. No hostiles were hiding there.

There were no snipers in the neighborhood.

Burke took the local P.D. and the state troopers into confidence. They would keep the streets clear when the operation began. They would keep an eye on known troublemakers and suspected criminals.

She went through a mental checklist. Everything was ticked off. She asked her task force to identify holes. They didn't find any.

She joined Bubba and stood quietly as he briefed his men.

'One house is a decoy, and one isn't,' he told her, when he had finished. She listened silently as he went through his plans.

'Those other dudes are joining us?'

Burke knew who he was referring to.

'Nope. They have helped us enough.'

Beldwin wasn't getting enough time with the laptop. He had sat through his permitted time and had randomly gone through several websites. Fiske hovered behind him, coming close several times.

Beldwin shrank inwardly from his stale breath but kept a game face on.

'This confinement getting to you?' the gunman grinned at him, displaying bad dentistry.

Beldwin shrugged. 'Hopefully, the boy will wake up soon.'

Fiske nodded absently, pushed Beldwin's hand away and moved the mouse down.

Checking on me. I need alone time. I need to know what's going on at the hospital.

His allotted time ended. Fiske shut down the laptop and took it away.

Beldwin rose from his seat, stretched casually and darted a glance at Merritt's laptop in the kitchen.

No one approached it.

Zeb took the Fourteenth Street and exited on the I-395 South. Bwana and Roger were with him. As were the twins.

They were heading to Manassas, to talk to Buster.

Burke had called the local cops and had smoothed their way. A cruiser had located Buster; he was sleeping on a park bench.

'What do you think you'll get out of him?' Burke had shouted over the roar of a chopper.

'No idea,' Zeb replied.

The twins asked him the same question when they hit VA-234.

'Buster is an addict too. We don't know how he knows the psychiatrist,' Zeb explained. 'Let's ask him.'

Zeb drove into the city, made his way to William Street and parked behind a cruiser.

A cop got out when they exited, greeted them, and pointed in the direction of the park.

'He's sleeping it off, in there. You'll find another cop near him.'

The sounds of kids squealing and laughing came from within the park. Families strolled inside; some were seated next to picnic hampers.

'Is he dangerous?' Zeb asked.

'Buster?' The cop laughed. 'Nope. That chair – that must have been because he was low on meth.'

He thanked the officer and joined his crew who was waiting for him impatiently.

Beldwin hung around the kitchen, kept himself busy brewing coffee, making sandwiches.

He checked on the boy a few times. He didn't show any signs of improvement. He still spoke randomly without any connection to his past. He turned and faced the wall after Beldwin started with his questions and gave him the silent treatment.

Beldwin stared at him for a few seconds. The boy stank. His room stank. He felt a momentary pang of pity.

He squelched it and exited the room. He shrugged when Merritt raised an eyebrow and followed the man downstairs.

'No change,' he said.

'How long do these states last?' Merritt asked, a question he had posed several times.

'You know the answer to that. Till his mind decides enough is enough.'

He watched the gunman sit in front of his laptop and drifted away to the living room.

There were more demands for Murphy and Burke's resignations from various news channels.

Beldwin put on a movie, settled back on the couch, and kept Merritt in the edge of his vision.

His patience was rewarded just as the movie reached a climactic shoot-out.

Merritt rose, stretched, and padded upstairs silently.

Beldwin didn't wait.

He hurried to the gunman's laptop, typed even before he was seated, and brought up his email.

He scanned his personal email for any messages from the hospital. There were none. His shoulders relaxed a fraction.

I still need to know.

He typed a coworker's personal email address.

'Hey, buddy, what's been happening? I'm giving a crack at

living off the grid. Didn't work, did it? Ha. Ha.'

He sent the email and was shutting down the browser when a chat message popped up. The email application came with an inbuilt chat messenger.

'Hey, Beld? Where you at?' It was the coworker. 'A drunk provided us some entertainment. He was asking for you. The cops hauled him away.'

Beldwin's fingers trembled. He darted a glance to the stairs. No sign of Merritt.

'What did he want? Did the cops say? Was Riggs teed off?'

Riggs was an administrator in the hospital; he signed off on their billing.

'He was cool. You enjoying the fishing?'

Beldwin almost groaned aloud in relief. The weight of his chest disappeared and sent his fingers flying.

'No fishing. Holed up in Winchester with a few friends. See you soon.'

He logged out, closed the browser, wiped the keyboard and went to the sink.

He closed his eyes and breathed deeply till his pulse slowed and the trembling in his fingers disappeared.

Everything's just fine. I was needlessly panicking.

Werner had several admirers. A Swiss miss, who was in reality a supercomputer in a research facility, a Chinese tigress, and a British computer, were just some of them.

It spent time equally with all of its fans. Equality of opportunity came easy to Werner. It was humans that struggled with that concept.

It was discussing pentaquarks with the Swiss machine when one of its alerts pinged.

Werner ignored it and continued the discussion. What could be more important than the attractive supercomputer at the other end?

The alert pinged again, louder.

Werner reluctantly disengaged from the conversation, promised to get back soon, and logged off. It couldn't be sure, but it looked like the Swiss miss had batted its electronic eyelashes.

Werner whistled in high spirits as it turned to the alert.

All thoughts of other supercomputers fled its mind when it

read the alert.

Beldwin had surfaced.

Chapter 35

Bwana shook Buster gently and when the drunk rubbed his eyes and opened them, crouched in front of him.

'Who are you?' Buster croaked.

His eyes flicked to Zeb, Roger, and settled on the twins.

He got to his feet hurriedly, lost his balance, and was helped back by Bwana.

'Sorry, ma'am. Ladies. Didn't know I had company.'

He reached into a dirty bag and drew out a bottle of water and drank deeply. He wiped his mouth on his sleeve and scrunched his face when the cop appeared.

'Buster, these people want to have a few words with you. They've driven a long way. It's important.'

'I ain't done nothing,' Buster shrank back.

Meghan came next to Bwana. 'We know that, Buster. We are looking for Doctor Beldwin. You know him, don't you?'

Her voice was gentle and calmed Buster.

'Sure, I know him.' He sneaked a look at the cop who moved out of earshot.

'How do you know him, Buster?'

Her green eyes compelled him to answer, but at the last minute, Buster backed away.

He wasn't going to lose his source of powder.

'Why do you want to know?'

'Some people might die, if you don't tell us.'

Buster thought of that for a long moment. Those green eyes were like one of them whirlpools. They came near to sucking him.

He shook his head and stepped back. No sir, he wasn't going to fall into that trap.

Another woman came to stand in front of him.

Buster stared at her helplessly. More brown hair. More green eyes.

He couldn't escape them. He gave in.

He and the doc were in the doc's car, two weeks back.

A strange relationship had developed between the two. They shot in each other's presence occasionally, in the medic's car in some remote parking lot.

He had learned that the doc was one of those who treated

people's minds.

'Mine's gone, pal. It can't be treated,' Buster had laughed.

They talked sometimes, stuff that made no sense to either, but gave some kind of comfort to each other.

That evening, doc and he were floating. Buster had told him of this new trash bin he had found behind a takeout. It was always full. It was like the motherlode to him.

The doc had nodded as if he agreed. Buster warmed to that. The dude was a stand-up guy. He knew the importance of a full trashcan.

The doc mumbled something.

Buster was playing with an orange sun that was revolving in front of him and he didn't pay attention.

The docs spoke louder. Buster turned slowly toward him. He felt light, yet his body was heavy, like one of those oil tankers in the sea.

The doc's head was on his chest.

'You saying something, buddy?'

'Decoys.'

'That's all I remember, ma'am,' Buster said apologetically.

Meghan asked him more questions, however it was clear, Buster didn't know anything more.

They thanked him, asked the cop to take him in, for his protection.

The police officer protested. That wasn't how things worked.

Zeb made a call which resulted in more calls and the cop's phone rang.

He took Buster to his cruiser.

Zeb belted himself, waited for his friends to seat themselves, reached out to the dash, when his fingers stopped.

His phone rang.

It was Broker.

His voice was taut, tense, sharp.

'Hold up a second,' Zeb said.

He put it on speaker. 'Go ahead.'

'Beldwin is in Lighthollow.'

Four hundred brake horsepower flooded through the SUV and sent it racing down William Street and carried it out of

Manassas as Broker ran it down for them.

'He has masked his IP address and is no doubt server-bouncing.'

'Track every house down in Lighthollow.'

'On it, Zeb,' Chloe replied. 'However, this may not be Lighthollow, Virginia. There are several other Lighthollows.'

'It is.' Zeb surprised himself with the conviction in his voice. The beast in him was sure. Bob wasn't in some distant state.

Bob was in Virginia.

The air in the war room could have lit a thousand light bulbs when they returned from Manassas.

People were returning from work, streets were busy, horns honked, and yet traffic had parted willingly for Zeb as if it sensed an ominous presence in the SUV.

Chloe whirled round at their entrance.

'We are down to three possibles. One is a pawnshop, another is a residence that has seen lot of traffic in the last few months, and the third is a boat repair outfit.'

She explained about Lighthollow, where it was, how they had narrowed the search down to those three locations. They had checked out all residents against various databases, cross-checked with employers, and social media. They had even checked residents' travel.

'You could do all this in the time we were driving back?'

'Werner did. Social media posts are public. Werner is hooked up with several databases, such as the DMV, that can easily verify identity in the first instance. The rest is a matter of digging into more databases.'

Chloe and the twins would have heaped scorn at Zeb's query, normally. The thrill of the hunt had wiped that impulse out.

Broker hadn't even looked up at their arrival. He was standing, hunching over Werner's screen, frowning.

Zeb joined him.

'Problem?'

'Why would you have a boat repair business in the middle of nowhere?'

'Why wouldn't you?' Bear countered. 'If you've got a rep, boat people will come to you.'

'They have a rep,' Broker acknowledged. 'Good reviews.

Not *that* far from the ocean.'

Zeb picked the sheets Werner had spat out; details of the owners, all three of which were companies.

Werner had tracked down their shareholders and had run identity checks against them. The results weren't conclusive and hence the supercomputer had flagged them up.

Pawn shop will have traffic. Lots of it. Will Bob want traffic? Residence and marine repair are quieter places.

He smelled gun oil and turned to see Bear and Bwana were back to cleaning their weapons.

Nine p.m. Four more hours to hard entry.

'Check the reviews,' he said suddenly.

Broker narrowed his eyes, trying to guess what he was leading to.

'The reviews,' Zeb repeated. 'Who posted them? Where from?'

Light flooded in Broker's eyes. He typed. The twins pulled up two other keyboards and followed suit.

'What about Burke?' Roger voiced a thought that had been running in Zeb's mind.

'Shouldn't we tell her about Lighthollow? She can put more resources.'

'Yeah, there's that leak, isn't there?' Roger answered himself after reading Zeb's face.

Zeb got a large printout of the repair shop and laid it out on a table.

It was a residence whose garage was converted to a large workshop. A driveway fed the house as well as the garage.

Lawn. Backyard. Hedge at the rear. Neighbors, though at a distance. Wide street in the front. Enough turning space.

A garage like that will have spray paint equipment.

'Covert entry will be a nightmare.' Roger pointed to the front of the house, at the lack of cover.

'What about the other house?' Bear wiped his hands on a rag and approached the table.

Zeb laid out two more sheets. The house as well as the pawnshop.

The house was smaller. The pawnshop had lots of glass in it. Windows. Display cases.

'Not that one. Bob will want closed walls, not glass cases,' Bwana said finally after they had studied the three layouts in silence.

'It can't be the residence either. Too small. Bob will have his four men with him and the two boys. Beldwin too. That's a lot of people in that one residence. My money's on the boat repair outfit.'

No one disputed him. Roger cocked an eyebrow at Zeb, but before he could speak, Beth drowned him out.

'It *is* the boat yard!' she yelled.

Meghan shushed her, turned around and explained. 'All those reviews are from the same few IP addresses. None of those reviewers are real people.'

'We need to check it out.'

'And we'd better do it fast,' Broker said grimly. 'Once Bob gets wind of the assaults in Winchester and Chantilly…' his voice trailed off.

He will flee, taking the boys with him. That'll be high risk.

Roger cut short Zeb's musing. 'Do we have a plan?' the Texan asked.

'Our SUVs have armor?' Zeb asked Broker, in turn.

'Yeah. You have something in mind?' Broker asked curiously.

'I have a plan.'

Chapter 36

Zeb explained his plan on their way to Lighthollow, in two SUVs. Bear, Chloe, Bwana, and Roger, in one. Zeb, Broker, and the twins in the other.

Zeb was driving. Meghan was in her preferred place, in the front, next to Zeb, acting as navigator and sarcasm dispenser.

The SUVs had all the equipment they needed, including the few specials Zeb had wanted. They all wore loose overalls, underneath which was their body armor. Around their necks were sound suppressors and night vision goggles.

Zeb and Bwana drove as fast as traffic permitted and when the night lights of the capital fell behind, floored it.

Lighthollow welcomed them at eleven. It was slumbering, the way small cities did, with very few cars on the streets, an occasional truck carrying deliveries for the next day.

It was quieter in the smaller streets inside the city. Zeb killed his lights, saw Bwana follow suit, in his mirror.

The first stop was the pawnshop.

Broker fired up two computers, and connected to Werner. The twins brought out two drones that weren't available in any hobby shop or any other commercial outlet.

The drones were equipped with infrared detectors, laser range finders, Doppler transmitters and more gadgets than Zeb cared to remember.

Broker and the twins launched into a list of features whenever the drones came up. Zeb cut them off each time. The drones could fly. They could detect. They could report back. That was all that mattered to him. *How* wasn't relevant.

They parked a street away, one SUV at either end of the street.

Zeb and Roger jogged at a fast pace along with the twins and reached the pawnshop.

The store was closed and shuttered and had a few lights on the outside. Its parking lot, at the front, was deserted.

Zeb kept watch while Roger helped the twins launched the drones.

'Got feeds,' Broker whispered in their ears.

A dog walker appeared in the distance. Zeb watched him and relaxed when he turned into a driveway.

One drone circled the front of the store; another flew to its rear.

'No infrared. No sign of life.'

They flew the craft for another fifteen minutes, confirmed that there were no humans in the store and set off to the second stop.

The small residence was ten minutes away and it took only two passes to confirm that there were three humans inside the house, no security setup of any kind was detectable.

'Not the place we want.'

'How long will we be at this place?'

Merritt, who was watching yet another news bulletin, craned his head toward Beldwin.

He studied the psychiatrist in silence and then chuckled. 'Got somewhere else to go, doc?'

Beldwin looked embarrassed and muttered something.

'We'll be here for another week, Doc. Then we'll exfil to another location.'

Not you though. We'll leave you behind. Dead.

The answer satisfied Beldwin who watched the TV in silence for some more moments and then posed another question.

'What if the boy never recovers?'

'We'll cross that bridge when we get to it.'

He'll die too, in that case. Both of them.

He watched the news for a while and then turned off the TV, checked on the men on the ground floor, and went upstairs.

The first story had four rooms that faced the rear. The boys were in two adjacent rooms.

Merritt was in one room opposite *the boy's* room. Next to the other boy's, was a bathroom and yet another room which Avram occupied.

Carlos and Fiske shared a large room, which had an attached bathroom.

Merritt spoke softly to Avram and Pico, who were on duty, checked in on the boys, who were asleep, and went to his room.

Another uneventful day, he thought as readied his bed.

The first drone rose uneventfully and blended with the night. It had dull, radar deflecting paint and circled the front of the third location. The second drone followed and eyed the backyard.

'Infrared sensors. All over the front yard.'

Zeb could feel Broker's triumphant grin as he looked at the feed. Broker was parked half a mile away. The other SUV was at the other end of the street, facing Broker's vehicle.

Zeb, Roger, and the twins were walking casually down the street. Just another pair of couples enjoying the late evening.

The drones whirred silently, saw everything and reported everything that they saw.

'One last confirmation needed,' Zeb said aloud.

Merritt didn't know what woke him. One moment he was in a dreamless sleep, the next, he was awake.

He glanced at the clock. Half past eleven. Not too late.

A loud report sounded.

Sounds like a shot. That probably woke me.

His hand snaked to his Sig in a practiced move and he got to his feet and listened.

More reports sounded. Shouts and yells came from the street.

A gunfight right on the street?

'Carlos? Avram? Pico? Fiske?' he called out softly.

They acknowledged. The men from downstairs replied. Beldwin appeared in the doorway of his room, disheveled. Merritt sent him back inside.

He took over from Pico who went down to check the security set-up. Merritt was sure whoever was shooting, weren't the cops.

They would have battered down the door by now. There would have been choppers in the air. Searchlights would have lit the night.

Fiske went to a front window and peered out cautiously. The street fight was still heated, but the sounds were growing fainter.

Gunmen firing at one another, from cars?

The drones circled and watched, relentlessly. Broker and Bear controlled them from inside one SUV and monitored the video. There wasn't much to monitor.

'Better and better. There's anti-Doppler in the house. The windows are laser defeating. There seems to be some kind of thermal masking. No idea how many bodies are inside. Whoever's inside is smart. Very smart.'

The lack of detail was good. It meant they were right to target the boatyard.

Bwana drove the second SUV which played sounds of a gunfight through a speaker on its roof. Lights came on in several houses and he knew 911 calls would be made. Those calls wouldn't be attended to.

Zeb had told Burke to instruct Virginia State Police and the local P.D. to ignore any gunfight calls. Burke had wanted to know more. Zeb had asked her to focus on the two assaults.

Broker nudged the joystick and moved one drone to cover the entire front of the house.

He zoomed in on one window whose shades had twitched. The cameras were similar to what satellites had, only smaller. From this close, the cameras would pick every blemish and pore on a person's body.

They picked out two faces and relayed them to the laptop in the SUV.

Werner grabbed those images and ran them against its databank and through facial recog.

Werner didn't take long. It came back with a message, which Broker relayed.

'Two faces showed themselves. One of those was in the hotel.'

The two couples were moving even before Broker had finished.

They turned and walked, a shade faster, to a rendezvous point behind a pickup truck on the street, away from the target house's sightline.

Zeb spoke just once.' We're on.'

Merritt walked around the house for several minutes, making sure everything was locked down tight. He cracked the shades at the front and the rear. The yards were silent and empty.

He peered at Pico's monitors and cameras. The pressure pads, the infra-red sensors – all showed no signs of intrusion.

Lastly, he checked the police scanners. There were reports of two cars shooting at one another in Lighthollow.

The cars were out of the city now and the cops were giving chase. A window had broken, but no one had been injured.

Gangbangers. He shook his head. *Get high. Live hard. Die early*.

They didn't have the discipline Merritt had.

He checked in on the boys. One had slept through the racket. The other asked Merritt if they were being attacked. There was hope in his voice.

Merritt said no, and enjoyed watching the light die in his eyes.

He went back to his room and checked his inner radar. It was quiet.

Most exciting night since the kidnap. Some hoods shooting at each other. The FBI should be ashamed.

He snorted, pulled back the spread and lay down and closed his eyes.

The accident occurred when he was deep asleep.

Chapter 37

He woke swiftly on hearing metal on metal, the sickening impact of two vehicles ramming into each other at high speed.

The sound was terrible. It was as if it came from his front yard.

'Just in front, outside,' Pico's voice came breathlessly from downstairs. 'Two SUVs just crashed into each other.'

'Are there cops?' he called softly.

'No. There seem to be injuries. Someone's coming.'

'Stay alert.'

Bwana and Bear had floored the vehicles and at the last minute, had jumped out.

The SUVs were heavy, were armor plated, had momentum, and each had a souped up engine under its hood.

The impact was spectacular.

None of them stood around to admire it.

Bear ran to the house, Zeb a foot behind. Their armor was under their loose clothing, the sound suppressors and protective goggles were stuffed down their necks.

Bear hammered the door. 'Open up. We got injuries,' he shouted.

He lifted his fist again.

The door opened.

A face appeared. Another came behind it. He could hear alarms sounding in the house.

An assault rifle was swiftly concealed.

Too late. Bear saw it.

A mouth opened to reply.

He dropped to the ground and flung two devices. Flashbangs.

He pulled mufflers over his ears, goggles over his eyes.

Light and sound flooded the house.

More light. More sound.

Night turned to day. Silence turned to cacophony.

Rifles chattered.

Zeb took out one gunman. Another stumbled into view.

His barrel turned smoothly. The shooter's face

disappeared.

They surged inside, crouching low, their eyes seeking, their weapons hungry.

Broker was prone, in the middle of the street, a McMillan TAC-338 rifle, cradled against his shoulder. One eye was glued to a scope, his finger rested lightly on the trigger.

He fired initial rounds and brought down the windows.

The flashbangs went off. Illuminated several gunmen in the living room.

Broker took them down. A shot at a time.

Trigger break. Target down.

'Four down,' Chloe called out softly.

She was behind him, scanning with NVGs. She was his spotter.

They didn't look behind, to the left or the right.

Behind and around was taken care of by the twins. They dispersed any onlookers.

FBI was their magic word.

Roger and Bwana had raced to the side and rear of the house the moment Bear and Zeb had set off.

One second to stand inside the cover of the side wall.

Peer around the side.

Backyard empty.

A peek up.

Rear of the house was empty. No faces at the windows. No gun barrels poking out.

The second-story window sills were about fifteen feet from ground level.

Four large windows.

They came to a decision without speaking.

They crouched and ran beneath the first ground floor window.

Bwana stood crouched, offering his back, in between windows.

Roger took a short run. Flew in the air. Used Bwana's back as lever. Soared in the night.

His left hand reached out. Grabbed a sill. Right hand had a gun.

It was a foolhardy move. It was suicidal. They didn't have a choice.

He raised himself. Glanced once. Lowered his head down again.

He didn't think of any hostiles. Bwana would take care of them. Hopefully.

He raised himself again. Got a better look.

Bed. Shadow on it. Shadow rising.

He raised his gun.

Lowered it. Shadow was unarmed

He broke the window, gun pointing straight at the closed door. Slipped a leg. Got his body inside.

Powered himself up with a left hand.

He grabbed the blanket back. Uncovered the shadow.

'Got one boy, here.' His voice was flat, emotionless.

The boy's eyes were wide. He drew a breath. His mouth opened wide.

Roger cupped a hand over his mouth.

'We are the good guys. We'll get you out. Do you hear me?'

He repeated his question again, half his attention on the closed door.

If it burst open – he planned moves in his mind.

Shove the boy down. Fire. Keep firing, till the hostiles went down, or till he died.

The door stayed shut.

The boy nodded.

Roger pushed him under the bed.

'Secure for now.'

Bwana had three flashbangs. He hurled one each through three ground floor windows.

At the first burst of light, he dived into a room.

It was empty.

'In.'

At the first flashbang, Merritt *knew*.

He donned his combat suit swiftly. Grabbed a getaway pack. Strapped it to his back.

Grabbed his Sig. Opened the door cautiously.

Waved Pico and Avram to the ground floor. Fiske was already downstairs.

His escape route was ready. He had planned for this

contingency too.

The gunfight below was thunderous. More flashbangs sounded. The attackers' shots were spaced, controlled.

An ace team. Not your neighborhood cops.

Merritt wiped the thought from his mind.

He opened the boy's room.

The boy was sitting up. He turned to Merritt.

Merritt thrust his barrel inside the boy's mouth.

'Get up.'

He heard a window crash. Not his. The one in the next room.

He shoved the boy to the window. One swift glance outside. No movement.

He grabbed the boy by his waist and crashed through the glass. Then they were falling. Landing.

Him on his left shoulder. The boy on top. He rolled over on his back. Pushed the boy away and rose to his feet.

He pulled the boy upright. One hand to his back. He pushed him to a run.

One second to the hedge. Another second to open the concealed entrance, and then they were in darkness

And safety.

Zeb headed to the stairs, leaving the fight to Bear, Broker from the outside and Bwana in a rear-guard action.

He laced the stairs in a steady stream of fire, as he climbed. Mag changes as fluid as the slither of water on slippery rock.

Reached the landing. Crouched. Turned. Aimed. No one.

Turned again. Caught a shadow. He ducked just in time as a burst of fire sang in the hallway.

Before he could respond, a door opened, answering fire came. A body fell.

'Zeb?' Roger asked cautiously.

'Yeah.'

'He's down. Bob got away. With the other boy. He escaped through the backyard.'

Zeb ran to the boy's empty room, saw the broken window and threw himself out.

He was vulnerable in the air. It didn't matter. Roger had his back.

He landed on his feet, one moment impact, motion the next

second.

He reached the hedge. Tried to find the doorway. Gave up. Kicked it. His foot throbbed from shock.

However, a door swung open.

He snapped a glance.

Didn't see anything. Just a narrow passage in darkness.

He won't be hanging around to shoot.

He took the risk. Bent low, snapped on a flashlight. No seeking fire came his way.

The passage in the hedge was wide and high enough for him to stand.

He ran. He strained to hear ahead. Got nothing but silence.

He upped his pace.

Fly! The darkness in him roared in warning.

He flew in the air, rolled, got to his feet, looked back.

The flashlight caught a reflection. A near-invisible wire. A trap.

He turned and continued running, his light now aiming at the ground and to the sides.

He crossed the second neighboring house, then another. He lost count. A dimness far ahead, beckoned him.

A flash caught his eye. To the side. He stopped.

Another wire strung in the hedge, lower than waist height.

He tested the hedge carefully, paying attention to the trip wire.

Another door swung open. He peered into the darkness, his flashlight piercing tunnels.

Another backyard. Another house. Still, dark.

Could Merritt have gone into it?

To his left the dimness of the hedge's exit. Ahead, another possible exit.

He wasted one second in thought.

'Beth, Meghan, check out the dark house.'

He turned to the left and ran.

Five feet, then ten feet. The exit receded behind him. The opening ahead, approached.

He thought he heard an engine cough.

And then he was airborne.

The explosion shook the night and carried him forward and dumped him just near the exit.

Where he lay still.

Merritt threw the detonator away on the next seat. That blast would distract the pursuers.

He tried the engine again.

The boy was snarling, muttering, shouting.

'Be quiet,' Merritt roared. He swung round, whipped his barrel on the boy's forehead.

The boy shrieked. Fell back. Tried to claw open the door. It was locked from the inside.

Merritt turned the key.

The engine fired.

He bared his teeth, pressed hard and swung the wheel.

Something impacted his window.

He glanced, startled.

A face stared back at him.

Zeb flung himself at the moving vehicle, his mind still reeling from the shock of the explosion.

One hand wrapped around the roof railing. Another sought his gun.

It was gone. He had lost it in the blast.

He hammered the glass with an elbow. He could crack it.

I have done it before.

He saw the pale face in the rear. The boy's eyes were wide in fright, mouth opening and closing in silent screams.

Bob swerved suddenly to dislodge him. Zeb clung on.

Elbow pointed in a spear.

It was one of the hardest bones in the body.

Zeb's elbow was powered by the darkness in him which bunched and tightened into a ball, then flew through blood and veins to once again become muscle and bone, which then met glass.

The window cracked.

From behind Bob there was movement.

The boy leaned forward. His hand reached around Bob and fingered the driver's door.

The doors unlocked.

Zeb tried the handle.

It swung open suddenly and smashed into him. His grip loosened.

Bob punched with his right hand.

Zeb managed to duck it.

Bob reached behind him. Brought his Sig. Pointed it at

Zeb.

Zeb let go, fell on concrete as rounds spat above and ahead of him.

Merritt stopped, engaged reverse gear and started backing up. It was time to finish this.

A door swung open behind him. A blast of icy air hit him.

The boy had escaped.

'You!' Merritt shouted.

The boy stumbled. Fell.

Merritt could hear sirens in the distance. His escape time was running out.

There was only one course to take.

He swore. Inched to the rear a few feet. His window rolled down.

His arm shot out.

The Sig bore down on the boy.

His finger depressed.

A shadow moved and threw itself in front of the body.

The attacker.

Merritt fired again. Center of mass. No time to aim.

The body jerked again and again.

Merritt tried to seek the boy behind.

The man covered him.

He changed a mag swiftly when the man moved.

Merritt couldn't help staring for a moment.

The man's face was bloody. He was moving slowly.

Yet, even through the few feet separating them, through the darkness, he could make out the man's eyes.

They were fixed on Merritt. Merritt couldn't turn his gaze away.

The man seemed to be relentless.

He seemed to bend. Something came out of his leg.

Too late, Merritt saw the gun.

He shifted to drive and accelerated suddenly.

The shot still pierced the pillar behind him.

He cursed aloud. Cursed the man. The boy. Darrell. Everyone he could think of.

He jammed the pedal and swung to the exit.

Rounds peppered him from behind. One burned his left shoulder. His left hand slipped. The wheel turned. The vehicle lurched.

A tree appeared in view.

Merritt blinked and tried to right the vehicle.

Not a tree.

A man. Tall. Dark. Implacable.

Merritt shot through the windshield. A white starburst appeared.

The man didn't move.

Another joined him.

Equally tall.

Merritt's lights bathed them in whiteness.

One black. One bearded. Something in their hands. Aimed at him.

He raced his vehicle at them.

He would go through them. He would pulverize them.

The two men didn't move.

Another starburst appeared in the windshield. One more.

The universe became white. Then cracked. A hole appeared. More holes appeared.

The vehicle ran drunkenly. Cool air blew through it.

Chip Merritt didn't feel it.

He was beyond feeling.

Chapter 38

The rescue's coverage hadn't subsided three months later.

The FBI still received glowing tributes. Media outlets talked about the three coordinated assaults on three houses.

The recovery of the kidnapped boys without the loss of a single innocent life.

Burke and Murphy, who just before the assault were castigated, were now national icons.

Burke gave several interviews and appeared on talk shows. She didn't want to, however, Director Murphy asked her to.

The FBI had to rebuild trust. Who better than Burke to do that?

She was followed by news vans. Reporters mobbed the hotel she was staying in. She changed hotels several times. It didn't help.

Chip Merritt's identity was unpacked, his planning was traced, more pieces in the jigsaw were filled in.

Merritt's planning and execution and the FBI's detection, felt like a Hollywood movie.

Book and movie deals were being discussed. Several A-listers said they would love to play various characters.

The vice president and his wife came on air, thanked the FBI and all those involved. They asked for their privacy to be respected.

The Fairman family gave similar statements.

The boys were never seen in public. They were never interviewed.

The boy still hadn't recovered.

Psychiatrists confirmed what Beldwin had diagnosed. The boy was suffering from a dissociative fugue. His circumstances were never disclosed.

The motive was still unknown. The FBI spun a story and the media lapped it up, however, Burke's task force was still investigating.

The other boy had been interviewed several times. He was equally clueless.

Beldwin had been found alive, hiding under his bed in the house in Lighthollow. He and another gunman were the only survivors.

Both sang. However, they too didn't know the motives.

Beldwin cooperated with the medical team attending to the boy. He would do anything to lessen his sentence. He spilled everything he knew.

He knew a lot. He didn't know why.

Zeb had a broken rib from the shots Merritt had fired at his armor. The rib healed fast. He had several cuts and bruises on his face when the explosion had flung him to the ground.

They mended.

'It's not like you're going to get male modeling offers,' Bwana said, after inspecting him critically.

'He never was in the running. Very few of us are blessed with superior looks,' Roger said loftily.

Burke and Bubba had spent hours with them, getting the details of their assault. Broker mentioned their strategy to the dumbstruck FBI team.

Bubba shook his head finally. 'That shouldn't have worked.'

'Yeah, it did, though,' Chloe replied drily.

Zeb had wanted to get back to New York, a week after the rescue. No one knew of their involvement.

Burke had persuaded him to stay till the motive was uncovered and the investigation was finally closed.

Werner swept through the boys' messages, social media, school work, yet again. It got nothing. The FBI and Zeb's crew reconstructed the lives of the two families. They found no reason for the kidnapping.

It was as if the motive had died with Merritt.

Darrell had hyperventilated the moment the news flashed on his screen. He was in a state of panic. Sheer will had kept him together.

He kept his jet fueled and ready for a quick dash to Colombia, where he had a villa and business interests. He canceled all business meetings and didn't step out of his residence.

He sent terse messages to his five partners. They wouldn't be meeting anymore. *They* would be wise to make arrangements to flee the country.

As days passed and the FBI didn't bust through his door, his panic started subsiding. He started thinking more clearly. The boy didn't seem to have revealed anything.

Maybe he hadn't recovered. Maybe he never would.

However, what if he had?

He could reach out to the family and find out. He had access. However, he didn't want to risk it.

He spoke to some other contacts of his and Mark spoke to his network in the law enforcement circles. No motive, they said. The Feds were still investigating.

A month passed and Darrell surfaced. He resumed as normal a life as he could. The jet was still ready. His passport was always with him; however, the urge to flee was lessening.

Late one night, he went to a park in Washington D.C. where he knew there would be WiFi access from the router of a nearby café. He was dressed in a loose overcoat, baggy hat, and dirty shoes. His social circle wouldn't recognize him.

He logged onto a fake social media page he had created, on a computer he had bought from eBay.

He sent a message to the boy. He used some words that would identify him. He ended the message with a line. *It, and more, can happen again.*

He got a reply a week later.

I won't talk.

The psychiatrists did their best, but the boy wasn't responding. The other boy spent time with him. It didn't help. As a fourth month passed, the family quietly resigned themselves to waiting and watching.

They resumed their lives to the extent they could.

The center of the political universe got back to normal.

It was an email in Zeb's inbox that got him thinking. It was about a remembrance service. He hadn't given any thought to the person since events had caught up, but now, he got Werner to look the person up.

The person had lived an uneventful life. There was not even a remote connection to the kidnapping.

However the darkness in Zeb was roiling.

He took the Lear and disappeared for a day, without informing his friends. They would have insisted on coming, and he didn't want them to waste a day if it proved a dead end.

He set Werner on a different search when he returned. Werner didn't take long. It confirmed the suspicion Zeb had.

That alone wasn't enough, however.

Zeb got it to look at old newspaper articles, for specific incidents. He then turned to the boys again. This time he looked at their lives differently.

He finally found what he was looking for three days later. It was buried within a lot of other material, but its simplicity astounded him.

The FBI, supercomputers from all over, various agencies, looking for clues, and not one of them found it.

It was right in front of them.

Darrell yawned, stretched, and went to his bathroom for a morning shower. It had gold fittings and a tub large enough to accommodate a family of four.

It had soft, fluffy towels that were imported from Europe. Its rug was from New Zealand.

He finished his bath, wrapped himself in a robe, and went into his bedroom.

His butler had laid out his shirt, a suit, and the rest of his clothing. He donned them, adjusted his cufflinks and heard his butler enter, carrying his breakfast and coffee.

He took the offered tray without turning around, drank his first cup of Jamaican Blue Mountain and placed the tray on the bed, and sat.

He yelped the next moment. The tray went flying. Toast and eggs and muffins scattered. Coffee spilled on the pristine sheets of his bed and darkened them.

Darrell didn't notice any of that.

He was staring at the man seated in a chair opposite. He was lounging casually, one leg crossed over the other.

The man was dressed in a casual jacket, T-shirt, and jeans. He had brown hair, cut short. He had brown eyes.

Those eyes pierced Darrell.

'Who are you? How did you get here?' Darrell yelled in shock which gave way to anger.

'You're trespassing, young man. You can be arrested.' He pressed a panic button on a nightstand, fumbled in a drawer and brought out a handgun.

The man didn't move. He didn't flinch. His eyes seemed to be amused.

Darrell frowned. No running footsteps. No butler. How had his stranger walked in?

'No one's coming, Senator. Everyone is preoccupied,' the stranger said easily.

Senator Darrell Winslow-Tulley, from Ohio, paled. His hands shook. He moistened his lips.

His house had the best in security. A specialist company manned all its cameras and responded promptly. There were former Secret Service men at the gate outside. Cops regularly patrolled his estate.

This man had entered his home despite all that.

Anger returned in a rush. Senator Darrell Winslow-Tulley wasn't to be trifled with.

'I'm calling the police, right now, young man. You had better leave if you don't want to see the inside of a prison.'

He kept an eye on the man, his gun firmly trained on the stranger, and picked up a handset.

There was no dial tone.

'Why don't you sit, Senator?' the stranger suggested. 'That gun isn't loaded, either.'

Darrell looked at him blankly, then at the gun. He broke it open. No rounds.

He flung the gun suddenly at the stranger and darted out of the room.

He turned to look back.

The man hadn't moved.

He slowed to a stop, returned, and sat on the bed.

'You are a child molester. A pedophile.'

Chapter 39

Darrell flinched at the words.

'You used your power and influence to get in contact with young boys. You molested them. You shared them with your friends.'

The brown eyes blazed for a moment before becoming expressionless.

'You promised to better the careers of their parents, in return for their silence. You killed those who refused to be quiet,' The brown haired man continued, remorselessly.

'I didn't–'

The stranger raised his hand. 'Save it.'

'You used your family trust to make endowments to various schools in your state. That gave you access to the schools. You gave scholarships to several students. Several of them got work experience at your companies. You got access to those kids.'

'You covered your tracks very well. Those boys who kept quiet – you rewarded their fathers or mothers with good jobs in your companies.'

'Almost all of them kept quiet. A young kid's words against that of one of the most powerful men in the country? You chair the Senate Appropriations committee. You are a billionaire. You can influence the system. You probably mentioned that to the boys.'

'One boy dared to speak out. Eight years back. You destroyed his family. You made sure his father never got a job. His mother was sacked from her firm. Dad committed suicide. Mom and boy were never heard of again.'

The stranger paused and drank from a cup which Darrell hadn't noticed previously.

'Good coffee,' the man acknowledged.

'You came across Shawn Fairman in Amherst. It was a school that had benefited from your endowment. You got him two week's work in your company in Ohio. You spent time with him. Maybe you molested him.'

'He protested. You promised a job for his dad in the capital. You knew his father was ambitious and wanted to move to D.C.'

'Shawn kept quiet. He was eleven years old. Your power scared him. A few disgusting hours in return for his dad's future – it probably felt bearable to him.”

‘You took him to a retreat. Another work experience, he told his folks. They didn’t suspect a thing. Your face is on TV almost every week. Why would anyone think you were a child molester?’

‘Five of your friends joined in that retreat. Shawn was smart. He aced his exams. He had a fantastic memory. He did something you never anticipated.’

‘He somehow recorded that evening. He hid it. The next time you met him, he told you about the recording. You threatened him.’

Another sip. ‘You came to an agreement. A job for his dad in D.C, in return for his silence.’

‘Arlene Slayton heard part of the conversation. You had met her a few times. She confronted you.’

Something swept across the stranger’s face. ‘You bought her silence. You paid for her sister’s treatment. The sale of her house wouldn’t cover the costs. You topped it up.’

‘You returned to D.C. You contacted Merritt and asked him to be ready for anything. You couldn’t resist your sick urges for long, however. You tried to meet Shawn Fairman when they moved to the city. He turned you down.’

‘By then he was friends with Barlow. You had gotten Merritt to monitor their messages. Merritt found the hotel appointment.’

‘You could have grabbed Fairman at any point. But you wanted a red herring. What better one than the kidnapping of the vice president’s son?’

‘Unfortunately for you, Fairman went into a fugue.’

Zeb waited for the senator to protest, deny, and threaten. He did none of that.

Darrell Winslow-Tulley was a handsome man. He was single, wealthy beyond belief and didn’t lack female companions. He regularly graced society pages in newspapers.

He looked a shell of a man. His face was devoid of color. His eyes stared sightlessly at Zeb. His hands twitched continually.

Zeb knew the basics of what had transpired from his investigation He was speculating about several details.

The senator didn’t refute him once.

Darrell thought wildly about calling for help. He could call Mark. Paul. The others. They would know what to do.

He half rose. The stranger looked at him curiously, as if he wasn't human.

Darrell subsided.

'The kidnapping was a message to Arlene Slayton as well as the other boys you molested. Nothing was beyond you. Keeping quiet was in their best interest.'

The stranger rose, went to a wall adorned with photographs. Darrell with the president. With past presidents. With his Appropriations Committee.

'We all were looking in the wrong places. Barlow and Fairman have eidetic memories. Their families didn't know it. Neither did their teachers. Both boys feared they would be bullied or treated specially and kept it even from their folks.'

'Slayton suspected Fairman had it and took him into her fold. I thought the kidnapping was something to do with their memories. One of them, or both, saw something they shouldn't have and were a walking flash drive.'

'I wouldn't have thought of the molestation angle. An email from Busman -- you know him, don't you?'

Darrell didn't reply.

'Busman sent me an email about a remembrance for Slayton. That got me thinking. It made me look into her sister. That string led to others. Slayton had written a line about a monster. Now it made sense.'

The stranger studied a ceramic plate. An Egyptian piece that had been in Darrell's family for generations.

'You got Senator Mark Randall to get the inside track on the investigation. He sat on the Senate Select Committee on Intelligence. He knew everyone worth knowing.'

'He was your mole.'

The stranger turned to Darrell, waited for him to make any response. Words were stuck in Darrell's throat.

Everything was stuck.

'You tried to find where Fairman had hidden his recording. You looked everywhere.'

The brown eyes pinned him down.

'It was right there in front of you. In front of all of us.'

'Fairman had split the recording into several parts and had spliced them separately into a recording of a school debating competition. That recording sat in the school's servers.'

'All of us looked at just the beginning and the end of that recording. No one viewed it in its entirety.'

'There was also a detailed statement. Similarly inserted in his course work. It has everything. Names. Dates. Places. Other boys.'

The man's gaze became a flame. 'Your molestation has damaged several young lives. It has ended many other lives. Shawn Fairman may recover, but will always carry the scars of your sickness.'

Darrell broke under the implacable voice. He ran around the bed.

He clawed at a bedside table. Gripped another revolver. Checked to confirm that it was loaded. Sobbed in desperation. He could get out of this too.

He turned. Pointed the gun at the stranger.

He was no longer where he was.

He turned again.

There he was. Against the dresser. He raised his gun.

What was that in his hand?

Senator Darrell Winslow-Tulley never found out.

The sun blossomed in the stranger's hand and enveloped the politician in its heat.

Zeb erased all traces of his presence. Werner had already tampered with the security system and wiped his entry and exit.

He looked at the body one last time. It had been too easy.

Those boys will suffer the rest of their lives. He didn't suffer.

He left the residence and went to the airport.

There was one last job to be done.

Storms returned home after a stroll in the evening. Killers went for evening walks too.

He tossed his backpack on a couch and went to the kitchen for a drink.

He stopped suddenly.

A brown-haired stranger was at the sink, glass of water in hand, facing him. His other hand rested on the counter.

'There's always a risk when a paymaster dies,' the stranger spoke without preamble.

'You should have changed identities and moved, the moment Merritt died.'

Storms's shock, anger, and incredulity began to be swiftly replaced by icy coolness.

Gun is in the backpack. Backpack's in the other room. There's one in the sideboard.

'You were confident of yourself, though. You had killed for years and hadn't come on anyone's radar. Your technique is perfect,' the stranger acknowledged.

'You made one mistake, though. It wasn't your fault. You didn't know I would be involved.'

'You didn't know I don't like killers of defenseless women.'

Storms sprang. He had worked it out in his mind.

Left hand would open the sideboard. It would grip the gun. He would fall, to put off the stranger's aim.

He would fire left-handed.

The plan worked.

The stranger stood motionless even as he moved.

Time became a liquid grey.

Left hand reached out. Left hand gripped gun. Knees bent to lower his body.

Still, the stranger didn't move.

Gun came down. Moved to cover the stranger.

Wait! When did that gun come in his hand?

It was two a.m. when Zeb entered the house in Cleveland Park, in the capital.

During the flight back, he had thought about courage.

He had thought about young boys and the weight they carried.

He had thought about sacrifice and family and what children did for their parents.

The security at the house was easy to overcome despite the recent events. The media mob had long since disappeared.

He stood for a moment in the living room and listened. There were normal sounds of a home at night. Electrical appliances ticking on and off. A faint sound of snoring.

He crept up the stairs, looked into a couple of bedrooms and entered the one he was seeking.

He kept looking at the shapeless hump under the cover until

it shifted. The person's breathing changed.
'Hello, Shawn.'

Shawn Fairman didn't move.
'I am a friend.'
There was no change in the shapeless hump.
'You'll find out in the morning. There's nothing more to fear. The senator will never trouble you again. Neither will his friends.'
A limb twitched under the cover.
'You recovered from the fugue a long time back, didn't you? When you were in captivity. You maintained the pretense to protect yourself and your friend.'
'And to protect your family.'
'Merritt tortured you and yet you didn't break.'
The shape shifted and Shawn Fairman's tear-streaked face appeared.
'I was scared. So scared. I was scared for Mom and Dad.'
Zeb leaned over him and remembered another young boy in another time, in another place, and the words came out unconsciously.
Fiercely. Deeply.
'As long as I am alive, you don't have to be.'

The deaths of a few senators, even ones as important as Darrell Winslow-Tulley and Mark Randall, didn't receive a lot of coverage. There were the usual bland pieces, eulogizing the dead, words of sorrow from other politicians. No one noticed that the White House hadn't commented on the deaths. No one cared. The media channels were still euphoric over the recovery of the boys. The people didn't care.
A few less politicians? Good.

The twins didn't give up.
They organized another bash to celebrate Clare's birthday. They organized it in the Presidential View Hotel.They invited a few more guests, one of them being Mark Feinberg, Beth's longtime boyfriend. They invited Roger and Bwana's girlfriends. They invited Meghan's current date.
Zeb looked at the last name on the invitee list.
'You do know what's going on, don't you?' Beth accused.
'I'm not dumb.'

'Could've fooled us,' Meghan deadpanned.

Sarah Burke dressed carefully for the event. She was nervous. She paid attention to her hair, her nails, what she would wear.

For crissakes, Burke. Get a hold of yourself. You have met the president. You have been chewed out by the director, several times. Get a grip.

She dressed in a simple, yet elegant black dress; her hair pulled back, and set off to the hotel.

If anyone at the hotel recognized them, it didn't show.

She started relaxing the minute Roger cracked a joke. They weren't a raucous bunch. They drank sparingly.

They felt comfortable. She fit in.

She had many things in common with many of them. She came from a cop family. So did the twins.

She loved science. Chloe did too. Bear had a droll sense of humor. Bwana laughed readily.

Broker? She felt warm inside.

Carter sat next to her, barely speaking. They accepted his silences. Ribbed him mercilessly.

'You should speak to him,' Carter told her suddenly.

Special Agent in Charge Sarah Burke felt herself going red. 'Am I so obvious?'

'He likes you. A lot.'

'Shouldn't he make the first move?' she asked her voice low.

'He would, normally. Not with you. He loses his composure around you.'

She ran a finger round the rim of her wine glass, her face still warm, considering Carter's words.

'You're different when he's around. Don't lose that.'

That decided it for her. She rose and headed to the cloakroom.

'Burke?'

'Yeah.'

'I would lose that hairband.'

She went to the cloakroom, washed her face, raised her hands to her hair and set it loose.

Go for it, Burke.

A space next to Broker had opened like magic when she reached them.

He was staring into his glass when she sat next to him. He

raised his eyes and smiled that smile.

She held out her hand. 'I am Sarah Michelle Burke.'

Zeb rose, hours later. Clare had left them earlier, after thanking the twins.

Bear and Chloe were cuddling. Broker and Burke were talking intensely, softly. The twins, Bwana, Roger, and their dates were in deep conversation with one another.

Zeb stepped out in the night and his eyes automatically flicked to his left. The Washington Monument rose above the city, as if standing sentinel.

He snapped a mental salute and for a moment the world fell away.

A pair of blue eyes looked down at him and smiled. So blue that he could, and had, drowned in them.

'What about you, honey? Don't you think it's time to move on?'

'You are all that I ever wanted.'

The smile grew deeper; the eyes blazed into fire and carried him home.

Coming soon

Dividing Zero

Gemini Series, Book 1

by

Ty Patterson

Chapter 1

'Daddy hits mommy.'

Meghan froze when she heard the words.

Beth, who was hurrying out of the kitchen with a plate full of cookies, stumbled.

The words were spoken by a green-eyed girl, whose blonde hair was neatly styled over her head. She wore a pink dress, had matching shoes, and usually her eyes were smiling.

They were sad now.

Madison 'Maddie' Kittrell, eight years old, was perched on a chair in front of Meghan. The chair went up or down at the press or pull of a lever.

She played with it, refused to meet Meghan's eyes, darted an occasional glance to the sides.

By her side were Liz McCallum, fourteen years old, and Lizzie's sister, Zoe, 'Peaches' McCallum, ten years old.

Maddie, Lizzie, and Peaches, were tight. They were besties. They were BFFs.

They grew up on the same street near Central Park, New York. They went to the same school.

Maddie wasn't from the city originally. She had come to the state when she was small. Her dad had a job in some company. Her mom worked somewhere else.

Maddie didn't know all that. She didn't care.

She cared that Mommy cried every week. That the sound of Daddy's blows terrified her.

That Daddy had turned on her a few times.

She hadn't told anyone about the beating. She carried it in her tiny heart. When she played with Lizzie and Peaches, she forgot everything.

Gramma, with whom Lizzie and Peaches lived, made the world's best cookies. Maddie was in Heaven when she bit into them.

One day it became too much for Maddie.

Her mouth was full of cookie. Her besties were with her. And yet, somehow, the tears started coming.

Lizzie made a fuss. Peaches made a fuss. Gramma hugged her tight.

Gramma smelled so nice that Maddie burst into more tears.

It came out finally. She couldn't hold it in. Mommy had told her not to tell anyone. Daddy told her too.

But these were her best friends. They were like family. Better than family.

She told them of that one time, recently, when Mommy's shoulder broke because of Daddy. Mommy had to go to work in a sling.

She had to apply makeup to cover the bruises in her eyes.

It started only a year back, Maddie said through great gulping sobs.

She would lie terrified in her room, hearing mommy cry. Hearing those horrible smacks.

Gramma became serious when she heard. Lizzie went white. Peaches started crying too. Silent tears.

Maddie couldn't help it. She cried more.

Something happened. Gramma looked at Lizzie. Lizzie looked at Peaches.

Gramma wiped Maddie's tears and told her to come the next day. They would go to the park.

The park was great. Maddie could play for hours in it. She agreed.

The next day, they set out. Maddie and Peaches skipping ahead. Lizzie talking about something serious with Gramma.

They played for a couple of hours.

Then Gramma made Maddie sit on a bench and told her they would go and meet someone.

Someone who was very dear to them. Someone who had helped them.

Maddie would have to tell them everything.

Maddie shook her head. She wouldn't tell.

She started crying again.

Daddy would go to jail. Mommy would cry.

She didn't want that.

She wished she had never told them anything.

Gramma hugged her again. That nice smell enveloped her again.

'Hush, honey. Nothing bad will happen. We trust them with our lives. They will not tell anyone. Just talk to them.'

Gramma produced a cookie. Cookies were magic workers. They could unlock tongues and change minds.

Maddie bit into the cookie and agreed.

They set out again.

Peaches told Maddie about the people they were meeting.

They had an office close by. It was neat. It had a hoop. A baseball bat. Ball gloves. It was better than their school playroom.

Peaches wanted an office like that when she grew older.

'Who are they?' Maddie tugged at Peaches' arm to slow her down.

'Beth and Meghan. Twins. They are our friends. They can do anything. They can find anything.'

'They found Mom's killer,' Lizzie added, when she overheard the conversation.

Maddie's steps slowed. She didn't want anything to be found.

'Nothing bad will happen, honey. They are good people. Just tell them everything, like you told us.'

Gramma urged. Lizzie nodded. Peaches pressed her hand.

Maddie agreed reluctantly.

They carried on. Peaches told her about Beth and Meghan. How wonderful they were.

There was a man who helped them sometimes. He didn't do much, Peaches said airily.

She didn't know why the twins kept him around.

They reached the office. It was a tall building. So much glass.

The guards inside sprang to attention when Peaches entered, along with Maddie, and the rest.

One of them rushed to an elevator and pressed a button.

The elevator whooshed up and opened into an office.

Maddie stopped.

It was truly like what Peaches had described.

Color. So much of it. So warm.

Orange. Gold. Blue. Couches everywhere.

Peaches squealed and ran and hugged a woman.

She was brown haired. Green eyed. She whirled Peaches around and set her down.

Another woman came. She too was brown haired and green

eyed.

Maddie was shy; however, Peaches pulled her by the arm and introduced her.

'My best friend,' she introduced Maddie.

The first woman bent and shook her hand gravely. 'Beth Petersen, ma'am.'

Maddie giggled. No one called her ma'am.

The other woman shook her hand. 'Meghan.'

'Want some cookies?' Beth asked.

Lizzie and Maddie nodded their heads simultaneously. No one refused cookies.

Meghan looked behind Maddie.

Maddie turned round.

A brown-haired man was bringing more chairs.

'He's the helper,' Peaches whispered.

Maddie looked at him, then at Lizzie. Lizzie's face had turned red. Gramma seemed to be smiling.

Peaches didn't care. She bit into the cookies Beth bought. Maddie followed.

They were delicious. As good as the ones Gramma made.

Maddie didn't know it; Gramma sent a batch over to the twins, whenever she baked.

The plate emptied.

Beth disappeared inside to refill. Peaches nudged her.

Maddie didn't say anything. Peaches nudged her harder.

'They are friends. You can tell them anything.'

Maddie nodded. Tears were in her eyes.

'Daddy hits Mommy.'

Check out the rest of the Warriors Series

'*Surely one of the best action writers of the day*' Amazon review

On Amazon On Amazon UK On Nook On Kobo iTunes
Find them on Ty's website: *www.typatterson.com*

The Warrior

You are Zeb Carter, an agent with a deep black U.S. agency. You are a master of the killing game. In your business, the mission's rules are the only ones that matter. You break a cardinal one; and the game changes.

The Reluctant Warrior

Broker, the ace intelligence analyst in the Warriors crew, is good at finding things. Like finding people who don't want to be found. When an investigation goes wrong, he soon finds that hiding is far more difficult when he's the one who doesn't want to be found. Dying is increasingly certain when he's the one on the run.

The Warrior Code

All that Zeb Carter wants is to be left alone. The only thing Beth and Meghan Petersen want is an opportunity to rebuild their lives. All that a ruthless gang wants is to kill them all.

The Warrior's Debt

New York. Two killers. Both hunters. Neither of them is used to being prey.

Warriors Series Boxset, Books 1-4

Ex-Special Forces operative Zeb Carter works for a U.S. government agency that doesn't exist. You wouldn't remember him if you saw him. Those who are dying to meet him - get there.

These four thrillers are his stories. Over 900 pages of high-octane action and edge-of-your-seat mayhem that's perfect for today's thriller fans!

Flay

Zeb Carter has battled terrorists, mobsters, and despots in the most violent hotspots of the world. Nothing has prepared him for the Flayer, a serial killer in New York. The Flayer plans to break the internet. But that's only one part of his plan. The second part will break the city.

Behind You

They warned Elena Petrova to drop her story. She didn't. They raped her. She didn't give up. They killed her and buried her body where no man could find it. Unfortunately for them, one man did.

Zeb Carter is back. This time it's personal.

Hunting You

You are Hank Parker. Armed intruders break in when you are dining with your family. They ask you a question. Tell a lie and watch them die. Don't Know isn't an option.

Warriors Series Boxset II

He works for a U.S. deep black agency no one knows of and goes on missions that never come to light. To his enemies, he is karma. Those who are dying to meet him, get there. Meet U.S. Special Forces operative Zeb Carter.

Author's Message

Thank you for taking time to read *Zero*. If you enjoyed it, please consider telling your friends and posting a short review.

Sign up to Ty Patterson's mailing list, and get The Warrior, free. Be the first to know about new releases and deals.

Ty's Amazon author page is here

The Warrior, Warriors series, Book 1

The Reluctant Warrior, Warriors series, Book 2

The Warrior Code, Warriors series, Book 3

The Warrior's Debt, Warriors series, Book 4

Warriors series Boxset, Books 1-4

Flay, Warriors series, Book 5

Behind You, Warriors series, Book 6

Hunting You, Warriors series, Book 7

Warriors series Boxset II, Books 5-7

Zero, Warriors series, Book 8

About the Author

Ty has lived on a couple of continents and has been a trench digger, loose tea vendor, leather goods salesman, marine lubricants salesman, diesel engine mechanic, and is now an action thriller author.

Ty is privileged that readers of crime suspense and action thrillers have loved his books. 'Intense,' 'Riveting,' and 'Gripping' have been commonly used in reviews.

Ty lives with his wife and son, who humor his ridiculous belief that he's in charge.

Connect with Ty:

On Twitter
On Facebook
Mailing list
Website: *www.typatterson.com*

Made in the USA
Middletown, DE
20 November 2016